# FORGOTTEN SPIRITS

# FORGOTTEN SPIRITS

## A NO ORDINARY WOMEN MYSTERY

by
Barbara Deese

NORTH STAR PRESS OF ST. CLOUD, INC.
St. Cloud, Minnesota

ISBN: 978-0-87839-768-6

Cover art by Jake Karwoski, Monster of the Midwest, LLC
Author photo by Karen Beltz

First Edition: September 2014

Printed in the United States of America

Published by
North Star Press of St. Cloud, Inc.
P.O. Box 451
St. Cloud, Minnesota 56302

"It is impossible to live without failing at something, unless you live so cautiously that you might as well not have lived at all . . ."

–J.K. Rowling

# PROLOGUE

DECEMBER, late 1990s

The six of them, three women and three men, spilled from the front door of the club, rosy cheeked and laughing. All three women were long-legged and striking. The one with glossy, dark-brown hair was draped in a fringed shawl. One wore a sleek platinum bob and a faux fur jacket. The third one had a pouf of hair the color of a red fox. Shivering in the chill desert air, she knotted her wool scarf over her coat.

The last of the three men to exit was almost as wide as the door. Swinging an arm over the blonde's shoulder, he said in his booming voice, "So a blond, a brunette, and a redhead go into a bar."

They laughed.

One of the men had a Burger King crown perched on his head, and three bright lip prints on his cheeks. He was the only one of the six who appeared to be inebriated. "I got one. What do Italians and alligators have in common?" he said, slapping the skinny guy on the back. Before anyone could guess, he said, "They wear the same shoes."

They all looked down at his shoes, laughing again.

"I shouldn't have had that last drink," the guy wearing the crown said.

The brunette nuzzled up to him as they moved down the nearly deserted street. In her heels, she was half a foot taller than her boyfriend. "It's your birthday," she said, starting them on another round singing the Beatles' birthday song.

The skinny guy in a leather jacket and pointy, alligator shoes drummed on the redhead's back with his fingertips. When they'd sung a few lines, he slipped his arm around her and pointed to a car parked ahead of them on the street. The yellow Lamborghini reflected lights from the sign above a seedy little bar. "One of these days we're gonna drive a car just like that," he said to her.

She stiffened imperceptibly. "Before or after we buy a house and have kids?" she asked.

"We're gonna have it all, my little fox. You'll see." He tugged her by the arm and led her to the car. They walked all the way around it, caressing the gleaming metal. "I think I like yellow," he said, "but we can get it in any color you want."

The blonde and the huge man struck a gangster pose against a big, black Cadillac Eldorado parked behind the Lamborghini. She pulled up her skirt to show the full length of her shapely legs and leaned against him. He held a pretend tommy gun across his big chest. The dark-haired woman and the man in the party hat pulled out imaginary weapons and staged a slow-motion gunfight, unable to contain their laughter. When the hilarity wore off, the three couples resumed their decorum and moved on.

Walking along the street in old downtown Las Vegas, they were nearing the corner where they would split up and go in separate directions, when suddenly, a man appeared from around the corner, running straight toward them, feet pounding and arms pumping. As he whipped his head around to look behind him, he bumped into the shoulder of one of the partiers, causing him to drop a bag, which rolled along the gutter. The running man crossed the street without looking back or losing speed.

The birthday boy lost his Burger King crown when he stooped to pick up the black insulated cooler bag with both hands. "I do believe that man just gave me a birthday present," he said, a grin spreading across his face as he showed them the broken strap. But before he could unzip the bag, a long black car screeched around the corner. The six of them froze. Tires squealed. Two blocks ahead, the running man picked up speed. A gunshot rang out. He lurched, and it looked like he might catch his balance, but then his feet faltered, and his momentum drove him forward several ungainly steps before he crumpled on the pavement.

"Holy shit!" said the skinny guy. The rest of them were speechless.

The dark-haired woman was the first to act. "Everybody get in my car!" she yelled. "It's just around the corner!"

Racing like their lives depended on it, all six of them jammed themselves into her car and sped off. The birthday boy didn't even realize he was still gripping the cooler in his hands.

If he could have known how much that cooler would change their lives, he would have chucked it out the window.

F at snowflakes drifted down slowly, but steadily, whitewashing old dingy snow with a sparkly new layer. Snow outlined red-ribboned garlands and turned shrubbery white around the stately mansions. Had it not been for the cars lining Summit Avenue, this historic part of Saint Paul would look little different from photos taken a century earlier. Picture perfect, and just in time for the Christmas season.

Walking their dogs, Catherine Running Wolf and Foxy Tripp chatted as they made their way down an increasingly slippery sidewalk.

Already overheated in thick wool mittens and felted wool hat, Catherine held both leashes in one hand so she could unzip her down jacket. "The guy was just standing on the street below, staring up at your window? You couldn't see anything that would identify him?"

"Nope. I can't even say it was a guy, although the silhouette made me assume it was a man with his hands in his pockets. I think he was wearing a stocking cap."

"If he was in silhouette, is it possible he wasn't even looking in your direction?"

Foxy stopped. Facing Cate, she said, "When I moved to the other window, I thought his head might have turned."

"That's creepy. How long was he there?"

"I don't know. I stepped away from the window and turned off the light. It took me a minute to get up the nerve, but when I crawled back in the dark to peek out the window again, he was gone."

Cate gave a little shudder. "I don't like the sounds of that! What are you going to do?"

"What can I do? It's not against the law to stand on the street and look at someone's house."

"But you said you were getting hang-up calls too. Did you check caller ID?"

Foxy's reddish curls bounced when she nodded her head. "Of course I did, Cate. It just says 'unknown caller.'"

"Maybe they're robocalls," said Cate. Carlton trotted along next to her, keeping pace as if he were an extension of his owner. The black lab had been particularly protective of her in the months since Cate's somewhat reckless decision had inadvertently put herself and others, including both of her dogs, in peril. "Or someone dialing the wrong number."

Foxy nodded. "Could be. Each thing is unnerving and can be explained, but together—"

"I know! It does sound sinister. I'm thinking you shouldn't stay there."

"That's ridiculous," Foxy said, too quickly. "I'm just letting my imagination go a little nuts. It's probably nothing." When Cate began to protest, Foxy pressed her lips together and then said she didn't want to talk about it any more.

Cate frowned. "You sure?"

When Foxy nodded, Cate said, "Okay, but you have to tell me if anything else happens. In the meantime, we'll just enjoy this gorgeous winter day."

Foxy looked around. "It is gorgeous, isn't it?" Slipping the leash onto her wrist, she scooped up a handful of snow and clumped it into a dense ball. "It's snowman weather!"

"What does a Nevada girl know about snowmen?"

"I wasn't always from Nevada." She tossed the snowball at a lamppost. It hit with a dull *thwack*.

Cate knew Foxy had spent her childhood a hundred miles or so north of the Twin Cities, in a small town where her mother still lived. Only a few days ago, Foxy had described a recent meal at the nursing home. It sounded like a dismal affair, an easily chewed meal of turkey loaf, mushy carrots, and gluey mashed potatoes with gravy, served family-style at tables of four. After supper, staff had gathered them all in the living room to watch a Perry Como Christmas video. Foxy had been shocked to see her former pastor there—a once powerful force in their small community, now confined to a wheelchair, where he'd dozed off with his head lolling on his chest. The whole scene made Cate grateful her own mother still lived independently.

They looked up when a horn honked, and watched a car slide through the intersection, unable to stop on the icy road. Other cars fishtailed as they braked to avoid a collision.

At the corner, they allowed ample time for cars to pass before crossing the street. Mitsy, Cate's patchwork dog, kept plugging along, but Cate could see she was getting tired. It had been over a year since the dog had sustained an injury while protecting her mistress, but her stamina wasn't what it used to be. "Let's turn around," Cate said.

Foxy, who'd devoted her life to healing not just humans but their pets, nodded and reached out to touch Mitsy's flank. "I can do some more Reiki on her."

"Would you?" Cate had her own way of communicating with animals, and had seen for herself how Mitsy responded to Foxy's ministrations. When they arrived at Cate's house, just half a block off Summit, she invited Foxy to come in.

Foxy ducked her head. "Thanks, but Bill's coming over at seven." She shifted uncomfortably.

Cate grinned. The whole book club had met Sheriff Bill Harley during a murder investigation. Although they'd come to trust him and even like him, the others were taken aback when Foxy told them last year that she and the Wisconsin sheriff were dating. As soon as they'd asked questions, she'd cut off further conversation by saying, "Would you all mind if we just didn't talk about it until I sort things out?" That approach, as far as Cate could tell, had only stirred up more conjecture.

Cate turned to face her, raising her left eyebrow. "He still drives all the way from Wisconsin just for a massage?" she teased.

Clearly, Foxy wasn't in a joking mood. "I have a legitimate massage business. We have ethical guidelines, so as soon as he asked me out, he stopped being my client. If I choose to do bodywork on him, it's as a friend. Just the way I volunteer with the seniors at Meadowpoint Manor."

Foxy could be so prickly! Hearing the rebuke in her friend's response, Cate mumbled an apology. "Wait a sec while I let the dogs in, and I'll walk you home," she added. When Foxy began to protest, Cate said, "I insist."

* * *

STANDING ON THE SCREENED PORCH, the man hunched his shoulders, bracing against the cold. He double checked the address and pushed the doorbell once more. When no one answered, he pressed the two other doorbells and pounded on the door with wind-chapped fists. Stepping over to the front window and standing on tiptoes, he tried to peer through the crack in the drapes, but the room lay in deep shadow.

Reaching into his inside jacket pocket, he pulled out a pack of cigarettes, slipped one out and wedged it between his lips. Rubbing his hands together, he thought about what it would be like to see Foxy face to face after all these years. She'd probably slam the door in his face.

He flicked his lighter, and the cigarette glowed as he sucked on it. Immediately he tucked his ungloved hands under his armpits.

Wind pierced his clothing, and he knew he didn't have the stamina to stand on her porch much longer. He hated to leave now, but the light on his gas gauge had gone on while he'd idled the engine in front of her house, and he couldn't risk running out of gas.

Exhaling, he watched the smoke curl in the air and turned his attention to the black SUV coming down the block. He'd seen it twice already. This time it slowed and came to a stop, double-parked in front of the house. Realizing the cigarette's glow made him visible, he stubbed it out on the conveniently placed ashtry when he saw the driver's head turn in his direction.

As soon as the vehicle drove off, he slipped off the porch, jumping into his car before the SUV made another pass. Shoulders slumped in disappointment, he went off in search of a gas station and a warm meal.

\* \* \*

Up ahead, Foxy's building, a once-stately Victorian home, now subdivided into apartments, came into view. When she took her daily walk down Summit Avenue, Foxy never failed to marvel that even though she didn't rub shoulders with the movers and shakers in Minnesota's state capitol, her modest apartment was in the same neighborhood as these amazing mansions, including the English Tudor governor's residence and the Georgian Revival next to it, which was owned by the college women's club.

Tonight she'd left lights on, and she could see her black cat, Elvis, stretched out on the windowsill in her second-story window.

Cate and Foxy walked a little more before Foxy noticed indentations in the snow on the sidewalk and up the steps of her house. They'd been made very recently. Since she shared the house with other residents, footprints in the snow should have caused no alarm, but as soon as she saw them, her hand tightened on the dog's leash.

She felt Cate's eyes on her.

"I'll go up with you," Cate offered.

Foxy shook her head. "I'm good." She noticed the concern in her friend's eyes as Cate scanned her face.

"Well then, I'll wait here. Just wave to me from your window so I know you're okay."

Foxy nodded. Molly Pat tugged on her leash. Terrier and owner added their own footprints to the scene as they bounded up the front steps and through the screened porch to the front door, where it took a moment for Foxy to fumble her key into the lock.

Upstairs, she used her second key to unlock the door to her own apartment, which took up most of the second floor. In fact, for the time being, the studio apartment in the back was vacant, and so she had the whole floor to herself.

Elvis barely showed his arthritis as he hopped off the sill, almost tripping her as he snaked around her ankles.

She hung up Molly Pat's leash, shook the snow from her wool coat and unzipped her boots before putting them in the front closet. After doing her ritual three turns, Molly Pat flopped down on her red plaid dog pillow near the kitchen. Only then did Foxy remember to go to the window. She saw Cate's upturned face and waved to let her know all was well.

But it wasn't. Watching Cate's departing figure, what stuck in her mind was the worry on her friend's face.

Something else gnawed at her sense of security, too. Cate wasn't the only one with intuitive powers, she thought, as she pulled wine glasses from the cupboard and sliced some cheddar cheese to go with the apple pie she'd baked earlier. The first time she'd served him this, Bill had said, "Apple pie without the cheese is like a kiss without a squeeze." It was a little corny and a little sweet, and now it had lodged in her brain, to pop up like an advertising jingle at the oddest times.

Just then, the thing she'd been trying to remember scuttled across her mind, and she knew she wouldn't fully relax until she'd checked it out. Her heart pounded as she retraced her steps, back down the stairs and out the door onto the porch. Intuition, she believed, was just a matter of noticing things subliminally and pushing them back into the subconscious, where they hooked up with other images until just the right mix of memories, observations, and analysis came together.

Flipping on the porch light, she saw it was there, precisely as her subconscious mind had recorded it, a single, unfiltered butt in the blue glass ashtray her landlady left there year round. Picking it up with all the disgust of a reformed smoker, she made a face. She snatched up the ashtray, stumbling over the leg of a wicker chair in her hurry to get back upstairs.

Having lived much of her adult life on her own, Foxy had never been a particularly fearful person. Back in the safety of her apartment, she took a couple of deep breaths. By the time she'd disposed of the cigarette butt and washed the ashtray, she convinced herself it meant nothing. In fact, when she thought about it, she was embarrassed by how quickly she'd turned a few phone calls and a cigarette butt into a big melodrama.

Looking at the clock, she smeared on some lipstick and set the table. By the time Sheriff Harley's vehicle pulled up, she had gathered herself together. She checked herself in the mirror before meeting him at the door.

"Foxy," he said, taking her hands and looking at her with warm eyes.

Enjoying the strength of his arms around her and the smell of her favorite aftershave, she closed her eyes. For most of her adult life she'd prided herself on handling, all on her own, whatever life threw her way, and yet sometimes, like this moment, she wondered what it would be like to give in and simply let someone take care of her.

He tossed his jacket on the bench by the door. Following her to the kitchen, Bill perched on a stool and watched her finish preparing their dinner of poached salmon and quinoa salad, food he once swore to her he'd never eat.

Sheriff Harley was clean-shaven and trim, definitely in better shape than when she'd first met him. He'd just turned fifty—four-and-a-half years younger than she was. Foxy took credit for introducing him to the ideas that donuts did not constitute a food group and cross-country skiing could be fun. When she actually stood back and took a realistic look at him, as she did now, she had to wonder why it was so hard for her to consider a more permanent arrangement.

She worked at the counter with her back to him. He stood, buried his face in her hair and kissed the back of her neck. She was almost embarrassed to feel a warm and familiar surge. She was almost fifty-six, for Pete's sake!

Okay, she was still in excellent shape for her age, but she was still her age! Never, in her younger days, could she have pictured having passionate sex with a man who had ear hair and age spots. Before she'd met Bill, she'd believed she was aging with grace, accepting the few extra pounds and softer jawline, the flat shoes and reading glasses. But once she'd gotten into this relationship, she'd become acutely aware of every little wrinkle, every consequence of gravity on her body, and she felt ridiculous. She couldn't pin those feelings on anyone but herself. Bill never judged her harshly. In fact, he treated her like an unexpected gift, wrapped up and left for him under the Christmas tree.

At dinner, she looked at him across the table, with the planes of his face sharpened in the candlelight. She considered asking him to spend the night. The trouble was, if he stayed over, she'd have to boot him out early in the morning so she could get ready for the book club lunch at Robin's.

She'd debated whether or not to tell him about the calls, but concluded he'd feel compelled to chide her for not having a real lock on the porch and an electronic security system. But the real reason she chose to say nothing was that he was sure to ask questions. That was a given, and being in law enforcement, there was no such thing as a casual question to Bill. Maybe he'd even go snooping into her background, something he promised he'd never do, even though he had, at his fingertips, the means to do it.

While they ate, Foxy made sure they kept the conversation light. Snuggling together on the sofa after dinner, they listened to classical piano music. His fingers stroked the back of her neck and wandered down the front of her sweater. Her body came alive wherever he touched. She again was about to ask if he wanted to spend the night when her phone rang. Regretfully, Foxy disentangled herself from his embrace and walked barefooted into the kitchen.

This time, the person on the other end did not hang up. Foxy knew immediately it was bad news.

"Yes, of course I remember you, Mr. Brady. What's wrong?"

He was blunt in delivering the news. "Sierra's dead. My daughter is dead. I thought you should know."

Dead? Foxy wondered if she'd misheard. It took a few beats for it to make sense. "Sierra? Dead?" she echoed stupidly.

She could hear him try to say something and then choke on it. "What happened?"

"She took her own life." His voice got stronger, more definite. "She was at home." He cleared his throat. "You do know she moved to Minnesota, don't you?"

"Yes, we've been in contact."

13

"The thing is, she killed herself at her home, well, in her garage. She'd been drinking, the police said, and then she went out to the garage and turned on the car engine. She died of carbon monoxide."

Foxy wondered if she'd misheard. "It must have been an accident."

Bill hovered in the doorway, his eyes questioning her.

She turned away and covered her mouth as tears spilled over.

Bill tucked his body up close to hers and began to rub her shoulders.

"She left a note." Mr. Brady forged on, determined to get his message out.

"A note?"

"She said she was sorry, but she couldn't think of any other way."

Foxy listened with growing sadness and confusion, as Sierra's father told her more than necessary about his daughter's death, from what she was wearing when her son, Beau, found her to the position of her body in the car and the boiled, red appearance of her skin. Perhaps focusing on the factual details was an effort to exorcise his demons, but by telling her, the demons had become hers too. She had no words of comfort to offer him.

Sometime in the late evening last Sunday, Sierra had eaten a meal of chicken and salad. She'd been drinking. In her intoxicated state, she'd gone out to the garage, gotten in her car and turned on the engine, he told her. She stayed there with the garage door shut. She'd been sick, but couldn't purge herself of the toxins in time. A nearly empty vodka bottle on her kitchen table explained her blood alcohol content.

She mumbled the obligatory words of condolence. "Is there anything I can do?" she asked, expecting him to decline offers of help.

"Yes, yes, that's the reason I'm calling. When she moved to Minnesota over the summer, she left some boxes for us to store. We went through them last night, and one of them is addressed to you."

"What?"

"She left a box addressed to you," he repeated. "We're down here in Rochester right now going through some other things. Beau found her. I told you that. He's still terribly upset." He went on, talking about Sierra's son. "We're taking him up to our vacation place in Alexandria for a few days. We're leaving here shortly, heading up there tonight, and I want to stop by with that box. We won't stay. Beau and my wife are taking this all pretty hard."

"Uh, sure. Of course." She began to give him the address, but he said it was on a slip of paper inside the box.

Clicking off the phone and wiping mascara smears off her cheeks, she turned to Bill, who enfolded her in his strong arms.

After she told him about the call, she found herself playing the scene over and over in her mind. It didn't hang together right. After a colorful life, Sierra had supposedly chosen death by a colorless alcohol and a colorless gas. It was peculiar to the point of being incongruous. Carbon monoxide, as a means of death, wasn't as ghastly as some, but suicide was cruel on so many levels. She pictured Beau coming home from spending the night with friends, as his grandfather had described it, and finding his still-beautiful mother slumped over the center console of her car.

Mr. Brady said the first thing the boy saw when he opened the door to his mother's car was her lovely face, now bright red, the hallmark of carbon monoxide poisoning. In his phone call, Beau told the police it looked like she'd gotten a nasty sunburn. He smelled the vomit and the smell of death and jumped back, turning around just in time to throw up on the garage floor.

Never in a million years could Foxy imagine Sierra doing that to her son.

C ate waited until Foxy waved from the window to let her know she was fine. Still, all the way home, Cate tried to quell her feeling that Foxy was in danger. Others, over the years, had mocked Cate's visions and hunches, but those flashes of insight had served her well at times and she knew better than to ignore them.

She found her husband at their heavy wooden table in the dining room, working on a stack of Christmas cards. A self-adhesive postage stamp was stuck to the forearm of his sweater. Cate picked it off and stuck it on his nose. Noticing the plate next to him with a sampling of the cookies she'd spent three days making, Cate sighed. "You're leaving some of those cookies for family, I hope."

Erik looked over his glasses at her. The silver hair that had, until recently, been only at his temples, was starting to insinuate itself into the rest of his dark hair. With a bemused smile, he said, "Catherine, honey, you do this every year. You spend days making enough cookies to fill a bakery. You guard them with your life when they're fresh out of the oven. You count them and put them in containers I'm not allowed to touch, and then you spend weeks protecting them from me."

It was hard to take him seriously with a Christmas wreath stamp on the end of his nose.

"And then, after the holidays, you look at all the leftover cookies and wonder why nobody ate them." He put a crisp gingersnap between his teeth and crunched down.

She pulled off her hat, letting her dark hair tumble onto her shoulders. "You're right." She kissed the top of his head. Then she reached out and snagged two frosted cut-outs in the shape of angels. After hanging her jacket and hat on a peg and kicking her boots into the mud room, she settled into the big leather chair in the den.

In an attempt to distill her earlier feelings about Foxy, Cate closed her eyes and waited for an image to appear in her mind. Breathing deeply, she tried to empty her mind of her surroundings. Suddenly, through her closed lids, lights swirled and flashed. She had a wave of dizziness. Her eyes flew open. "Erik, did you do something with the lights?" she called out.

"Nope. You must be hallucinating," he teased.

Hallucination, vision or aging eyes—whatever it was, the flashing lights made her reach over, snatch up the phone and punch number two on speed dial. She needed to talk over her unsettling premonition with the person she had always turned to.

Cate and Robin went all the way back to college days. Their friendship had lasted over thirty years, and they'd been fortunate enough to marry men who were close friends. Robin was also one of the No Ordinary Women, the name they'd given to their book club years ago.

Robin knew Cate's hunches could be wrong, but there was no denying Cate had some ability to see beyond what others saw. It came, her father had believed, from the fraction of her blood that was Cherokee.

Of course, there were those times her intuitions had been utterly or partially wrong. Over the years, Robin had accompanied her on more than one wild goose chase, following some idea that proved erroneous.

Robin picked up on the fifth ring, saying she was putting her phone on speaker so she could keep cutting fruit for the compote she was making for tomorrow's book club luncheon.

Cate wasted no time telling her about Foxy's hang-up calls and the shadowy figure who'd been watching Foxy from the street.

"She could stay here," Robin said. When Cate said she'd already offered her a place to stay, Robin responded, "Well then, I think she should ask Sheriff Harley to sleep over."

Cate snorted. "I think he's on his way. They have a date tonight and she's fixing him dinner, but if it's a sleepover, she's certainly not letting on."

Robin giggled. "A sleepover? You mean they're going to do each other's hair and paint each other's toenails?"

Cate made a face. "Thanks so much for planting that visual in my head." One of the wonderful things about their friendship was that one of them would be worried or unhappy, and the other would throw in a ludicrous comment to lighten the mood, while still understanding the seriousness of the situation.

"My pleasure. Did I mention they're both wearing baby doll pajamas?"

"Now that's a disturbing picture!"

"Here's an even more disturbing thought," Cate said. "Maybe I'm letting my imagination get away with me, but is it possible Bill's the one making those hang-up calls?"

"Bill Harley?" Robin laughed. "Oh, come on, Cate. We know him!"

"We know he's good with animals, which I never disregard, and he seems like a nice guy, but what's to say he's not checking up on her?"

"You don't mean 'checking up on her.' You mean 'stalking.' Does he strike you as the jealous type?"

Cate crunched on a frosted angel wing. "Not jealous, exactly, but I think there's some hurt, and even anger, just under the surface. And let's be honest, how well do we really know him?"

"Hmm." Robin hesitated before asking, "Is your intuition telling you something?"

"About Harley?" Cate shrugged. "I admit he's not a likely suspect, but we have to consider every possibility, don't we?" She laughed at herself. Looking around her home, with its clean lines and rich woods, her dogs asleep in front of the stone fireplace, and her husband at the table munching on cookies after an early dinner, Cate felt foolish. Here in the safety of her home, the idea of danger seemed preposterous. She brushed cookie crumbs off her sweatshirt and put them on a napkin. "Maybe we're making too much of it. The two things could be unrelated."

"That's why I'm wondering what Foxy's really worried about." Robin said. "It isn't like her to worry. She's usually kind of a cool customer."

Erik appeared at Cate's side with a stack of addressed envelopes, sealed and stamped. "I'm going to bed. Got an early morning." As an anesthesiologist, his early mornings were absurdly early to Cate, who had always been a night owl.

After dropping the envelopes in the basket for outgoing mail, he gave her a one-armed hug and kissed the top of her head. He smelled like gingersnaps. "Good night, Robin," he yelled so she could hear him over the phone.

Robin returned the greeting as Cate held the phone to Erik's ear. Cate watched him climb the stairs.

Robin said, "We've known Foxy for years, but she's a quiet one, isn't she?"

"Or maybe she's just quiet in comparison to us."

"Yeah, I suppose it's hard to get a word in edgewise sometimes. But really, what do we know about her?"

Cate rested her head back in thought. "We know she grew up in a small town up north—Pine something. Her parents were Christian fundamentalists."

"I got the impression the whole community went to that one church, didn't you?"

"Exactly, and it sounds like it was pretty repressive. The way she tells it, running off to Vegas as soon as she graduated was the only way she could break free. We don't know much about her time there except that she was some kind of dancer, right?"

"A showgirl! How could I forget? Remember when she dropped that on us? My God, we were speechless!"

"I remember," Cate said, twirling a finger through her hair. "Remember how Grace's mouth fell open and stayed that way? I wish we could get Foxy to tell us more about those days."

"What exactly does a showgirl do?" Robin asked. "I know she wasn't a stripper, but some of those showgirls are topless. Do you think she was one of those?"

Cate snorted into the phone. "I've never gotten up the nerve to ask, but somehow I can't picture Foxy going topless."

"Okay, she probably didn't go topless, but she was a showgirl. They do those big, theatric productions. It's genuine dance, I know. Foxy said she studied ballet for years."

"I picture showgirls wearing feather headdresses, bikini tops, rhinestone G-strings, that kind of thing. Can you picture Foxy—?"

"They put rhinestones on G-strings? Wouldn't that be painful?" Robin asked.

"The rhinestones wouldn't be—Robin, do not derail me! What else do we know about Foxy? I know she was either married or in a serious enough relationship to refer to the guy as her 'ex.' Do you remember his name? It started with V. Vito or Victor, maybe. And they didn't have any kids, obviously."

"Vincent?" Robin suggested. "Vladimir? Like Vlad the Impaler."

"Yes, I'm sure that was it," Cate said dryly. "Foxy was married to the guy who inspired Count Dracula."

"Vishnu? Uncle Vanya?"

"Stop it." This was all part of the banter they'd perfected in their long friendship.

"I think she made a pretty clean break after she and Voldemort broke up."

"Stop it!" Cate said again, but she was laughing. "Whoever she was with, I think she got out of Dodge when they broke up, and never looked back."

"She still keeps in touch with that one friend from their dancing days. You know the one she went to see in Portland last year?"

Cate remembered seeing a handful of pictures from the trip Foxy and Bill Harley took together, when they'd spent time with Foxy's friend Tina in Oregon. "Tina."

"Right. She didn't move with any of her friends from Vegas. Instead she came back to Minnesota. I wonder why if she hated her upbringing so much. She hardly ever talks about family."

"No, not so much. There's just her mom in a nursing home, and her brother, Matt," Cate said. "If I didn't have company coming, I would've taken her up on her invitation in a heartbeat."

"To all go to Matt's resort?"

"Uh huh. Ever since she brought it up, I've been picturing us all at this peaceful log cabin in the woods with no one around but the book club and Foxy's brother." Instead, Cate would be stuck with a houseful of relatives, some of whom were meeting each other for the first time.

"I know. I'm still tempted. Do you think she's going up there anyway?"

"I have no idea."

Robin pulled them back to their previous conjecture. "Why do you suppose Foxy didn't move back to her hometown? I don't get the impression she wanted to be close to her mother. Am I nuts to think she might be running away from something . . . or someone."

*Well, that's something to consider*, Cate thought.

* * *

IN HER COMFY BUNGALOW in Portland, Tina Wilbert lowered the living room blinds and checked the locks on both doors. Her usual Zen-like calm had vanished with Wylie's call. She paced from one room to another and wished she hadn't given up drinking. She closed her eyes and tried to remember Sierra Brady when she was alive—beautiful, dark-haired and vibrant, a bit of a risk-taker.

Opening the closet in the spare bedroom, she rummaged through an assortment of plastic boxes until she found the one containing show bills and photos from the old days. An inch down, she found the photo used in one of the casino's slick advertisements. Foxy and Tina, as the two shortest dancers in the troupe, stood on either end of the dance line. Sierra, with her regal height and bearing, posed front and center. Her long, dark tresses were wrapped up inside an elaborate gold headdress. They'd all hated the weight of those headpieces. That particular one, she remembered, was nearly eighteen pounds.

*How things have changed*, thought Tina, running fingers through her hair, which she still wore in a blonde bob. They'd all stayed fit, she, Sierra, and Foxy, and took care with their appearance, but that spark, that dazzle factor, was gone. They'd used it all up on stage, given it away to one roomful of strangers after another, saving none for themselves.

The six of them had been close once—three showgirls, a blonde, a brunette, and a redhead, and the guys in their lives—Tina and Big Al, Sierra and Wylie, Foxy and Vinnie. Now two of the six were dead. And of the three couples, not one had stayed together. It had taken only a few months for them all to come apart.

When Foxy left Vinnie, she'd hung up her dancing shoes and moved to Colorado. For a while Vinnie quit gambling and cleaned up his act. He'd tried his hand booking talent at some of the smaller lounges downtown, but that lasted a matter of months. After all, Las Vegas was no place for a recovering gambler to . . . well . . . recover.

After her boyfriend, Big Al, dropped off the planet, Tina had moved to the northwest coast. Sierra was a little younger than Foxy and Tina, but she'd been the first to retire from dancing. By then, she had a baby to think about. Sierra and Wylie had always been off again-on again anyway, and at some point, the off again had become permanent.

The three former showgirls had been in touch sporadically, and sometimes with difficulty, over the seventeen years since then. Oddly, none of them had married, or in Foxy's case, remarried. And although Sierra had had various boyfriends, she'd never been serious about anyone other than Wylie, but theirs was an unsustainable love-hate relationship.

As if it had happened yesterday, Tina recalled the night of Wylie's birthday celebration. They'd driven at breakneck speed to the apartment Tina and Al shared. They'd slammed the door behind them, in full-blown paranoia after having witnessed someone being gunned down on the street. Wylie, looking like a deer in headlights, remembered he was clutching the cooler. He unzipped it then, and his mouth fell open.

They hadn't even counted all the hundred-dollar bills when Foxy had said, "If we keep it, it's going to come back and haunt us all. Nobody loses that kind of money and just forgets about it."

Tina had agreed, but Sierra had been quick to argue, "Well, nobody finds that kind of money and lets it go, either." They talked for what seemed like hours, but Sierra wouldn't budge, and by throwing her vote in with the men, who'd all three voted to keep the money and divvy it up, Sierra had cast the die for all of them.

Now it looked like Foxy had been right. Tina's gut told her Sierra, like Big Al, had finally been done in by that fateful night so long ago.

She looked at the glossy photo once more before returning it to the box, which she wedged back into the closet. Back in her living room, she sat in her rattan rocker and watched rain battering down on the back windows. She loved three of the four seasons in Portland, but this weather put her in a siege mentality. When she'd left the desert for the Northwest, her new state's wholesome reputation and amazing gardens had looked like paradise to her. The greenery didn't happen without a whole lot of rain, though, and when it rained and rained like this, she wished she'd spent a winter here before making the decision to buy a house.

She sighed. Tucking her hands under her arms to keep warm, she murmured, "Poor Sierra!"

**R**obin Bentley enjoyed the early morning hours when she was up before Brad. A golden band appeared under the eastern sky's pink glow. The black-and-white world gradually took on color. As she watched, the new snow changed from gray to indigo to lavender.

Sitting at the kitchen counter, she sipped her coffee and opened her laptop. She looked again, as she had for the past week, at the photos their older daughter, Cass, had posted on her Facebook page. Cass was in love. Again. The dust had barely settled from her last breakup, when she'd gotten involved with this new guy, and after only five months together, she was on her way to spend Christmas with him and his family in the Denver area.

Cass was beaming in the photos, taken only last week. Sitting on a picnic table in the Cascade National Park with her boyfriend, she looked as happy as Robin had ever seen her. He, on the other hand, looked smug and aloof. Wind-tousled hair obscured her face in some of the photos, while his remained perfect. His expression looked practiced and insincere.

When Brad got on her about making too much of the group of photos, Robin had said, "I'm a photographer, and I can tell a hell of a lot from a photo." Finally, they both conceded the other had a point and let it drop. Maybe, as Brad suggested, Robin was just mourning the fact their girls would soon be on their own, not just away at college, one on either coast, but perhaps moving far away for good, and having families that would keep them too occupied to visit often. It was hard to think last year might have been their last Christmas together as a family, and she hadn't even known it.

Their younger daughter, Maya, wouldn't be home until the day before Christmas Eve. Having been sidelined by a persistent case of pneumonia during mid-terms, she'd stayed at her off-campus house, shared with five other students, to finish up a paper and work on the essay part of her application for a summer internship in Chicago.

Both her daughters accused her of "lurking" on the Internet, but she saw nothing wrong with clicking on their Facebook pages. Maya's profile picture was a goofy one of her bare feet, dirty soles facing the camera. Cass had updated hers to one of the picnic bench photos. She was no longer Cass, but half of a couple, Robin thought, with a pang. Maybe checking out the new boyfriend's page was lurking, but she did it anyway, and saw that his photo was of him alone.

She refilled her coffee and decided to quit obsessing over her daughter's relationship, and tackle a task she'd been putting off for too long. Her publisher wanted her to update her bio to be used in promoting upcoming book events. Most people assumed the photography or the writing that went into her books was the hard part, but for Robin, it was writing her bio that actually proved most difficult.

She typed a few words, searched her online thesaurus for their synonyms and typed those too before deleting everything. All she needed was to come up with some new, succinct yet tantalizing phrases about her life. The problem was, what people found interesting about her were the things she wanted to keep private.

The exception was her membership in the No Ordinary Women book club. Although the five women had come together for the sole purpose of discussing books, deep friendships had developed over the years. And then two and a half years ago, they'd found themselves up to their bifocals in a real live murder mystery and had fallen too readily into the role of amateur detectives. They'd gotten rather good at it, too—if good meant stumbling upon murders and darned near getting themselves killed in the process of tracking down clues.

"Robin Bentley is a smart and sensible woman who routinely makes stupid and irresponsible choices and still manages to stay alive," Robin typed. She read her words and her smile slipped away. She clicked the keys again, adding the words, "So far."

As she highlighted the words to delete them, she heard the ping indicating she had a new e-mail. "If you're up, would you mind giving me a call?" the message said.

Robin was certain Foxy's polite request hid something more serious. She and Cate had once joked that if Foxy's house were on fire, she'd dial 9-1-1 and say, "I'm sorry to bother you, but I'm having a little fire problem here. Do you suppose you could send someone over—I mean, if it isn't too much trouble?" Whatever Foxy had on her mind, it must have to do with what Cate told her last night.

True to type, as soon as Foxy answered the phone, she began by apologizing to Robin for taking her away from her husband.

"Don't be silly." Did people think she and Brad spent their days gazing lovingly into each other's eyes, or clutched in passionate embrace? "Brad was at the hospital last night with an older mom who miscarried twins at three months. He's still asleep," she explained.

"Oh." There was a long pause before she said, "I was wondering if you want me to come over early." Her voice was tight with anxiety. "You know, to help get things ready."

Robin looked at the time on her computer. Almost eight thirty. "Is everything okay?" Even though she said she was fine, Robin didn't believe it for a minute. She told Foxy to come any time after eleven.

After hanging up and closing her computer, she refilled her coffee cup and looked over her To Do list, a thorough action plan for the book club's Christmas lunch. She'd already queued up four hours of music and arranged cookies on a silver platter. The plum pudding was covered in muslin, ready to be steamed again. She crossed those off and looked at the remaining items, all requiring attention closer to lunchtime.

\* \* \*

CATE SLEPT LATER THAN USUAL. Her waking dream made her skin prickle. Foxy had been twirling in the snow, her hair flying around her like a copper halo. She spun faster and faster until the snow formed a snow globe around her. Suddenly, Foxy stopped twirling and stared directly at Cate. Her mouth formed the word HELP, but no sound escaped her glass prison.

Cate flung her legs over the side of the bed, trying to squelch the sensation of dread. By the time she was up and dressed, it was almost ten o'clock. Erik's breakfast dishes were in the sink. She recognized the sound of the snow blower, and looked out the front window to see Erik pushing it down the driveway, taking the heavy snow in narrow swaths to avoid clogging the machine. The white plume thrown into the air coated his stocking cap and frosted his eyebrows. His icy cheeks were bright red.

It was still more than an hour before she was supposed to pick up Foxy for the lunch. She wanted to talk to Foxy, but hesitated. Erik would call her a mother hen and tell her to respect Foxy's privacy. Maybe, she reasoned, Bill Harley had slept over and they weren't taking any calls. Cate grinned at the euphemism. In those early years of marriage, she and Robin had often said to each other, "I won't be taking calls." Still, she picked up the phone. There was a text message from Foxy, saying she'd left early so she could give Robin a hand.

"Good," Cate said out loud. At least Foxy wasn't alone.

\* \* \*

THEIR BOOK THIS MONTH WAS *A Christmas Carol* by Charles Dickens. Robin had pored over cookbooks and searched online for just the right menu items to go along with the theme. When she finished wrapping the pastry puff around bite-sized chunks of beef tenderloin, she stuck the tray in the freezer.

She and Brad had spent days on Christmas decorations, and the place looked festive. She'd wrapped gifts and tucked them under the tree. Last year the cats had circled incessantly, round and around under the tree, tails erect, knocking most of the needles off the expensive, "freshly cut" fir. Then they'd climbed partway up to knock off more needles and a few ornaments and to chew the arm off a Christmas elf. That's when Brad threatened to find a tree made of barbed wire. They decided instead to invest in a good artificial tree.

Foxy arrived exactly at eleven. She didn't give any hint she wanted to talk about anything. "It's so beautiful," she said, looking over the Christmas decorations. "I don't even bother putting up a tree anymore."

A brief, sad memory came to Robin, of the Christmas she'd spent on the lam with her father. She was ten. They were sitting in the dinette of a rented house. A few wrapped gifts lay around an aluminum tabletop tree atop a gray Formica-and-chrome table. Her father's smile was tentative as she unwrapped six Nancy Drew books, some knee socks and a pretty blue sweater that matched her eyes. She wanted to make her father's smile look less sad. She handed him the last gift, a cylinder of rolled paper tied up in a ribbon. It was a painting she'd done herself. He unrolled it and saw their broken family, magically reunited in watercolor—mother, father and small girl with yellow hair. And then he turned his face to the wall until his shoulders stopped shaking.

A familiar constriction of her throat made her push the memory aside. "Let's see what's left to do," she said.

Foxy followed her into the kitchen. As they worked together, Foxy got around to telling her what was on her mind. A friend of hers had died, a showgirl named Sierra. Robin couldn't recall Foxy ever talking about her.

Wrapping her in a hug, Robin said how awful it was. Remembering what Cate had told her last night about the phone calls and the man watching her house from the street below, Robin said, "Are you afraid to be alone, I mean after news like that?"

"No," Foxy said too quickly, giving her a funny, sidewise glance. She removed water glasses from the cupboard and set them on the table. "I'm a big girl. I don't know if it was the right thing to do, but I sent Bill home last night so I could work through my thoughts about Sierra on my own, but then I woke up way too early and had all this time on my hands. That's all."

Robin wasn't buying her friend's almost flippant response, and wasn't sure how to proceed. Foxy had a pattern of opening a window into her feelings and then closing it. She handed Foxy a box of sherry glasses to set out.

A loud, high beep came from the living room and a gray blur of cat flew past the doorway. Foxy squeaked and dropped one of the etched glasses. It shattered on the tile floor.

Robin raced into the living room and made the sound stop.

"What was that?" Foxy said from several feet away. Her eyes were huge.

"Sorry." Robin ran a hand across her forehead as she walked with Foxy back into the kitchen. "I put a motion detector on the Christmas tree." She reached into the utility closet for a broom. "It's in the cats' DNA to climb trees, artificial or not."

Foxy sighed. "Why do you think I don't put up a tree anymore?"

Robin explained Brad had placed a miniature motion detector near the bottom of the tree that emitted an annoying series of beeps when one of the cats put so much as one paw on a branch.

Foxy shook her head. When she tilted the dustpan into the kitchen garbage can, she winced at the tinkling of broken glass. "I'm so sorry! I suppose these are priceless antiques."

"Not at all."

Foxy leaned against the counter and crossed her slender ankles in front of her, ready to say something, when the beeper went off again. Two gray blurs streaked past them and up the stairs.

Robin snorted. Back in the living room, they found only one ornament on the floor, a little mouse made of felt, not much different from the catnip mice Robin bought for her furry companions. "Enough of that nonsense," she said, turning off the detector.

"Could I see that?" Foxy turned the motion detector over in her hands. It was white plastic and looked similar to the night light she'd installed in the hallway outside her apartment. "This looks pretty fancy for a beeper."

"We're not even using its full technology," Robin said. "Brad wondered why it was so expensive and then we read the directions and found out you can hook it up to the computer and conduct surveillance from a remote place."

"Wow!"

"I know. It's invasive. The clerk was telling Brad how you can check up on the babysitter or see what your kids are doing when you're not home."

"What a strange society we live in! That's horrible!"

"It doesn't seem so immoral if your kids have four legs and fur coats, though, does it? If cats ever unionize, I'm sure they'll outlaw spy cameras," she said.

Foxy, who'd been preoccupied and cheerless since she'd arrived, started laughing. And just as quickly, her laughter turned to tears.

Robin put an arm around her and gave her shoulder a squeeze. "Listen, we're all here for you. You know that."

Foxy inclined her head to rest against the top of Robin's. "I don't want to ruin your beautiful meal. Can we please not talk about this today?"

"Oh, c'mon, Foxy, you've just had some bad news, and you need to talk about it. What's more important? When the others get here—"

Foxy shook her head vehemently. "No, not over lunch. Promise me."

Robín acquiesced. "We'll eat, open presents, and then we'll talk, okay?"

B y the time the others arrived, Foxy had sponged her face with cold water, reapplied makeup and had found her smile. Robin had to wonder how many times, in her former profession, Foxy had had to stuff down feelings and put on her show face for a roomful of strangers.

The women of the book club were all seated at the table. Grace wore the cowl-necked sweater she'd been kitting for months. "I'm going to be gauche and cover myself," she said, looking at the bowl of butternut squash soup in front of her and draping a large napkin over the cream-colored wool.

"Are you feeling okay?" Robin said to Grace, noticing the dark circles under her eyes.

Grace rolled her eyes. "I'm exhausted. You would be too if you slept with Fred."

Robin raised her eyebrows.

"Wait, that didn't come out right. Fred snores. That's all I meant, and yet I'm the one who's going to have a sleep study to see why I wake up tired every day."

"Might as well rule out anything else," said Robin.

Louise gave a little moan as she lifted her spoon to inhale the rich aroma of the soup. She took a sip and moaned again. "This is liquid velvet." For all the years Louise had lived in Minnesota, she still had a hint of southern in her speech.

"It's nothing elaborate, I swear," Robin said. "It's just squash and chestnuts, a tiny bit of cream, some—"

"Nothing elaborate?" Grace swiped her hand in front of her to indicate the dishes, decorations, linens, and food. "It makes me tired just thinking about putting all this together."

"You always make a sumptuous feast," Louise said.

There was a time Robin might have felt guilty about this comment, as if preparing a nice dinner were not only decadent, but socially irresponsible. After all, there were women who didn't have the time or money to entertain, and who fed their families by picking up takeout on the way home from work.

Never mind that her own childhood had had its hardships, or that she'd worked hard to support Brad in med school. The only time she'd ever questioned her lot in life was when she'd had good fortune. Then a few years ago, a young immigrant woman at her church had said to her, "You say, 'why me?' only when you have plenty, yet for the bad, you don't grumble. You must take all, good and bad. It is what God gives." It had been an epiphany to Robin.

She looked around the table now and knew she was fortunate indeed to claim these women as friends.

"Please don't tell me you replicated all the food in the book!" Grace snatched up her copy of A Christmas Carol, opening it where she'd placed a sticky tab, and read. "Heaped up on the floor, to form a kind of throne, were turkeys, geese, game, poultry, brawn—" She interrupted herself to say her annotated version defined brawn as boar's meat. She continue, "great joints of meat, suckling-pigs—"

"Stop," Cate begged. "I will not sit on a meat throne, and I refuse to eat suckling pig!"

"Wreathes of sausages, mince-pies, plum-puddings, barrels of oysters, red-hot chestnuts, cherry-cheeked apples—" Grace stopped and said, "Dickens sounds like a food critic for the Times."

"He was," Robin said, straight-faced. "Well, the London version anyway. They called it The Best of Times and The Worst of Times."

Grace looked at her over the top of her reading glasses. There was a collective groan.

"The Victorians were way over the top, but I love doing this at Christmas," Cate said, fingering the grosgrain ribbons festooning the centerpiece of holly and red roses.

Louise, who routinely helped herself to an endless supply of treasures at the antique store she owned, wore a gem-encrusted comb in her champagne-colored hair. "I love that era! The dresses with the wasp waists and voluminous skirts, the gold lockets and lace gloves—Gawd, it was all so grand back then," she drawled.

"Okay, Louise, you can be the ghost of Christmas Past," Grace said. "I'd like to toast the Christmas Present and our hostess." She raised her glass of sherry and they all clinked. "And, Cate, how about if you use your powers to tell us about Christmas Yet to Come."

All eyes turned to Cate, who raised an eyebrow. Her fingers automatically curled around the turquoise amulet that always hung around her neck.

They waited expectantly.

Cate inclined her head and with a dramatic flair, said, "At her next checkup, Robin will be told the doctors can do nothing to cure her sick sense of humor."

"Hey!" said Robin.

Still looking very serious, Cate said, "Grace will have to make the decision whether or not to retire early, and Louise will postpone a business decision." She bit her lower lip.

"Go on," said Foxy.

"Foxy's love life will get . . . complicated." Quickly, she added, "And she'll live happily ever after."

Foxy skewed her mouth to the side. "I don't believe in fairytale endings."

Cate stared into the candle. "Okay then, your life will have normal ups and downs like the rest of us. But after the holidays, you'll have a long rest."

"A long rest?" Louise slapped her palm on the table. "Good Gawd, you make it sound like she's gonna take a dirt nap." She switched to a Jersey accent, or at least her southern version of one. "Youse sayin' she's gonna sleep wit' da fishes?"

Foxy's veneer looked like it was about to crack.

"Of course she doesn't mean that," Robin said, fixing Cate with a look. "Who doesn't want to rest after the holidays, right? What about your own future, Cate?"

Cate dabbed her lips with her napkin. "You know I can't read my own destiny. If I could, it would mean I've made all my dumb decisions on purpose."

The oven timer buzzed, and Robin excused herself. She came back with clean china plates, each one holding an individual beef Wellington, a Duchess potato, and a mound of glazed carrots with walnuts. On each side plate, she placed two bacon-wrapped sea scallops with a sprig of rosemary.

When they'd finished the main course, Robin turned the warm, freshly-steamed plum pudding out on a platter, doused it liberally with brandy and touched a match to it. Even in the afternoon light, they could see blue flames dance around the dark mound. It smelled heavenly. Robin cut generous portions, passing each plate to Cate for an added dollop of hard sauce.

"It's just like the book," Grace managed to say, even though her mouth was full of the sweet, spicy dessert.

Robin said, "It's as authentic as I could make it. All the recipes called for raisins instead of plums, and I finally discovered real plum pudding is not pudding and it isn't made with plums, but raisins."

"Someone should teach proper English to those Brits." Eyes twinkling, Louise gave an indignant shake of her head.

Once the table was cleared, they retired to the living room to open presents—flannel scarves, leather journals, glass wine stoppers, bracelets, and etched vases. When there was nothing left to unwrap, Foxy's fingers twirled around strands of curling ribbon in her lap, a far-off look in her eyes.

Robin knew she was preparing to unburden herself.

In the entryway, a cell phone rang. Foxy blinked, shook her head and rushed to find her purse among the four black handbags near the door. Clawing through it, she snatched up her phone.

* * *

IT WAS TINA.

Foxy had hoped to escape the unending speculation about Sierra, if only for a couple of hours, but it was not to be.

"First it was Big Al, and now Sierra." Tina's voice was tight.

It was true. Sierra had not been the first of them to die. The first had been Tina's former boyfriend, the one they all referred to as Big Al. For months no one had a clue where he'd gone, and then one day Vinnie called Tina out of the blue to tell her Big Al was dead.

"And you think there's a connection?" Although Foxy had wondered that herself, she found it even more unsettling that Tina saw the connection too. Whatever Tina's former boyfriend had been up to in the months after their breakup, he'd somehow wound up dead, the victim of a hit and run. His body had been found in the old downtown area of the city, not far from where they'd found the money a year earlier. There had been sixty-two dollars in his wallet, the newspaper reported, and a Nevada driver's license. The driver of the car that hit him had never been found. At the time, there had been a flurry of phone calls among the five remaining friends, and

37

the concern had quickly escalated to paranoia. But then years passed and the subject of Big Al's death didn't come up any more.

"I'm absolutely convinced she didn't take her own life," Tina said, "And I don't think the killer's going to stop with her, do you?"

They'd been through this all last night. "I don't know what to think." Foxy, certain her friends were listening in the other room, struggled to stay grounded. "Please, let's not jump to conclusions," she pleaded.

"You'll jump to the same conclusion when I tell you this. Sierra told me she was afraid someone might kill her. She got pretty obsessed about it in the past few weeks."

Foxy said, "Just a minute," and took the phone into the sunroom for privacy. "Is that why she moved to Minnesota?"

"No, it happened after she moved. She thought someone was stalking her."

"Why would she think that?" In their dancing days, they'd all dealt with overzealous audience members who fantasized about one showgirl or another. Sierra had had more than her share of obsessed fans. The bouncers dealt with those guys.

"It started out with hang-up calls."

Foxy's mouth went dry.

"At first she thought it was her son's friends pranking him, but then a few days before she died, she woke up in the middle of the night and felt a presence—that's how she put it. She felt a presence next to her bed. She screamed, and when her son came in to check on her, nobody was there."

"What?" It came out as a hoarse whisper.

Evidently Tina and Sierra had talked about that incident at length, and Sierra had refused to call the police, saying it would be pointless. With no signs of tampering and nothing missing, she'd said, they'd blow her off as just one more hysterical woman, afraid of sleeping alone.

"She never said a word to me," said Foxy, stung by the exclusion.

"She didn't say anything to Wylie or Vinnie either."

"Do all of you talk to Vinnie?" It came out louder than she'd intended.

"We talk sometimes."

"I really need to get back to my friends," Foxy said.

\* \* \*

ROBIN SAW FOXY'S SHOULDERS slump. Her voice carried into the living room.

"Vinnie!" Robin said to Cate. "I knew it started with a V."

When Foxy returned, Louise asked what was wrong. Foxy eased herself into the chair as if she were in physical pain, her mouth twisting to one side as she looked at the four pairs of eyes focused on hers.

"What is it, sugar? You can tell us," Louise persisted. "What we lack in worldly experience, we make up for . . . well, by giving a damn."

For so many years Foxy had tucked her past away from them all. Robin wondered if she would ever let her guard down. But then, looking at their concerned faces, Foxy must have decided there was no longer any point in keeping secrets. With no further coaxing, she began talking as though she couldn't get the words out fast enough. They bubbled out of her in fits and starts. First she told them about Sierra's death, and then backed up to tell about Sierra's life, starting with the more recent years.

After dancing in Las Vegas, Sierra had worked in California for years, and then suddenly she'd moved to Minnesota over the past summer and rented a house in Rochester. Her son, Beau, was in high school. Foxy thought he was a junior or senior, not the ideal time to pull a kid out of school and move across the country so he'd have to finish out high school with strangers.

"Sierra just up and moved one day," she continued. "She told us about it after the fact, and never really explained why. I was so excited having her here in Minnesota after all these years, but when I said I wanted to get together, she kind of blew me off." Foxy explained how she'd arranged meetings twice, once in Rochester and once in St. Paul, but both times Sierra had cancelled at the last minute. "I kept trying, though," Foxy said, unable to hide her emotions.

As she talked, it became apparent Foxy had talked to her friend Tina in Portland after hearing the horrible news about Sierra, and after piecing together what they knew, they'd become fearful. Robin, for one, wanted to know why.

Foxy clenched her fists on her thighs, and said, "I don't care what Sierra's father believes. He says she left a note, but when he told me what it said, I thought it could have meant a lot of things other than a suicide note."

Cate jumped in. "What did it say?"

"Something like 'I'm sorry. I have no other choice.' But how could she kill herself? She'd never leave her son. I just don't believe she'd do that, and neither does Tina."

Louise, an anachronism in her pre-Victorian jewelry and clothing, checked the time on her cell phone. She leaned forward, fixing Foxy with a look. "You think it was an accident, like maybe she was sitting in the car with the engine running and fell asleep or passed out or something?"

Foxy looked at her with wet eyes. "I think someone killed her."

Her audience of four glanced around to see how others heard that comment.

Louise reached out and took Foxy's hand. She spoke slowly, her Southern accent more drawn out than usual. "I think we're all a little jumpy after getting involved in those two little incidents—"

"You can say the word, Louise," Grace interrupted. "Murders." She stifled a yawn, which was out of context, considering the gravity of what they were discussing. "We got involved in murders. Solving them, I mean."

Louise nodded sagely. "Yes, sure. But, honey child, there are explanations other than murder."

Grace nodded. "She's right. We can't jump to conclusions."

They all asked questions at once. Had Sierra been working in Rochester? Was there a new man in her life? Could she have gotten married recently? Did she have family in Minnesota? What was to become of the boy? Had Sierra been ill? Might she have moved to Rochester to be close to the Mayo Clinic?

Foxy answered as best she could, but for most of the questions, she had to admit she simply did not know. She had no idea if Sierra was working in Minnesota. She'd never married, although there'd been a few men in her life over the years. The only boyfriend Foxy actually knew was Wylie, but Wylie and Sierra hadn't been together for years. She thought they were still in contact, though.

Grace asked about the funeral, suggesting a trip to Rochester might answer some of the unknowns. Robin suggested talking to the son or Sierra's parents might shed some light. "Alexandria is only a couple hours away," Louise reminded her.

"There's not going to be a funeral, just a memorial service in a couple of months," Foxy told them, explaining that Sierra's parents, who had to be in their seventies, were still staggering from the kind of heartache no parent ever recovers from. And now, in the midst of their grief, they had to make arrangements for their grandson. Foxy didn't know if the parents still lived in Iowa and had a summer place in Alexandria, or if they'd retired to the quiet little resort town. Either way, poor Beau was going to have major adjustments to living with grandparents. As were they. "You hear about that all the time—retired people raising their grandkids—but can you imagine?" Foxy said.

"What about the father?" asked Cate. "I can't keep all these names straight."

"It's Wylie. Wylie and Sierra were a couple, Tina was with Big Al, and I was with Vinnie."

"Why wouldn't Wylie take Beau?"

Foxy shook her head. A tear rolled down her cheek, and she caught it with the tip of her tongue when it got to the corner of her mouth. "Wylie hasn't been in the picture for a long time. I totally understand why he and Sierra broke up, but I always thought it was wrong he didn't stick around for Beau."

Cate tipped the last of the wine into her glass and swirled it, mesmerized by the blood-red cabernet. Robin knew that look. Cate was trying to get under the words and understand the bigger situation.

Robin studied the faces of her friends. Their compassion for Foxy was obvious. So was frank interest in a past that was so different from their own. But what Robin was witnessing went beyond mild curiosity. She felt a chill when she recognized they had already been swept into the intrigue of Sierra's death.

A loud clattering in the kitchen startled them. Robin leapt to her feet to see what new mayhem the cats had perpetrated, and instead saw Brad picking up a stack of cups he'd knocked over. "How long have you been in here?" she asked, noticing the conversation in the other room had shifted, suddenly and deftly, to recipes.

Pivoting to face her, Brad ran a hand through his hair. "Just long enough to be concerned."

She laughed, not out of mirth, but to put him at ease. "There's nothing to worry about, Brad. Foxy was just telling us about an old friend of hers who died."

"So I gathered."

She hugged him and put her mouth close to his ear. "She just needs to talk about it, that's all."

"That's all? You forget I know you, Robin Bentley. When did you ever leave it at that?" He pressed his lips together and stared at her with weary eyes.

He had a point. In the first year of their marriage, she'd gotten involved volunteering with a missing persons support group. Her intense interest in the subject ran deep, and had led her, over the years, to many a sleepless night. Her volunteer work was, of course, a way of dealing with her own father kidnaping her in the midst of a custody battle, and Brad had understood that her supporting others whose children were missing had been an important part of restoring normalcy in her own life.

At some point, though, she'd needed to get beyond her own trauma, and just about the time she'd decided to pull back from the volunteer work, events had sucked her back in. She and her friends had found a body below the waterfall on the Bentley's property in Wisconsin, and Robin had been thrust right back into sleepless nights. Not to mention she'd very nearly lost her life. Twice.

Brad's eyes were still focused on hers. If she'd seen excitement on the faces of her friends at the prospect of getting involved in another murder investigation, Brad was surely seeing it on hers.

She struggled to meet his gaze when she told him, "Don't worry. We're not going to get involved in anything stupid."

"When have I heard that before?" He ran his fingertips over the stubble on his jaw. His Adam's apple bobbed in his throat.

"Please don't worry. I know our book club has gotten into a little trouble in the past, and I appreciate your concern." She stopped long enough to pull him toward her so she could kiss him on the cheek. "I really do hear you, but for all we've done that was stupid, you know my friends and I always help each other out of whatever mess we get ourselves into."

His shoulders sagged. "Jesus, Robin, not again!"

**H**e drove around the block, looking for a parking spot. On top of the "NO PARKING" signs, the streets were totally hosed up because of the snow, and he was getting more pissed by the minute. He finally found a place a block and a half away from her house, where one whole side of the street was empty and parked as close to the curb as the massive snowbank allowed.

If possible, it was even colder than yesterday. He'd taken off in such a hurry, he hadn't even thought about dressing for goddamned Antarctica. Slipping and sliding on the sidewalk, he made his way back to Foxy's house. Once more, he went through the screened porch to ring her bell, and once more, no one answered. It occurred to him she could well be home and refusing to answer the bell.

This time, though, he wasn't leaving until he had her in his sights. If it got any colder, he might just have to call her and if she didn't hang up on him, he'd let her know he wasn't leaving until he saw her face to face. He rattled the door handle and pounded, but it was futile. Pressing a button on his cell phone, he realized the battery was dead. He checked his pocket for cigarettes, and then remembered leaving the pack in his car. Sitting down in the wicker chair, he waited. He watched a cadre of snowplows go past, scraping the streets and piling up even more snow at the curb.

After a while his face was numb and his toes were burning with cold, and he cursed his own stupidity for coming unprepared for the weather in this god-forsaken place. Standing to scan the streets before leaving, he was relieved there was no black SUV in sight.

He was pretty sure his feet were frozen. He slipped and slid back to where he'd left his car, or at least to the place he remembered leaving it. But there wasn't a single car parked on that side of the street. He swiveled his neck back and forth, looking to see if he'd gone down the wrong street, but no, it had been right there, where that— He approached the big white mound, which, on closer inspection, was a mess of fluffy and hard-packed snow laced with mud and ice where his car had been.

He clawed at the mound that encased his car until his hands were raw, realizing he wasn't going to dig the blasted thing out with his bare hands. What he needed was a jackhammer. "I'm so screwed," he muttered to himself as he made his way back to Foxy's. He waved and yelled at the lone man up ahead who was pushing a snow blower, but the guy didn't look up.

After going back to the front door and determining she still wasn't home, he tromped around between the houses where someone had worn a crooked path in the snow. At the corner of the house, he hooked around to find the back door steps covered in a foot of snow. He pounded and tried the handle, but it was just as tightly locked as the one in front.

Turning his attention to the single small window just to the left of the door, he peeked through it and saw a shovel leaning against the inside wall. So close and yet so far. He groaned, and then, as an idea occurred to him, he pulled out his Swiss Army knife. "Little Miss Foxy," he said through chattering teeth. "You are in more trouble than you know." His fingers ached from the cold as he opened the knife and slipped its blade through the crack at the top of the little window. As he'd hoped, it was held shut with a simple latch, which he knocked aside easily with his blade. The window opened right away. Standing on the tips of his icy toes, he stuck his hand through the opening and felt around. The lower edge of the window frame cut into his armpit, but he pushed harder until finally his fingers touched the round doorknob. With a little more exertion he was able to turn it until he felt and heard it click.

Once inside, he took a moment to get his bearings. He was standing in what appeared to be a mudroom or storage room. It had a musty, old-house smell. The shovel and a broom, he now saw, leaned against the wall under a pair of jumper cables hanging from a bracket. Terra cotta pots full of dirt were stacked precariously in the corner. A makeshift set of shelves held pantry items—paper products, oversized cans, jars, bottles. He spied a bottle of Canadian whisky, the seal unbroken. Not his drink of choice, but it would go a long way to warming him up from the inside out.

One hand was on the shovel handle, but his eye was on the bottle. The idea of going back into the wintry weather made him remember how brain-numbingly cold he was. Shivering, he looked at the crumbling concrete stairs leading to the basement, and the wooden stairs inviting him to go upstairs into the warmth. He grabbed the whisky and started up the wooden steps.

* * *

THE SUN LOWERED IN THE SKY and street lights went on, and still Foxy talked. Surrounded by her friends, she looked at Robin's Christmas decorations and reminisced out loud about the Christmas she'd brought Sierra with her to Pine Glen. Foxy hadn't spent a holiday with her family in a while, and her parents were pushing pretty hard for her to come home. She'd agreed, bracing herself to get an earful about her life in Sin City.

Since she and Vinnie had just started dating, it was way too soon to do the whole family thing, so she'd asked Sierra to make the trip with her. "I don't know what I was thinking," Foxy said to her book club friends. "It wasn't a disaster, exactly, but I can't say anyone had a jolly Christmas. I warned her right up front that my family was already praying for my soul and would probably be praying for hers, too." She laughed drily. "But Sierra had this romantic idea about having snow at Christmas." Foxy's eyes threatened to spill over with tears as she remembered that trip. "I had ulterior motives inviting her," Foxy admitted. She'd wanted to play matchmaker. Her brother Matt had dated most of the eligible girls in their small community, and since he and Sierra were close in age, she'd thought they might hit it off.

Louise interrupted. "Y'all were living such glamorous lives. What made you think Sierra would be interested in a Minnesota boy?"

"Life wasn't as glamorous as you might imagine," Foxy said. She stared down at her plate. "To be honest, I wasn't thinking so much about what Sierra might be looking for. I just wanted an ally in the family. Matt was the sweet, wholesome kid my parents raised him to be, and I guess I thought if he married Sierra, y'know someone like me, the pressure would be off of me." She wouldn't meet anyone's eyes. "I can't believe how selfish I was."

Robin said, "They were both consenting adults."

Even though she'd always felt responsible for her younger brother's well-being, Foxy conceded he'd been old enough at the time to make his own decisions. "Sierra thought Matt was pretty hot, actually," she said.

Sierra was an exotic mix of Irish, Puerto Rican, and Lebanese, and, according to Foxy, people couldn't take their eyes off her. "All Matt said about her was that he thought she seemed 'nice enough.' Don't you think that's an odd way to describe a gorgeous, leggy creature like Sierra?"

They nodded.

Foxy, though, confessed she hadn't given up trying to get them together, even after that trip. When Matt moved up north to take a job as an outdoor adventure guide in Ely, she'd tried once more. She and Sierra had flown into Minneapolis, where they'd rented a car and driven to the resort where Matt worked, up near the Canadian border. They'd stayed for two whole weeks that summer, and Foxy studied Sierra and Matt together, eager to detect any sign of a spark. Matt took them hiking and fishing and taught Sierra how to paddle a canoe. "One day Sierra even played shuffleboard in a string bikini and high-heeled sandals," Foxy said, "but nothing came of it. He was a perfect gentleman, but the chemistry just wasn't right."

Grace chortled. "I raised my boys to be respectful, but I don't delude myself. They're still men, and even though they're respectful, that's a lot of temptation to resist." She looked at her friends, raising her hands as if entreating them to agree with her. "I mean, what young man wouldn't be thrilled to have a sexy dancer throwing herself at him?"

"A gay one," Louise said, and immediately put her fingers to her lips. "I'm sorry, Foxy. I forgot we're talking about your brother."

Foxy sighed loudly. "No, you're exactly right. My brother hid it for years. By the time he actually told me a year or so after that visit, I'd figured it out. I didn't care about him being gay. I guess I got my way, because from then on he was my ally in the family. I had his back, too. When he came out to our parents, I went with him as backup."

"I'm guessing that didn't go well," said Louise. She repositioned her jewel-encrusted comb to catch a stray lock of hair.

Foxy gave a mirthless laugh. "You guess right. At first they tried to talk him out of being gay, and when that didn't work, they sent him to the pastor to talk him out of it. Pastor Paul had that "love the sinner, hate the sin" creed, and he did his best to pray poor Matt straight." Foxy spoke softly about her brother, but it was easy to see she carried a sense of outrage still as she said, "Matt came away from the experience convinced he didn't deserve to be loved."

When there was a pause, Robin turned the topic back to Sierra. "If you and Sierra were so close back then, what happened?"

Foxy shrugged. "We all moved away, and—I don't know, it just changed. Sierra got more and more—" She searched for a word.

"Reclusive?" Louise suggested.

Foxy stared at her fingernails, which she kept short because of her work as a massage therapist. "Not reclusive," she said to her hands. "I guess our lives just changed in different directions. She was awfully wrapped up in her son. And maybe it's because she was a mother, and I never—" She stopped to blow her nose. "After we all went in different directions, she stopped sharing things like we used to. She didn't tell much about her life in California, and didn't want to talk about the time we were all together in Nevada, either. I don't know . . . it was almost like she thought our dancing days were shameful. Whatever it was, it drove a wedge between us."

"What's shameful about dancing?" Louise said. She put a hand over her heart as she spoke. "Honey, if I'd been gorgeous and talented enough, I'd have taken great pride in doing what y'all did." The others agreed.

"We never talked about why things changed between us. It's a shame, because there aren't many people who could understand that part of my life."

Grace said, "You know you can always talk to us."

Foxy gave a small, sad smile and shook her head. "What can I say about being a Las Vegas showgirl to people who could never, in a million years, imagine doing such a thing? I mean, Sierra and Tina were my partners in crime."

Cate raised an eyebrow, which did not escape Robin's notice.

Taking a deep breath, Foxy seemed to come to a decision. "Okay, there's more to it. I think Sierra's death might be related to something in her past. In our past, actually."

The women were utterly silent.

"It could be nothing. Maybe she even died accidentally, but Tina and I both think it's related to something else that happened the night we went out to celebrate Wylie's birthday. It was a lifetime ago."

The next part of her story poured out of her. Wylie and Sierra were seriously dating at the time, and several of the dancers and their boyfriends decided to go to the Flamingo for cocktails. Sierra was pregnant at the time, although Foxy couldn't remember if anyone else knew it. It was after their last show, which meant it was sometime after two in the morning. From the Flamingo, six of them had left together and went on to another casino off the strip. It was in the old downtown, closer to where they all lived. Even though they weren't looking for trouble, they had been drinking, especially Wylie. Vinnie, Foxy's husband at the time, was also feeling no pain.

The book club women had known almost nothing about Foxy's "ex" until now, and eagerly listened to what she had to say about Vinnie.

"Vinnie and I had our problems, obviously, or we'd still be together." Foxy held her hand up, as if warding off any comments. "But that night everyone was just having a good time. Wylie was a harmless drunk. I don't know where he got it, but he was wearing a stupid paper Burger King crown that night. Outside the casino, there was this yellow Lamborghini, and we started goofing around, posing in front of it like we were the kind of people with money to buy a car like that." A tear ran down her cheek. "God, we were so innocent!"

Robin couldn't imagine where this story was headed, but she, along with the others, hung on her every word.

Foxy finally got around to telling them about the man who careened around the corner on foot, dropping a cooler bag, literally at their feet, and dashing out into the street where he was shot dead while they watched.

"How awful," said Robin and Cate together.

Foxy shifted as if she couldn't get comfortable. "We were all catatonic. We just stood there, horrified." There was pain in her voice. "We actually saw a man get murdered, and we didn't do a thing." She sniffed and looked away, adding, "No, that's not true. We ran away."

They sat in stunned silence.

Finally Cate spoke. "What was in the cooler bag?"

Foxy didn't meet their eyes. Shrugging, she said, "I don't know. Wylie never told us."

Robin shot a look at Cate, who raised an eyebrow at her. "He never told you?" Robin asked, incredulous.

"Well, actually, he claimed it was a chicken salad sandwich, but nobody believed him." Foxy laughed nervously and stood up, effectively ending the conversation.

They all sensed the party was over. Louise stood to leave. Grace got up too, and reminded Robin about their early morning choir rehearsal before worship.

Robin groaned. She'd been so engrossed in Foxy's story, she'd forgotten all about it.

As Foxy zipped up her boots, Robin said, "Wait a minute. I want you to take something." She came back with the motion detector, pressing it into Foxy's hand. "I'll feel better if you'd take this. Put it somewhere in your hall or your porch. Not in your apartment, or your animals will set it off."

"Really?" Foxy said, but the way she gripped the plastic device told Robin she'd done the right thing.

"Really. You'll sleep better knowing it's there."

"I'm just down the street if you need me," Cate reminded her. "And you'll have Molly Pat, the Nancy Drew of the dog world, to keep you safe."

Foxy laughed, but her eyes welled with tears. "Thank you," she said huskily. She wrapped a scarf about her and made her way down the shoveled walk and into her car. Cate and Robin watched until the engine purred to life and she drove off.

Cate let out a pent up breath. "I hope you're not kicking me out too."

"Are you kidding? If you have as many thoughts bouncing around in your head right now as I do, it's going to be a long evening."

They sat together on the loveseat facing the Christmas tree. The sun had completely dropped from view.

"I don't know where to begin," said Cate, leaning back, her long legs stretched out in front of her.

Robin curled her legs under her and pulled an afghan from the back of the loveseat to drape over their laps. "That was quite a story," she said. "But I don't think it's the whole story, do you?"

Cate shook her head. "Nope. She's holding something back."

"She talked about how terrified they were that they'd been seen, and yet they grabbed whatever the dead guy dropped. Did she really expect us to believe they never found out what was in the cooler? I mean, why even bring it up if she was just going to lie about it?"

"I'm thinking the same thing. I've never thought of Foxy as a liar, but she's definitely hiding something. Either she did something she's ashamed of, or she really believes whoever killed that guy will track her down and kill her too."

"Or both."

"Or both. Does that even seem plausible to you?"

Cate considered before answering. "It does seem far-fetched, but then who would've guessed any part of what Foxy just told us? Just because something sounds weird doesn't mean it can't happen."

Robin nodded. "Life is weird. Just think about our last couple of years, Cate. Who'd have predicted the messes we got ourselves into?"

Grinning, Cate said, "Yeah, but we get points for getting ourselves out of them, don't we?"

Robin chuckled. "Exactly what I told Brad."

The two of them spent the next hour cooking up scenarios, each one more outrageous than the last, to explain Foxy's behavior, beginning with whatever was in the cooler.

"I think it was jewelry," Robin suggested. "They saw the cat burglar get killed by the man he robbed, and it took the victim-slash-murderer seventeen years to figure out who the witnesses were and now," she said, lowering her voice ominously, "he's picking them off one by one."

"Why would he kill the witnesses if he's the one who got robbed?"

"Because they saw him kill the thief. Maybe the killer isn't really a victim. Maybe he's part of a huge ring of international jewel thieves, who won't quit until they find the, the—"

"The Pink Panther diamond!" Cate said.

"Exactly!"

"No, I think it was a mob hit. I think the guy ran off with some-one's head in the bag." Cate pulled the afghan up under her chin.

Robin made a face, but eagerly added, "Yes! And they recognized the face! Foxy and her friends are the only ones in the world, other than the mobster who killed him, who know what happened to Jimmy Hoffa!"

"Right! And now she's in the witness protection program."

They stopped talking when Brad passed the open door.

Robin lowered her voice. "Maybe it was money, lots of it, and they split it, but now one of them wants it all and is killing off the others."

Suddenly sobered, Cate said, "That's actually possible. There's a name for that, where you get a bunch of people to buy shares, and then as each investor dies, their share gets split among the survivors."

"Right! It was in that book by Robert Louis Stevenson." Robin searched her memory. "It's called a tontine."

"Yes! And you know what happened to the investors in *The Wrong Box?*"

**B**efore going inside, Foxy paused on her front walk. She saw tracks in the snow where the young men who rented an apartment next door routinely cut through between the buildings. She felt suddenly alone. With the upstairs renter gone and the landlord on a cruise, the house felt cavernous and a little spooky. But of course she had her pets. Molly Pat would let her know if something was wrong.

She walked up the steps. Passing through the porch, she glanced to make sure the blue ashtray was empty. Sniffing the air, she detected no odor of cigarettes. She let out her pent-up breath and mounted the stairs. Even before she reached the second floor she could hear Elvis howling. He had a large repertoire of words, as far as cat vocabularies went, and what he was saying now was no pleasant greeting. She had a sick feeling as she unlocked the door and opened it. Elvis stood in the middle of the living room, his black tail bushed out like a Halloween cat's. It was the feline equivalent of having the hair stand up on the back of the neck, which was exactly what Foxy experienced, looking at him.

Molly Pat rushed to lick her outstretched hand and whined. "What on earth?" Foxy muttered. "You two act like you're possessed."

After a few minutes they were all a little calmer. Foxy grabbed a throw blanket and plunked down in her new, lime-green recliner. Closing her eyes, she did her best to shake off all thoughts of Sierra and her appalling death.

Elvis jumped into her lap. As she ran her hands over the cat's fur, she remembered the day she'd found the scrawny kitten almost nineteen years ago. More accurately, the kitten had found her one night when she'd stepped out the back door for a cigarette between sets. She'd watched him slither through the narrow opening of an overfull Dumpster and come out with something in his mouth. That cat was no bigger than the rats she'd seen hanging around the garbage. The next night she'd waited for him and tossed him some shrimp from the buffet. The black kitten waited at the back door for a handout each night for a week, and since she could hardly leave him there on her nights off, she took him home.

Her husband, Vinnie, named him Elvis. Sometimes they called him the King. When it was time for her to leave Las Vegas, the alley cat was pretty much all she took with her, and although it seemed unkind to deprive Vinnie of the cat's company, it was the way it had to be. She figured Elvis was as sick of life on the Strip as she was.

The King was definitely in his Fat Elvis stage now. In cat years, he was much older than she was, and sometimes she looked at him and felt a pang, imagining the day he wouldn't be around. Only recently, she'd noticed Elvis was sporting a few gray hairs on his face. As for her own gray hairs, she'd colored them with henna for so long she almost forgot she had any.

Foxy turned on the TV for distraction, but the only words she heard were in her head as she played and replayed the phone call from Tina in an endless loop. Until Tina had called her during the book club lunch, Foxy could pretend her fears were unfounded, but now there was no such delusion.

Replaying that call in her head, Foxy felt prickles of fear crawling up her neck. From where she sat in her recliner, her eyes played across her living room. She peered into the shadow made by her bookshelf. The flickering of the television as it flashed on the walls made her jumpy. She shut off the television and opened the refrigerator. Even though she'd had wine at Robin's house, she decided to pour herself a glass of chardonnay.

Sleep didn't come easily to her that night, but after sipping a glass of wine and listening to music, Foxy finally succumbed, only to be wakened by Elvis pawing her arm and yowling. She opened one eye to look at the clock. It was three eighteen. "I'm not feeding you in the middle of the night," she scolded.

The cat's ears perked up. He turned his head toward the back of the house. Foxy strained to hear whatever had caught his attention. "It's just the guys next door, Elvis. Please let me sleep."

She shut her eyes and began to drift back to sleep. In that strange state between consciousness and unconsciousness, she sensed the cat staring at her from the foot of the bed. And then she remembered Sierra was dead. After getting hang-up calls. Paralyzed by the thought it might not be Elvis looking at her, she lay perfectly still, listening to the beating of her heart. When she was able to move again, she flung the bedding aside, leapt to her feet and snapped on her bedside lamp.

She was alone in her room.

* * *

WAKING FROM A FRETFUL SLEEP, Tina held the phone to her ear and looked at the alarm clock on her nightstand before answering. When she heard who it was, she said, "Wylie, it's after one in the morning." She waited for him to say something and watched the rain coursing down her bedroom window.

Wylie's voice was heavy with despair. It was fair to assume he was taking Sierra's death even harder than she was. He rambled on about how much he'd loved Sierra, and how guilty he felt that their last phone call had gotten ugly. "She even asked if I was stalking her.

How could she actually think that, after all we've been through? I mean, for the love of God!"

Wylie and Sierra had been crazy about each other once, but they could never stay together for more than a few months. And yet they hadn't been able to live apart for more than a few months, either. "She didn't really suspect you. She was just looking for any explanation other than—" Words caught in her throat. "Other than the mafia."

After a long pause, he said, "I know. Vinnie said something like that, too."

"Are we crazy to think her death has anything to do with that night? It was so long ago." Tina was now wide awake. She turned on lights. Padding into the kitchen for a glass of water, she shivered as she felt a gust of cold air.

The night they'd witnessed a man get gunned down passed before her eyes, as it often did. She wanted to rewind the movie in her head, back to the moment they exited the casino. Wylie had made a joke about a blonde, a brunette, and a redhead. She was still blonde, Foxy was still a redhead, and Sierra was dead.

"Well, Vinnie took it seriously," Wylie said. "especially when I said Sierra thought she was being stalked."

"Foxy thinks she's being stalked, too!" Tina blurted out.

A long pause. "You didn't tell her about Sierra's stalker, did you?"

"Of course. I had to warn her." Sitting at the kitchen table, Tina scratched her ankle, noticing a new varicose vein. Her toes, stuffed for too many years into all sorts of dance shoes, sported callouses and painful twisted joints.

Wylie used his big, angry voice. "Didn't you say she's dating a cop?"

"A sheriff," she corrected. "I know, but maybe he can help us."

"Yeah? And maybe he can hurt us. If he starts snooping around, he's just gonna stir things up. He asks a few questions of the wrong people, and pretty soon some mobbed-up cop in Nevada gets us all killed."

"I had to tell her about the stalker, Wylie," she said again.

There was a grunt on the other end.

"Foxy warned us, way back then. Don't you think we should warn her?"

"Yeah." His voice cracked. "I suppose you're right. I told Vinnie too. He knows better than anyone what those people can do."

"I know." Sierra remembered all too well.

"They hurt him bad. Thing is, they didn't get what they were after. You think they're gonna let that go?"

"They did let it go. For years." Bare branches of her Pacific willow slapped against the kitchen window. The damp winter air seeped into her bones. "Even the mob would've given up by now!"

"You got a better explanation?"

Well, that was really the crux of it. Maybe Sierra really had committed suicide. Maybe she'd just picked up some small town stalker with a crush on her who killed her. Maybe it had nothing to do with the rest of them. And maybe Big Al's death had been a simple hit and run. As long as Sierra had been the only one being stalked, there were explanations that didn't involve her and Wylie and Foxy and Vinnie.

But now, no matter how she looked at it, there was only one story that bound them all together. When they'd counted out the cash in the cooler bag, each of them had walked away with over a hundred thousand dollars. Not chump change to anyone.

She still remembered the look on Vinnie's face when she and Foxy tried to convince the others to turn the money in to the police. From the moment he'd laid eyes on all that cash, the gambling fever was in his eyes. Tina had seen it and so had Foxy.

When all was said and done, Sierra was the only one who'd come out of it unscathed.

Unscathed! Tina tried not to picture her beautiful friend the way her son had found her.

It had taken Tina years before she'd put it all behind her, and now, with Sierra's death, the fear and mistrust were back. "Listen, I'm going to pack up and go stay with a friend for a while," she said. When Wylie asked where he could find her, she said, "You don't need to know."

O n Sunday morning, Grace lay in bed, sorting dream from reality and wondering if she'd concocted Foxy's story about her days in Las Vegas. She opened one eye to see her bedside clock. She could go back to sleep another fifty-seven minutes until the alarm went off, but if she were to get up now, she'd have an entire leisurely hour before having to get ready for choir practice.

If Robin was willing to get up for choir after throwing that lovely party yesterday, Grace figured she could drag herself out of bed. Grace's eyelids were heavy and her body begged for more sleep. However, there was little hope of getting any sleep now, with Fred, dear Fred, lying on his side facing her, his mouth slack as he snored loudly. He used to snore only when sleeping on his back, but lately he could make an unbelievable racket in just about any position. She wondered, only for a split second, if he'd still be able to snore with a pillow over his head.

Readjusting her ear plugs, she covered her own head with a pillow. His snoring managed to penetrate even that. It was like sleeping with a chainsaw!

Last week when she'd floated the idea of separate bedrooms, Fred had looked at her with a bemused smile, and said, "Sweetheart, you may not realize it, but I'm not the only one snoring." She'd said it couldn't possibly be as bad as the noises he made, and he'd responded, "I should record you some night. You would not believe the sounds you make."

It had been embarrassing. If what he'd said was true, she not only had to put up with his noise, but would be too self-conscious about making unladylike sounds in her sleep to get any sleep at all. Last night, she'd decided to borrow Fred's own idea. She'd dug up his digital recorder, put new batteries in it and hung it on their bedpost. Fred had never even noticed it.

She glowered at him now as he slept, lips puffing out with each exhalation—*Puh, puh, puh,* followed by a pause and then a loud snort, over and over. Snatching the recorder from the bedpost, she threw on robe and slippers and shambled into the kitchen. Measuring coffee into the filter, she couldn't believe she was upright. She felt like she could sleep through anything, and yet, obviously, she simply couldn't sleep through Fred's one-man percussion concert.

As the coffee brewed, she took the recorder into the family room, pressed a button and listened. She heard a bit of rustling, which sounded like her adjusting her pillows, and then silence. She fast-forwarded, and this time she heard labored breathing. She advanced the recording some more, and there it was, a remarkable cacophony of noises, all produced by the resonating chambers of just one man. Had she not heard him herself, she would have thought she was listening to a herd of wild boars. Hearing the flush of the toilet upstairs, she turned off the recorder. Looking for someplace to stash it, she saw her open purse and slipped it in.

Yawning, she poured two mugs of coffee and emptied a sugar packet into his and handed it to him. They read the Sunday paper while they ate their oatmeal. The *Star Tribune* was fat with Christmas ads, which Fred deposited in a messy pile in the middle of the table. Grace took a pen and marked various offerings in the Variety section, anything that might remotely appeal to her boys when they spent time at home for the holidays.

The Twin Cities of Minneapolis and St. Paul offered an impressive number of cultural events on a daily basis—theaters, galleries, music, museums, visual arts, lectures—basically anything you'd find in New York, Chicago, Los Angeles, or Boston. For years, Minneapolis had been second only to New York City in the number of either theaters or theater tickets sold per capita.

Brett was in an a cappella group in college, and so she circled some choir concerts he might enjoy. Chad's tastes ran more to graphic arts and history. She highlighted a play at the History Museum and an exhibit at the Walker Art Center.

Her husband looked over the top of the business section. "You got up early." There was an edge to his comment, and she reminded herself he'd been under a lot of work pressure.

"I had trouble sleeping."

He grunted. "You've been looking awfully tired lately. Maybe you should have your thyroid checked." He gulped the last of his coffee and stood to refill his cup.

She tried to keep her tone light. "Nope, my thyroid checks out just fine."

They swapped newspaper sections. After a few minutes, Fred said, "Did you ask the doctor about sleep apnea? You were kind of noisy again last night."

"I was noisy?" She shook her head wearily. "As a matter of fact, I did ask the doctor, and she thought I should do a sleep study. I set it up for January, but the clinic called yesterday and there's an opening Tuesday night. I said I'd take it."

He nodded, smiling. "Good."

She wanted to chip away at his smugness. Smiling back at him, she said, "When I told her your snoring was keeping me from sleeping, she said we both need to do a sleep study."

He looked at her over his glasses for a long moment, and said, "Probably not a bad idea," before he resumed reading the paper.

\* \* \*

FOXY WOKE TO THE SOUND of her phone and remembered her creeping fear last night when she sensed someone in the room. She didn't think she could deal with another hang-up call today. She rolled over and groped on the nightstand for her reading glasses, so she could see who the caller was before answering. With relief, she saw it was Bill Harley.

"Good morning, beautiful!" he said when she answered. "How are you feeling today?" They talked for a bit. He asked how she was handling news of Sierra's death, and she lied and said she was getting over the shock. Then he told her about his plans to drive to a place near Somerset, Wisconsin, later in the morning to pick up venison from his hunting buddy.

Still not fully awake, she couldn't figure out why he'd called to tell her that.

"If you're interested, I could stop by your apartment to give you some venison. Just tell me what you want—stew meat, ground venison, tenderloin . . ." He let his voice trail off when she didn't immediately answer.

"I've never cooked with venison before." For some reason, it felt like some kind of test.

"No problem. You use ground meat for chili, and cook up stew meat just like you would with beef. With venison steaks, the only trick is heating up the plates before serving."

Foxy hesitated. "I don't know, Bill." She wanted to tell him her place was haunted. The words were on the tip of her tongue. There was a long and awkward lull in the conversation as she thought about just what she did want to say.

He took her silence as a rebuff. When he spoke again, he sounded rather formal. "Maybe you just want to meet me halfway for lunch. Hudson's as good a place as any."

She peeked at the time, surprised it was already nine-thirty in the morning. She rarely had a chance to oversleep. She didn't have to open her planner to know she had no clients on a Sunday, and no other definite plans, but she said, "Uh, give me a chance to wake up and check my schedule," she told the sheriff. "I'll call you back in a few minutes."

She padded into the bathroom, where Elvis was pawing at the baseboard in the corner. She saw nothing there that should captivate his attention, but then cats were funny that way. Either Elvis was entertaining himself with imaginary gremlins, or—she made a face at the thought—there might be a mouse trapped between the walls.

She suddenly felt a sort of emotional vertigo, as if she were standing on shifting tectonic plates that represented different parts of herself. Sierra Brady was dead and Bill Harley wanted to meet for lunch—the two things could scarcely coexist in her mind, much less in her life. She felt a strong need to get away from there, but there was an equally strong desire to retreat into memories of another time, the time she and her friends were young and sparkly and full of hope. She thought about her box of old photos in the basement, and knew if she looked at them right now, she'd fall apart completely.

The last time she'd looked at old pictures, she'd thrown away all of her wedding pictures, and then cried off and on for days. That left photos of her with her friends, including Sierra. Sierra's death, Foxy thought as she wiped her fingers across her eyes, had dredged up memories she'd worked hard to quarantine.

As she scuffed into the kitchen, she felt resolute that she needed, once and for all, to embrace the life she'd made for herself. She called Bill back to tell him she'd be happy to meet him for lunch. "I haven't been out yet, but I'm sure it's frigid out there," she said, and immediately wished she hadn't used that word. That's probably exactly what he thought of her after she practically pushed him out the door two nights ago, saying that she needed to be alone.

What was it about her, she wondered, that compelled her to suffer in silence? The news of a friend's death might send other women into the arms of the men in their lives, but with Foxy, fear and grief had always made her want to wrap her own arms around herself and retreat. All things considered, she was surprised Bill had bothered to call her today at all.

"Frigid, but sunny," Bill replied, sounding a bit too sunny himself.

Before agreeing to drive across the river into Wisconsin, she opened her living room blinds to see if more snow had fallen during the night. The roads were plowed and sanded. The sky was clear and glacial blue.

"Sunny's good, and you gotta eat anyway, right?" Bill cajoled her.

She laughed. "Sunny is good. Eating is good." They talked just long enough to arrange a rendezvous at a favorite restaurant in Wisconsin.

Elvis, having finished his breakfast, now sat in front of the door, lashing his skinny black tail back and forth as Foxy fixed herself some tea. A low rumble came from the cat and his tail thrashed more vehemently. Foxy stepped over him to get close to the door.

All was quiet. She held her breath and felt prickles of fear as she listened, convinced someone lurked in the hallway. Only a few heartbeats later, at the exact moment Elvis whacked his tail against her leg, she heard muffled footsteps and the creak of a floorboard. Only one floorboard creaked, and it was between her room and the top of the stairs. She stepped back, her heart thudding so hard she thought she might pass out.

She looked around for a weapon. The only one she could think of was the shovel in the back entry. If the intruder weren't in the blasted hallway, she could run down and get it. She eyed the knife rack, but the thought of slicing and dicing her stalker meant getting close enough for him to grab the knife away.

Only then did she remember the motion detector she'd borrowed from Robin and placed at the top of the stairs, concealed by an African basket and an artificial plant. At that very moment, the device began to squeal.

She didn't scream. She didn't dial 9-1-1. She didn't call Bill back to tell him she was scared senseless, and to send the police. Any of those things would have been more intelligent than what she did. In that split second, fear and anger drove her to snatch up her big cast iron skillet and throw the door open. Wielding the skillet over her head, she rushed into the hallway with a battle cry that died in her throat.

To her left, a man in black retreated down the hall. He was tall and skinny. The hood of a sweatshirt covered his head. Foxy noticed he walked with a slight limp, as if one knee didn't straighten all the way. He slipped through the open door of the vacant apartment in the rear without turning around.

She sucked in air as if she'd been held underwater and then let go. Her arms dropped impotently and her feet were glued to the floor. Any doubt she was being pursued had vanished. Staring at the closed door, she knew, even without seeing his face, who her stalker was.

B ig storm coming," Millie said to the choir members as they
trickled down the stairs to assemble in the church basement.
The choir director was from Oklahoma and, although she remained calm in the face of tornadoes, almost any dusting of snow
flung her into driving anxiety.

Her comment devolved into general grumbling about the
weather, as if Minnesota shouldn't have to deal with snow yet another winter. As if God might finally hear their cries, take pity on
them and dump all the snow on Florida or Hawaii instead.

After sitting up with Cate until midnight, Robin resented Millie
scheduling an extra rehearsal before church in preparation for the
Christmas cantata.

Coming up behind her, Grace said, "You outdid yourself yesterday. I wouldn't have blamed you if you'd decided to sleep in."

"I'm really not at the top of my game this morning," Robin admitted. "I was groggy when I grabbed what I thought was my prescription bottle, and realized later I'd taken the cat's pills for
diarrhea."

Grace guffawed, but then bit her lip. "Are you okay? Can that
hurt you?"

Robin shook her head. "I called the nurse hotline. I'm fine."

"No side effects?"

"Well, I do have a crazy craving for tuna."

They laughed and went to the coffee cart to fill Styrofoam cups. Standing with their backs to the wall, they both commented on how sleep-deprived they were. "'Tis the season," said Robin.

Grace stifled another yawn. "Yeah, I haven't been sleeping well lately. I'm so tired of being tired."

Robin, having noticed the dark circles under her eyes yesterday, was glad Grace brought it up. "Are you feeling okay? Maybe you should tell your doctor." Ever since her bout with cancer, Robin had been much more vigilant about her own health and that of her friends.

"I don't need to. I know exactly why I'm tired. It's Fred's snoring. It takes me forever to fall asleep and even when I do manage to, his dang snoring wakes me up again. It gets really bad around three or four in the morning." She rummaged in her purse and pulled out an electronic device a little smaller than a cell phone. "I taped him," she said.

"You're kidding."

"Nope. I've been telling him for months but he doesn't believe how bad he is. Now I have evidence." She grabbed Robin's sleeve and tugged her around the corner into an unlit hallway behind the kitchen. Pressing a button, she held the device up for Robin to hear.

Robin tilted her head and listened. Her eyes widened. "Oh, my God, Gracie! That's terrible!"

Grace's head bobbed up and down. "Isn't it? I wasn't kidding, and I don't even have it at full volume."

"No wonder you're exhausted."

"Exactly! He snerks and snorks and whiffles and grunts the whole night long!"

All Robin could do was shake her head.

Looking vindicated, Grace said, "He claims I snore, too, but there's just one person making noises on here, and I can assure you, it isn't me."

Millie clapped her hands and called them all to line up. Grace dropped the recorder back into her purse.

People continued to talk as they picked up music folders and tucked purses in the cubbies of a lockable cabinet. Grace leaned over and touched a finger to Robin's face. "Hold still. You have something on your upper lip." Robin saw her look of mischief before Grace said, "Never mind. It's just a whisker."

Robin leveled a look at her.

There were no risers in the basement but Millie always had them line up exactly the way they would upstairs. Robin and Grace took their places side-by-side in the alto section. Millie announced the first song, and people continued to converse as they leafed through their folders to find the appropriate sheet music.

"Okay, let's settle down," Millie said. "Sing ah, ah, ah, ah, four beats to each note, C-major scale up and back down." She started them on the note, and they vocalized to her beat as Millie's hand chopped the air a little higher with each rising note.

Suddenly Millie's hand stopped moving, and her head spun to face the cabinet where they'd stashed their purses. The annoyance on her face was obvious as she sought the source of the ragged and grating noise.

Robin burst out laughing, as Grace's mouth opened wide and she made a mad dash to the cabinet, where she seized her purse and ripped it open. Soon the recorded snoring stopped, but Robin and Cate did not. Even if no one else had figured out what had happened, Robin had tears in her eyes from laughing.

Millie's lips were tight. "We have a Christmas program to put on, and we really don't have time for your shenanigans. Honestly, you two!"

It was not the first time Robin and Grace had gotten on Millie's bad side, with such minor infractions as Robin's Birkenstocks peeking out from under her choir robe, or Grace dropping her music folder on her way into the sanctuary, but this was surely the worst. Clenching her teeth together to control her laughter, Robin tried not to look at Grace when she stepped back in line.

The rehearsal did not go well after that. Millie seemed to be convinced they'd played the recording just to mock her and occasionally scowled in their direction.

After worship service Robin threw an arm over Grace's shoulder and said, "Gracie, if I tell you something, promise you won't be mad."

"Why would I get mad at you?"

"Because that second time you played the recording, I'm pretty sure I heard more than one person snoring." It was for her own health, Robin pointed out to her, to do everything she could to get a good night's sleep.

Grace sighed. "Yeah, I heard it too," she finally admitted.

"Not that there's anything wrong with it," Robin hastened to add.

"I may snore, but during that last hymn I think I heard meowing coming from somewhere near where you were standing?"

"Ha ha."

"Not that there's anything wrong with it."

\* \* \*

FOXY TRIPP STARED at the closed door with her mouth agape. She could not have been mistaken. She knew that walk—a long stride with a slight limp that had been caused by a horrific beating. There was no one else it could have been. Knowing that did nothing to calm her frazzled nerves. In fact, it threw a zillion new complications into the mess. The frying pan dangled from one hand as she raised the other hand to her chest, sure her heart was about to explode.

Within seconds, her fright began to turn to fury, and without pausing to consider the rashness of her decision, she marched down the hall.

She was still scared out of her wits, but she was not about to let that stop her. Action was required. Pounding on the door, she yelled, "Vinnie, you weasel, open the door before I call the cops!"

She heard scuffling on the other side, and the door opened a crack. Her ex-husband, Vinnie, stared out at her. His eyes widened when he saw the raised skillet, and he quickly slammed the door again.

"I'm not going away!" she yelled. She figured if he was half as frightened as she was, he'd probably throw himself out the window into a snowbank.

But soon the door opened again, just enough that she could see his face. "Is he with you?" he asked.

"Is who with me?"

"Him. Your lover."

"What? No!"

He pushed his face through the opening and craned his neck around. Seeing no one else, he stepped back to let her in.

Foxy did what she always did when frightened. She squared her jaw, put her hands on her hips and confronted him head on. "What the hell are you doing here?"

"Let me explain."

Foxy was shocked to see his puffy eyes underscored by purplish smears. Either he hadn't slept in a while, or he was ill. In any case, he'd aged. He took a step closer and she smelled the booze. Her stomach was one big knot.

"What happened to the sheriff?"

"Oh, God! You're spying on me? Vinnie, what the hell?" She looked past him into the empty apartment. The only thing the former tenant had left behind was a broken chair. The seat and back cushions were lying end to end on the carpeted floor, as though he'd slept on them. A bottle lay on its side next to the cushions. She was relieved to see there was still plenty of liquid in it. The whole scene was so pathetic, her anger and fear started to dissipate, just a little. "For the love of God, Vinnie, what're you doing here?"

"I came to see you. I know this looks crazy."

"Damn straight!"

"I've been thinking about you a lot lately, and I just wanted to talk to you face to face, you know? He ducked his head the way he used to do when he'd screwed up something. I waited for you outside, and—" He reached his arms out to her. "It's a long story, Foxy. Please let me explain."

She was speechless.

"Please," he begged.

She and Vinnie had loved and betrayed each other. They'd trusted and mistrusted and hurt each other again and again. And now, when she thought she was finally over him, he stood in front of her, appealing to her humanity and sense of fairness. "You broke into my house!"

"I did, but—"

"You broke into my house!" she said more forcefully.

His Adam's apple bobbed when he swallowed. "Yeah, that was dumb."

He was shivering, she noticed, and she remembered the landlady had turned the heat way down in the empty apartment, not cold enough for the pipes to freeze and burst, but cold enough to make for a miserable night, if he'd indeed spent the night here. The leather jacket he wore over a hooded sweatshirt would not have kept him warm enough.

"Vinnie, you are an idiot!" She hadn't seen her ex in years, and their last interactions had been distinctly unpleasant. But looking at his sorrowful expression, she couldn't bring herself to hate him. She wanted to call the cops and have them haul his sorry ass off to jail, but ultimately curiosity won out. She wanted even more to know what had possessed him to break into her house and hide in the empty apartment. "It's twenty degrees warmer in my apartment," she said curtly. "Follow me. I'll give you ten minutes to explain, and after that you're out of here."

He dipped his head. "Thank you, Frances. That'd be nice." Few people knew her given name, and fewer ever called her that. She'd always been Foxy, the nickname given to her by her father because of her red hair.

"C'mon." She turned on her heel and sensed Vinnie following her.

When Sheriff Harley pulled up to the restaurant, he didn't see Foxy's car in the parking lot, but he was still early. Entering the building, he removed his sunglasses and let his eyes adjust to the darkened area around the bar. The hostess seated him at a table near the four-sided fireplace, facing the parking lot so he could watch for her. He ordered black coffee and waited.

Pier 500 had become a favorite place of theirs since they'd begun dating. Bill and Foxy had spent some fine afternoons in the spring, summer, and fall, eating and then strolling along the St. Croix River near the Hudson Pier just across the street from the restaurant.

After the second time the waitress filled his cup, she asked if he was ready to order. He checked his watch. Foxy was fourteen minutes late. Not like her at all. She'd left no phone or text messages either. Nada. He hated to bug her if she was running late. Even more, he hated the thought she might have been involved in an accident. Just last month he'd been on the scene of a car that spun off the road and into a pine tree. The driver was a seventeen-year-old girl on her way home from school. She'd died on the way to the hospital. Unbidden, the image came to his mind of the crashed car, with Foxy rather than the high school girl inside.

The server, a dark-haired beauty, came by to see if he was still waiting for his friend. The question annoyed him more than it should have. He told her to bring some Brie cheese curds, Foxy's favorite item on the menu, while he waited. She'd introduced him to some interesting dishes since they'd been going out, and he had to admit he'd actually developed a taste for some of them.

He gulped down coffee, and went back over their earlier conversation. The death of her friend had been a blow to her. She was shaken and grieving, and he'd held her in his arms as she cried. But then it went wrong, and he couldn't figure out what he'd done to offend her. After she stopped crying, he'd asked if she'd like him to spend the night with her so she wouldn't be alone. "Alone is what I do best," she'd said with a sad smile. He'd insisted she didn't have to be alone, that he loved being with her—what the hell was wrong with that? But she said she'd rather sort through her feelings on her own, and then she'd sent him packing.

It took him a day to get over it. Her way of coping with grief and loss had nothing to do with him, at least that's what he'd told himself before he'd called her this morning. Running their morning conversation over in his mind, he didn't believe she needed to check her schedule. She was hiding something, he'd bet on it.

He slammed a hand on the table when he realized he was examining her every word and inflection as if it were evidence in a crime. That trait might serve him well in law enforcement, but it could be toxic to a relationship.

Remembering past relationship failures, he let insecurity seep in and suddenly he felt like a damn fool sitting there by himself. He was well aware Foxy was a catch. She was beautiful, smart, and she even loved dogs, so what on God's green earth did she see in him?

The cheese curds had vanished by the time a different server passed him with a loaded tray of food destined for another table, food he'd given up in an attempt to lose weight. The enticing smells made his stomach growl. With longing eyes, he watched each plate as it was set before the five diners.

Checking the time obsessively, he waited until she was thirty-five minutes overdue before calling her. When he was prompted to leave a message, he pushed the button to end the call. Concern rippled around the edges of his mind. He didn't know whether to hope she'd been in a minor traffic accident or had forgotten their date. After a few more minutes, he signaled his waitress over and ordered the huge Reuben sandwich he'd smelled as it went past a few minutes ago. And, since he wasn't on duty today, he figured he might as well order a beer too.

\* \* \*

Vinnie, still looking sheepish, followed along behind Foxy. Once inside her apartment they both stood inside the door, awkward and unsure what to do next. Elvis slunk up to sniff Vinnie's pant leg. The black cat retreated several inches and then took a couple wary steps toward him.

Tears shone in Vinnie's eyes as he stretched out his hand. "Elvis? The King's still alive?"

She nodded, feeling a lump in her throat.

Skittish, but curious, the cat sniffed his outstretched hand. Finally he allowed Vinnie to stroke his tail, but he dashed off and hid under the loveseat the second Vinnie bent to pick him up.

In that moment, the tectonic plates shifted again and the past and present became one.

Unsteady, Foxy went into the kitchen, refilled the teakettle and set it on the stove. Pulling a paper towel off the roll she began wiping water spots in the sink, stalling for time to pull herself together. Vinnie's behavior in breaking into her house was bizarre, to say the least. There was, however, one circumstance that might lessen the rashness of that act. When she'd last been with him, he'd been erratic, easily enraged and frequently depressed. Later, when she was studying massage, she'd learned he may have been suffering the aftereffects of a brain injury from his brutal beating. *It all comes back to that moment,* she thought. *Still.*

Following her into the kitchen, Vinnie said, "I wanted to call you, but last time I did, you said not to bother calling again."

"There was a reason for that, Vinnie. You made some pretty crappy comments about my being a massage therapist, if you'll remember."

"Aw, c'mon, Foxy. It was a joke. We all used to laugh about the ads in Vegas, like they weren't fooling anyone about what they really did. You laughed too, remember? 'Petite, cute massage therapist. Hot, deep, sensual, the ultimate treat.'"

"Yeah, I get it. You thought I'd turned to prostitution."

"I never thought that, Foxy, I swear. I was just givin' you a hard time."

She planted a hand on the counter. "Right. By asking me what I charged for a happy ending? Not funny, Vin."

"Jeez, you're still bent out of shape about that?"

"No, I just didn't need the aggravation. I kept asking you to knock it off, but you just kept going. I've always hated that."

He dropped his head. "Yeah, I guess I do that."

"Let me ask you, Vinnie. Did you ever think about leaving me a message before coming?"

He shook his head and ran a hand through hair. "I didn't want to." His stubble was salt and pepper and didn't look intentional, more like he'd forgotten to shave. As long as she'd known him, he'd been fussy about his appearance, and she hoped that hadn't changed.

She prodded him to explain why he hadn't left her a message.

"See, I'd already decided to drive up here, so I—"

She whipped her head around. "Drive up? From where? I don't even know where you're living these days."

He looked surprised. "I moved to Kansas City a while back. Didn't Tina tell you?"

Now it was Foxy's turn to be surprised. Why had Tina kept that from her, and what else was she holding back? "What are you doing in Kansas City?"

"Are you serious? I'm not allowed to move without consulting you first?" He crossed his arms. His expression wasn't belligerent. In fact, he seemed to be amused. "I'm a licensed social worker now. I work mostly with people with addictions. A lot of my clients have gambling addictions, as a matter of fact."

That was the last thing she expected to hear from him. "Wow!" Why hadn't she anticipated him growing up? So, Vinnie really quit gambling, she thought with a pang. And then the resentment set in. Too little, too late. How different their lives would have been if he'd given it up the first time she told him he had a problem!

"Do you mind if I sit?" he asked, heaving himself onto a barstool.

Standing on the other side of the pass-through counter, she asked more questions, and nothing in Vinnie's manner seemed evasive as he tried to fill in the gaps. He'd left Kansas City on Friday morning and had driven straight to her house, he explained. He'd arrived, apparently, when she and Cate were out walking their dogs. As any normal person would do, he went to the front door and rang the bell, knowing he had the right apartment because a label with her name—her maiden name, he pointed out to her—was tacked below the doorbell inside the porch.

He said, "I stood there in your porch, trying to figure out what to do. People were walking and driving past, and I felt conspicuous standing there—well, cold too. I sat in my car for a while, but I was running low on gas, so I drove around looking for a gas station. After I filled the tank and stopped for something to eat, I drove up and saw a light was on upstairs. I figured it was your apartment." He looked out the front window. "And it looks like I was right."

She came and pulled up a barstool next to his, crossing her arms, still challenging him to explain himself. His story squared with her movements two days ago. So far, so good.

"I had to park down a ways and walk back. It was like a skating rink out there."

Foxy leaned over to see his feet and started to laugh. "Alligator shoes? Not real good on the ice and snow, Vin."

His grin was the one she remembered, self-deprecating, sweet. "Yeah, I figured that out."

"I was down there a few houses," he said, gesturing with his thumb, "and then he drives up—the sheriff. I watch to see where he was going, and guess what? He goes up to your place and lets himself in." He put his elbow on the counter and propped his head on his fist, trying to look nonchalant. "You know people can see into your apartment when you get near the window? Well, they can see shapes, anyway."

Foxy felt herself flush. And then she pictured the figure standing on the street looking up at her window. That had been three days before Vinnie claimed he'd arrived in St. Paul.

"So, you and the sheriff, are you . . . an item?"

She met his eyes. "Vinnie, when did you really get here?"

"Night before last," he answered matter-of-factly. "Tina told me about your boyfriend. She said he's a nice guy."

"He is." Foxy blinked. Emotions threatened to bury her. She felt betrayed that neither Tina nor Vinnie had bothered to mention they'd been talking about her, as if they were residents of a world she no longer inhabited. She'd closed the door on that life when it had become too hazardous, and now the ugliness was seeping into her life again. And try as she might, she couldn't tell if she and Vinnie were both in danger, or if he was the danger.

Not to mention her astonishment that she was sitting here talking to her former husband, which led to a whole mess of other feelings. Vinnie was still tall and slender, but he'd gotten a little gray at the temples and his jawline and chin had softened with age. In his piercing dark eyes, now lined with small wrinkles, she could still see the man who used to make her weak-kneed with longing.

It was as if more than one Vinnie now coexisted in his body, like Russian nesting dolls. She could see the young boy whose parents had left him to fend for himself way too often while they ran a successful furrier business. His expression was both tough and little-boy-scared.

She saw, too, the old man he was becoming, a little stooped in the shoulders, a little more deliberate in his movements, with arthritis and a gimpy leg. His hands were chapped and wrinkled. But despite the signs of age, he now had a vibrancy he hadn't exhibited in the last years when his addiction had really taken hold.

For a heartbeat, she pictured hugging him. Her mouth remembered the feel of his mouth, and her insides tightened with other memories. But then she remembered how he'd sworn off gambling more than once. She was reminded of the conviction she'd formed years ago, that if she ever were to let him back into her life again, she would spend the rest of her years waiting for the other shoe to drop. When it came to Vinnie and dropping shoes, it was like dealing with a damned centipede!

She got up, popped some bread in the toaster and searched through her basket of teabags until she found the Lemon Zinger he used to favor. He followed her, hovering nearby. He was close enough she could smell booze and stale smoke on his breath. When he coughed into his closed fist Foxy wondered again if he was unwell.

He sat at the counter to eat his toast, slathered with butter and sprinkled with cinnamon sugar, just the way she used to make it for him. Even after two cups of tea, he shivered now and again. Sitting next to him, Foxy clasped her hands in front of her, surprised how quickly they'd settled into familiarity.

He kept his eyes straight ahead when he said, "God, Foxy, how did it come to this—me sneaking around, afraid to talk to you, afraid you'd shut me down? We used to be so good together." He started to shiver again.

"You know what happened. Why don't you take a shower while I make you a real lunch. We'll talk later, okay?"

His eyes teared up again. "Thank you."

The sound of running water triggered memories she'd long ago banished, of Vinnie shampooing her hair in the shower. He always started with his thumbs circling her temples and his fingertips caressing the top of her head.

Harley! Her eyes flew open. She'd forgotten all about meeting Bill Harley for lunch! Again she had the sensation of two worlds, kept separate for so long, and suddenly sharing the same space and time. The minute Vinnie had walked through her door, she'd fallen into that alternate life where her plans with Bill didn't exist. Swearing to herself, she grabbed the phone and saw his text message.

She called him immediately. "I'm so sorry! Something came up. Somebody stopped by, and I completely forgot."

Offering no words of absolution, Bill Harley let her babble on, which was how she knew he was pissed. Or hurt—yes, probably more hurt than angry. And he had every right to be.

"I suppose I could drive to your place and drop off the venison, like I offered earlier." His voice was cheerless.

She hesitated. "Uh, no, that won't work. Maybe . . ." She was trying to figure out how she was going to end the sentence when the bathroom door opened and Vinnie, clad only in a towel, stood in the hallway, bellowing, "God, that felt good!"

Foxy muffled the phone against her chest, hoping she'd stifled the words in time. She held her finger to her lips to let Vinnie know to keep quiet. "It's complicated," she said feebly into the phone, once more apologizing to Bill for forgetting their lunch.

His response was decidedly frosty. Neither of them suggested rescheduling their date.

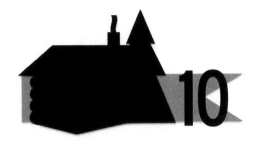

**W**hile Vinnie dressed again in the clothes he'd been wearing, Foxy scrounged in the refrigerator for something to eat, coming up with leftover lasagna and a green salad.

Sitting at the kitchen table together, he tried to explain to her how he'd come to be in the unoccupied apartment across the hall from hers. "Something happened, and I wanted to tell you in person. See, I've been thinking about you a lot lately, and—"

"When you say something happened, are you talking about Sierra?"

"You heard?"

"Sierra's dad called." As soon as she mentioned him, her eyes flicked over to the box Mr. Brady had dropped off last night, now sitting in the corner of her living room. From the moment Mr. Brady called, Foxy had the sensation she'd fallen down the rabbit hole. The box in the corner was just one more surreal element. Of all the things Sierra might have left her, for the life of her, she couldn't figure out why she'd want Foxy to have a case of wine.

"He called you?"

Foxy's anger blazed suddenly. "How did you know about Sierra before I did? I get the impression you're all talking to each other and leaving me in the dark."

He hung his head. "When Sierra's boy found her, the police called his grandparents, Sierra's mom and dad, to find out who the father was. The family expected Wylie to step up and raise his own son, but Beau is almost grown up and—"

"So Wylie called you?"

"Right. I guess it was Thursday, and he thought it was a bad idea to tell you. Because of your boyfriend, you know. He's convinced that business back in Vegas is going to bite us all in the ass because you're hanging out with that guy. " He spread his hands out. "But all I could think was how much I wanted to talk to you."

Foxy pressed her lips together, and then, before he could say anything else, she ordered him to eat before his food got cold.

He picked up his fork and ate.

"I don't get this nonsense about my dating Bill. What's he got to do with anything?"

Vinnie's mouth was full. When he could answer, he said, "Fine, blame me for being paranoid. For all I know, your boyfriend, the sheriff, is a standup guy, but let me ask you this. Did you tell him about the money we took?"

She pressed her lips together.

"Did you mention Al and Sierra were murdered?"

"We don't know that." With a slight shake of the head, she looked away. "But that's what I've been thinking too."

"I think you didn't tell your boyfriend because you don't trust him."

"I didn't say that!"

"Maybe not, but your actions say it all."

The phone rang.

It was Bill again, calling to apologize for hanging up too quickly. "I know you're going through a rough time," Bill Harley said. "Wanna talk?"

While she thought of an answer, Foxy shut her eyes, but the image she had of Bill's face, hurt but still hopeful, made her sick to her stomach. "I know I screwed up, Bill. I'm truly sorry, and I want it to be right between us, but the thing is, I'm on my way out right now. I'd love to talk, but can we—?"

"Are you okay?" His voice was suddenly concerned.

"I'm fine."

"You said you're going out?"

She knew he wanted to know where, but there was no way she could explain any of this to him over the phone.

"I'd rather you didn't. The roads aren't good," Bill said.

She was stuck between being touched by his concern and feeling smothered. The man hadn't been worried about her driving when he'd asked her to meet him in Hudson, had he? In the dead air that hung between them, Vinnie clear his throat loudly. She didn't muffle the phone in time.

Suddenly Bill's tone changed as he apologized for bothering her. "Be safe," he said. and hung up.

She planted her hands on the counter and took two deep breaths before walking back into the living room. Sinking down across from Vinnie, she asked him, "Did you do that on purpose?"

"Do what?"

"Clear your throat while I was talking on the phone."

"You're mad at me because I cleared my throat?"

"Yes, because I think you did it on purpose."

Vinnie's expression was blank.

"Never mind."

"Oh," he said as it dawned on him. "Was that your boyfriend?"

She hated the way he kept saying that word. Glaring at Vinnie, she said, "Yes, and I don't want him getting the impression there's anything going on between us because there isn't."

He threw his hands up. "Fine."

"You were about to tell me why you came here."

He began trying to explain his half-baked decision to cancel his appointments and drive to Minnesota. "I was worried about you, you know? When Big Al got himself killed, we all wondered if it had to do with the money. You can't have forgotten all those phone calls. You were as certain as I was that he'd been knocked off by the mob, maybe a bookie."

This conjecture was old business. In the beginning all six of them had speculated ad nauseum about whose money they'd found in the cooler bag, and whether the rightful owner would know they'd taken it and split it six ways. Then Vinnie got beaten up and wound up in the hospital. After that, they'd scattered to the four winds, where they tried to build new lives.

But then Big Al got run down on the streets of Las Vegas. Foxy preferred to believe Al's death had been a simple hit-and-run. Now, it all came back to her, and she felt a familiar flutter of fear in her throat.

As Vinnie described his recent actions, Foxy kept recalculating. Had Vinnie been stalking her or was he just being Vinnie, acting out of misguided passion, making knee-jerk decisions without considering other, saner options? Without doubt, he'd committed a criminal act breaking into the house. What else had he done?

But if Vinnie was not the one making the calls and hanging up on her, as he claimed, then who had? And who'd been standing below her house on the sidewalk, staring up at her house, if not Vinnie?

Picking up his dishes she turned her back to him while she washed them. With the water running, no one spoke, giving her time to think. Someone other than Vinnie had been stalking her, she was sure of it. Even though he was bundled up, the man standing below her window had not had Vinnie's proportions. Whether the phantom caller was trying to figure out if she was at home or was simply calling to instill fear in her, she didn't know, but either way, that person intended harm, and Vinnie was not throwing off those vibes at all.

She shuddered, thinking about last night. Maybe Elvis was picking up on Vinnie's presence across the hall, or maybe it was another
presence altogether. She felt her panic rise. She wanted to tell Vinnie, but not until he explained how and why he'd wound up in the
vacant apartment.

Vinnie grabbed a towel and dried the plate she'd just washed,
and Foxy felt nostalgia sweep over her. Trying to stay in the here
and now, she said, "Vin, I'm just trying to understand. You came on
Friday around supper time, and I wasn't home, right?"

He bobbed his head as he thought. "Right."

"So you waited on the porch and smoked a cigarette. I saw the
Lucky Strike butt in the ashtray."

He looked chagrined. "I'm not too good covering my tracks, huh?"

"Not so much." They wandered to the living room. Sitting side by
side on the loveseat, Foxy twisted her unruly hair into a bun and secured it with the black lacquer chopstick she'd left on the end table.

She kept asking questions, moving his account past Friday and
into Saturday—yesterday. He told her how he'd returned while she
was at Robin's only to discover the city plow had dumped a load of
snow on his illegally parked car.

"You're lucky they didn't tow you." It made sense that someone
from out of state would fall victim to St. Paul's snow emergency rules.
They were aggressive about keeping roads clear for the plows, even
if it meant burying some cars and towing others.

"There was no way I could dig it out without a shovel. I thought
you might have one. When I didn't see one by the front door I tried
the back.

Vinnie's stories always seemed plausible, at least on first impression. When he got to the part about using a knife to open the window, Foxy got a chill to think how easily he'd gotten in. She'd been
living with false security all along.

An old fear settled in. There was no safe place, no one to protect her. There never had been. She pulled away from him, folded her hands in her lap and watched his face intently. "You didn't take the shovel, though, did you?"

"I was cold. I just needed to warm up."

She encouraged him to continue.

"That back entry isn't the most comfortable place. But I did find a bottle of whiskey."

She stared at him and the pieces fell into place. "You broke in to get a shovel to dig out your car, but you stole a bottle of booze instead?"

"You don't need to jump down my throat. I'll replace the damn thing." He gave the old look he used to give her, like she was his warden or something, but then his features softened into a look of contrition. "Yeah, I saw the whiskey, and decided to find a warmer place to drink it. I guess I drank just enough not to give a rat's ass about shoveling my car out."

She sighed heavily. "Yeah, I get that you drank yourself into a coma, but—"

"Ah, c'mon, Foxy, that's not the way it was. I wasn't tanked at all, but as soon as I started to get warm and comfortable, I got sleepy."

She shook her head, amazed after all these years at the way his mind worked. "And then?"

"And then I guess I fell asleep. It was dark when I woke up. My cell phone needs a charge, so I couldn't tell what time it was when I heard you come back."

She felt her face pinch up into what Vinnie used to call her "school marm" expression. "And yet, for some reason, you didn't come down the hall to tell me you were here."

His laugh was mirthless. "Yeah, right! Can you imagine what would've happened if I'd jumped out of the apartment when you came up the stairs? For God's sake, think about it! I would've scared you out of your skin!"

"As opposed to what happened when you decided to lurk outside my door and set off the motion detector?"

Elvis jumped onto his lap and put a paw on his chest. "Is he telling me to shut up?" Vinnie asked.

As annoyed as she was, Foxy chuckled.

"You gotta believe me. I didn't mean to scare you."

It was all so typical of Vinnie, she had to believe it.

"I had it all figured out. As soon as it was light, I was gonna slip down the stairs to the front door and ring the bell, like any self-respecting visitor. When that alarm went off, I almost had a coronary!"

They faced off, she not wanting to let him off the hook, and he not willing to concede he'd mishandled everything. It was all too familiar. It made her stomach hurt to think of how much energy they'd spent over the years in just this kind of standoff.

"Vinnie, why did you really come here?"

In the years they'd been together, she'd gotten pretty good at spotting his lies. There was always some tell, like a quick flick of his tongue across his lip, or a downward cast of his eyes. Most often, he'd used anger to divert her from a subject he didn't want to discuss.

What he did now was to look her in the face, a little too deliberately, she thought, and say, "Honey, I already told you. I wanted to tell you about Sierra in person."

"I already knew about Sierra."

The look on his face confirmed she was right to grill him. He sat back, stretching his long legs in front of him. "You know how you said that money was going to come back and haunt us?"

She nodded.

"Well, I think you were onto something."

\* \* \*

ROBIN HAD DECIDED to forego mailing Christmas cards this year, but was having an attack of remorse for sending out a mass e-mail. She decided to address a few cards left over from last year to those on her list who didn't have e-mail. When the phone rang, she side-stepped the laundry basket full of wrapped presents and caught it on the fourth ring. She saw the caller was her older daughter, Cass, who was finally checking in, as Robin had asked, to let her mom know she and her boyfriend had safely arrived at his parents' house.

"Mom?" Cass's voice sounded like it came from the child she hadn't been in more than a decade. "Are you in the middle of something?"

With someone else, this might have been a polite opener, but with Cass, it meant something was wrong. Robin was immediately on guard. "What is it?"

"I'm okay." Her voice was shaky. "Well, not okay, exactly. We got to Nick's house, I mean his parents' house, yesterday afternoon, but we had a really awful drive."

"You didn't have an accident, did you?"

"No, we didn't have an accident, Mom," she chided. "The roads weren't great, but that wasn't the problem. Nick and I fought the whole way there. As a matter of fact, I think we just broke up."

"Oh, honey, everybody has fights."

"Mom!" Cass's tone was sharp. "We broke up, okay?"

Her heart sank. Over their lifetime, she'd done all she could to keep her daughters from harm, but there was no way to protect them from broken hearts. Robin asked what had happened.

Her daughter didn't answer.

"Honey?"

"I'm here. I can't even talk about it."

She waited a beat, and Cass said, "Nothing happened."

Robin knew her response had to be neutral. "I see."

"Well, obviously something happened," Cass said, as if she hadn't just declared she couldn't talk about it. "I was nervous enough meeting his parents without him pecking away at me. Everything he said just made it worse."

Robin could hear sniffling and nose blowing. "Maybe he was nervous, too."

"Mom! Please do not take his side! It's like he was going through a checklist. Intelligent, check. Professional parents, check. Blonde hair, check. Orthodontics-enhanced teeth, check. And then he started to coach me on how to behave and what to wear, like I was going to embarrass him in front of his perfect parents. He just went on and on, and so I finally asked if he was ashamed of me."

Robin had always had a penchant for stepping in and trying to fix everything with her daughters. Over and over she'd discovered it was counterproductive, so this time she said nothing. Instead she pictured confronting arrogant, pretty-boy Nick and telling him he'd never find anyone that could hold a candle to Cass Bentley.

"I actually thought we'd wind up getting married and having kids! He may have a doctorate, but he has got to be the biggest, most self-centered dumbass on the face of the earth! And I'm an even dumber ass for thinking he was anything other than a colossal, arrogant prick."

"I'm so sorry." Robin took a deep breath, and reminded herself this was the hyperbolic language of breaking up. In time, Cass's rage would subside and everything would seem less tragic. "Just hop on a plane and come home, honey. We'll cover the cost. You know we would love it if you'd spend Christmas here."

The wrenching sob at the other end reached into Robin's chest and squeezed her heart.

"It's not gonna happen, Mom. I already called the airlines. Planes are stacked up from here to Chicago, and people are crazed trying to get wherever they're going for the holidays. There aren't even any rental cars to be had."

"How about a bus or a train."

"Nothing's going anywhere or it's all booked. You think I didn't check already?"

"Oh, sweetie!"

She sniffed. "He made it perfectly clear he's just not as invested in the relationship as I am, and he—" Her voice got a hitch in it. "And here I am, stuck here with his stupid, pretentious family. It's beyond awkward. It's agony." She started to sob.

"We need to get you back here, honey. Let me brainstorm on it. I'll call you back after I've talked to Dad. We'll figure out something, okay?" An idea was already bubbling around in her head.

Cass's voice got small again. "Okay."

As soon as they hung up, Robin planned what she would say to Brad.

* * *

"ABSOLUTELY NOT!" BRAD SLAPPED his magazine down on the arm of his recliner. "I know you think you're invincible, but you are not driving out west by yourself. It's a thousand miles, at least." He took a gulp of his drink.

"Actually, it's just over nine-hundred, but—"

"You're missing my point. The whole idea is nuts." He leaned forward, tented his hands under his chin and looked her in the eye. "You know I'm right."

Sinking onto the hassock next to him, Robin sighed. "I just wanted us all to be together for Christmas."

He picked up the remote and clicked from basketball to the weather channel. "Do you see that?"

"I see the Denver area should be clear by tomorrow afternoon. I've got it all mapped out. If I take I-90 and drop down on 83, I'll miss the storm altogether. Look." She pointed at the television screen. "If I run into snow at all, it would be around Sioux Falls, and if I had to I could hang out there until it passes." They watched the time lapse projection of the storm. It appeared to be heading south of the Twin Cities. "Look, just light snow. Good grief, Brad, I drive through heavier snow than that all the time."

He was silent for so long, she knew she'd lost the argument. When she pictured poor Cass, forced to spend Christmas with an angry ex-boyfriend and his judgmental family, her heart was heavy. She dreaded having to call her back and tell her nobody would be coming to her rescue. She stood to make the call.

"I'll go," Brad said.

"What?"

"I said I'll go. I'll leave first thing in the morning."

"Really? Good, we'll go together."

"No. You stay here."

"Brad, it's not necessary. You can hold down the fort. I know how much you've been looking forward to two weeks off. When did you ever take a two-week vacation? You've been talking about sitting around in your pajamas and doing nothing."

He shook his head. "I'm going." When he made up his mind about something, it was almost impossible to dissuade him.

"The least I can do is go with you. You can sleep in the car."

"And the least I can do," he said, standing to face her, "is to be there for my daughter. For once."

Robin stared at him.

"You've always been there for the girls. You're their rock. I don't have to tell you the burden has been uneven."

"It wasn't a burden," she assured him, but she couldn't argue with the fact she'd been there for their daughters. In the early years when Brad was obsessed with building up his practice, none of them expected him to be a very involved father, and the pattern had become ingrained.

"I can count on both hands how many concerts and plays and soccer games I attended. How many did you go to, not to mention parents' weekends and other college events you went to all by yourself? You've done everything for them. Let me be the hero this time."

She hadn't considered until now how her devotion to her girls might have pushed him away. "Thank you!" she gushed.

"Look, you've busted your butt with all the Christmas preparations. Now you can just kick back. Read a couple books, rent some movies, hang out with your friends."

After shoveling out his car, Foxy and Vinnie trudged back to the house, rosy-cheeked. He looked silly in her faux fur hat with a brim, but at least his lips weren't blue. She'd wrapped her heaviest wool scarf around his neck and dug out a spare pair of mittens.

Carrying a shovel over her shoulder, Foxy shook her head. "A thin leather jacket, flimsy gloves, and alligator shoes! For crying out loud, Vin, what were you thinking, coming to Minnesota in December dressed like that?"

He didn't answer immediately, and when he did, he gave an embarrassed shrug. "I was just thinking about you."

She didn't want to meet his eyes. Her own stung, and not just from the cold. Not only had she handled things with Bill Harley clumsily, pushing him to the back burner the minute Vinnie had shown up, but now she'd offended Vinnie as well. She felt like a clod.

He didn't seem to hold it against her, though. They chattered away, their breath forming clouds that rose from their mouths and hung in the chill air.

"Sun dogs!" Foxy said suddenly, raising her mittened hand to point at the glowing parentheses around the sun. "That means it's cold."

"I don't need no stinkin' sun dogs to tell me it's cold!" he said, taking the shovel from her and throwing an arm over her shoulder.

She laughed.

He pointed to the sky. "They look like pieces of a rainbow."

"Kind of the same thing. The sunlight bends when it passes through ice crystals in the atmosphere. That's what my father taught me. He used to call them sun ghosts."

"Can we knock off all this talk of ghosts for a while?" He pulled her close and said, "This cold doesn't bother you, does it?"

"You really aren't made for Minnesota, are you?" she teased.

He bit his lip and let his arm drop.

Once more she seemed to have found a tender spot and pushed on it. The thing was, they had enough history between them that almost anything had the power to wound deeply or spark an argument. She leaned against his arm to let him know she'd intended no harm. Feeling an old longing, she reminded herself how easy it would be to light other sparks.

Neither of them noticed the black Acura SUV parked at the end of the block, or the man in a stocking cap hunkered down behind the wheel.

Leaving the shovel on the front porch, they went upstairs, where Foxy heated water for tea, and Vinnie pulled the phone charger out of his pocket and plugged his cell phone back into the outlet above the kitchen counter.

"I don't have any clients for the next two days," she said as she handed Vinnie a mug of tea. "I was planning to run up to see Mom. I try to get up there once a month or so."

"How is she? Did she stay on at the house after your dad passed away?"

Foxy shook her head. "Not for long. She's in her own little world half the time. She's in long-term care at a nursing home in Pine Glen. They built it a few years ago where the old skating rink used to be."

"What's Matt up to? Still at the resort?"

"He's okay. He's still up in Ely. In fact, I'm planning to spend a few days with him after seeing Mother." She filled him in on her mother's health and Matt's love life, which was currently nonexistent. He'd had a few catastrophic relationships before Patrick. They'd been together seven or eight years, but recently Patrick had moved out, she told Vinnie. "Matt doesn't want to talk about it. I think he's depressed," she said, adding that she wanted to check up on him.

What she didn't say was how desperate she felt to get away from her apartment. It wasn't logical, but the feeling was persistent. Even before the call from Sierra's father, she'd felt a menacing presence. Cate had picked up on it too.

"I miss your brother." Vinnie had always spoken wistfully about Matt and her parents, as if she'd grown up in some kind of Norman Rockwell family. But her upbringing had been about as dysfunctional as his had been, and she didn't want to get into their pointless and well-rehearsed dispute about whose childhood was more screwed up.

She didn't know what to do, and so she changed the subject by saying, "Tina told me you got married again."

"Mm hmm." Elvis pawed at his thigh. Vinnie scooped him up and set him in his lap. "I suppose she told you it didn't last."

"She did."

"I guess I'm not made for marriage either."

She looked up sharply. "What do you mean, 'either'?"

"Not made for Minnesota. Not made for marriage."

She relaxed back and said, "Oh."

Setting his cup down, he ran his hand from the top of the cat's head to the tip of his tail, over and over. Elvis purred loudly and nuzzled his head into Vinnie's hand with each stroke.

Seeing the reunion of Vinnie and the cat tore at her heart. "More tea?" she said brusquely.

He declined. Leaning back, he rested his head on one hand. "Your turn. What's up with you?"

"Me?"

"You and the cop. Think you'll get married? I mean, is he the real thing?"

She closed her eyes for a second. "The real thing? I don't know. He's a thing. I mean we've been seeing each other for a while now," she said lamely.

"Did you just say he's a thing? Christ, Foxy!"

She couldn't believe she'd so easily disparaged a man who'd shown her nothing but kindness. He deserved better. Bill had been honest and reliable, and she'd stood him up. And for what? So she could sit here having sexual fantasies about a man who was neither honest nor reliable? "Just drop it."

They abandoned their monosyllabic conversation in favor of silence.

Foxy left Vinnie petting the cat, and picked up their mugs to set in the sink on her way to the bathroom. Shutting the door behind her, she looked at herself in the oval mirror over the sink. Her eyes were puffy and her skin had the pallor she got whenever she was sick. She hadn't slept well for two nights, and she couldn't imagine tonight would be any better.

Tears welled in her eyes. No matter what happened next, it would be wrong. Sending him back to sleep in the cold and vacant apartment across the hall seemed unkind. But if not across the hall, then where? She couldn't imagine sleeping in the same bed. She didn't trust either one of them enough to do that. But how well would she sleep knowing he was on her too-short sofa in the next room?

"Want me to go with you?" he said as if he could read her thoughts.

She saw his hopeful expression and it caught her off guard. "To my mom's?" She stalled for time. On one hand, it would be the most natural thing in the world and provide driving relief and companionship. On the other. . . well, familiarity cut both ways.

If she sent him away, whether to a motel or to Kansas City, she'd be alone, and right now being alone didn't have much appeal. There would be no more phone calls from Bill Harley, no chance he'd come rushing to her side if she saw shapes in the shadows of her room, or sensed the presence of someone or something in the room with her in the middle of the night.

The soft tinkling of chimes filtered through her thoughts like the soundtrack of a creepy movie and she gasped before realizing it was the ringtone on Vinnie's phone. When she came from the bathroom, Vinnie was leaning on the counter, talking in a low voice. His phone was still attached to the wall outlet by a short cord.

He mouthed something to her, and it took her a minute to figure out he was telling her who he was talking to—Wylie, Sierra's old boyfriend.

"Yeah, we're heading out in the morning to visit her mom up north," Vinnie said.

Squaring her jaw, she shook her head vehemently.

He nodded back at her just as vigorously in the affirmative.

"I don't know, long term," Vinnie said to Wylie. He turned so she couldn't read his face. "Right now, we aren't safe here." There was a long pause and then he said, "Yeah, the dude was sketchy. Set off my Spidey senses." Another pause. "Definitely. I think we all need to be on alert."

Be on alert. Foxy could hear only his side of the conversation, but his words made her think about the Homeland Security sign posted on the highway leading to the airport. Since it had gone up following 9/11, she'd never seen it at any level other than orange, indicating a high level of alert. What would it take, she'd wondered more than once, to drop the alert level to yellow or raise it to red?

He traced his finger on the countertop in small, circular patterns. He was trying not to show emotion, but Foxy knew him too well. He was nervous as hell. "I never saw his face, but he was a big guy, you know, broad in the shoulders . . . Uh, huh . . . No, I couldn't tell. He was wearing a stocking cap."

She sat on the barstool and watched his expression change from disbelief to worry. "No, don't come here. We won't be here." There was a pause, and then he said, "Maybe up to her brother's resort. You remember the place . . . yeah, the Twin Loons, but why can't you just tell me over the phone?" he said.

Foxy wrapped her arms tightly around herself. For all his upfront honesty, Vinnie had obviously held back an important little detail.

"Really! Just a minute." Vinnie said over the phone. He turned to Foxy and said, "Tina was so spooked she took off. She won't tell Wylie where she went."

"Doesn't she trust him?" Foxy asked as soon as he hung up.

"Not really. He's acting a little weird. He says he figured out something and has to tell us in person."

Foxy frowned. "That's just great! And he knows where I live." If Foxy had needed convincing earlier, she was a believer now.

* * *

"I THINK FOXY AND BILL are going off together," Cate told Robin over the phone. "When we said we couldn't join her at her brother's place, she canceled the trip, but she called a little bit ago to say she's going to visit her mom, and asked me to check on the pets in case she doesn't get back 'til the next day."

Robin chuckled. "Cate, I didn't know you were such a hopeless romantic. Why can't she just be going to visit her mother?"

"Because when she does, she never stays overnight."

"Maybe she just wanted a fallback. It's not a bad idea considering the weather."

"Uh huh, but listen to this. She called me back just now, and suddenly the plan's changed. Now it turns out she's going up to her brother's place after all, and she's definitely going to be gone for a few days. When I started asking questions, she said she couldn't talk because she had to call her clients to reschedule. She said she's not seeing any more clients until after the new year."

Robin let the words settle. After the day of revelations from Foxy, she didn't think Foxy would be taking off on a lighthearted romantic romp. It sounded much more like Foxy was fleeing in fear. "How did she sound to you?"

"Excited. But here's the kicker. I heard him coughing in the background, but when I asked if she was going alone, she said she was taking Molly Pat."

Robin couldn't quite hook into Cate's enthusiasm. "Aren't you even a little worried about her after everything she told us? I mean, the guy in the background might have been holding her at gunpoint for all you know."

Cate snorted. "Where do you come up with this stuff?"

"Um, Cate," Robin said, "have you learned nothing in the past couple years about our uncanny ability to attract trouble?"

She barely paused to take a breath, let alone consider that Robin might have a point. "The only thing she was anxious about was getting on the road."

"Cate, you were so worried about her, and now you think everything's just ducky."

"I was worried, but not any more. I figure if she's being stalked, she picked the right person to protect her. I think hanging out with the sheriff for a few days is the smartest thing she can do. Bill Harley will guard her with his life."

Robin pondered her friend's reaction and decided she was giddy with relief to have Bill Harley on the scene. Cate had been anxious ever since she'd dreamt about Foxy trapped in a snow globe and calling for help. It seemed odd to Robin that Cate would dismiss it, but then, the dream didn't have to come true. For each of Cate's premonitions that came to pass, there were ten more that didn't. Cate claimed it was impossible to discern which to heed and which to ignore. "Yes, I'm glad she's with the sheriff, but I'm confused. Do you think they're going to see her mother or her brother?" Robin asked.

"Could be either one, or maybe they're going to hole up at Bill's place in Wisconsin. Either way, I know she'll be safe with him."

Vinnie had insisted on sleeping on the sofa. Both slept fitfully, and at five-thirty in the morning they gave up on trying to sleep. Sitting on the sofa, they debated which car was more reliable. It was a toss-up, since Foxy drove a six-year-old Saturn and Vinnie a Mustang that was only one year newer but had more miles. Since both of their black cars were covered in the same chalky salt residue as every other car on the road, they'd be pretty much unrecognizable if anyone should be following them. The tie-breaker was Foxy's experience driving in the snow.

Yesterday after Wylie's call, they'd put it all out there and tried to examine what they knew. Like Sierra, Foxy thought someone was following her. And now, Vinnie said a menacing man was scoping out her apartment in a black SUV. The more they talked, the more they knew it was time to get the hell out of Dodge.

"Just because you're paranoid doesn't mean people aren't out to get you," Vinnie said.

"Thank you. That's so reassuring." Foxy already felt a little queasy. She should've known Vinnie would say something to make it worse. She was already regretting the plan but hadn't come up with a better one.

It was still dark when Foxy pulled her car into the alley to load. Her winter emergency duffle—with blankets, flares, candles, matches, and protein bars—was already in the trunk. She tossed in another bag with warm clothing, hats, and mittens, and tucked a pair of Sorrels on the floor in the back seat. The last thing to go in was a large Ikea tote filled with wrapped Christmas presents for her mother—a robe and slippers, hand lotion, a new hairbrush and two CDs of relaxation music.

She didn't like to think of her mother spending Christmas Day with no family, but last Christmas her mother had gotten so agitated and confused she had to be medicated. The nursing home director had explained some of the residents got over-stimulated when their routines were disrupted around the holidays. Throw in a jumble of decorations, energetic music, sugary foods, and a room full of strangers, and some of them just couldn't cope. Foxy reluctantly agreed from then on she would have private celebrations with her mother, avoiding the days when too many activities were planned.

Elvis purred and snaked around Vinnie's ankles, and then Foxy's, back and forth, in and out, as they tried to get ready. Jasmine hid under the bed. Finally, Foxy had everything they needed, including the dog's four little booties with non-skid soles and her red, fleece-lined hoodie. At the last minute, she took off her heavy wool jacket and exchanged it for her down coat, which had a hood trimmed in faux fur.

Foxy breathed a sigh of relief as soon as they got moving. After some argument, she agreed to let Vinnie drive the first stretch. He took a circuitous route on side streets, claiming he just needed to get the feel of the car before they got on the interstate. Foxy thought he was using diversionary tactics in case they were under surveillance. He slipped and skidded at each intersection and swore each time he overcorrected. When Foxy offered to take over, he said, "No, it's coming back to me." By the time they reached the freeway entrance, he appeared to have gotten the hang of it.

Cars idled on the ramp, drivers inching forward toward the traffic control light that would allow them to enter traffic, where at least in theory they could move quickly. But today rush hour had begun early, and traffic on I-94 was a mess. Even though the pavement was mostly clean of snow, cars were bumper to bumper. As Foxy and Vinnie watched, a pickup truck darted around them, tried to slip into the small space a few cars ahead of them and suddenly lost control. Clipping the bumper of a van, the truck left the road at a sharp angle and wound up nose-down in the ditch.

"Black ice," Foxy said, and Vinnie grunted.

"You know about black ice, don't you, Vin?" she asked.

He grunted again. "We get ice in Kansas City, too, you know. Besides, I've driven in the winter here before, in case you don't remember."

She wasn't ready to remember. Neither of them had known it would be their last trip together. She'd been full of joy and trepidation as they drove to her parents' house. Of course when they got back to Vegas, it wasn't long before events sucked the joy right out of their marriage, leaving a place in her too painful to think about.

After a few miles, Vinnie asked if she wanted the radio on. They decided on a classical station.

Foxy drew air in through her nose and sighed heavily as the memory of that visit pushed its way to the front. They'd driven a rental car that time, and Vinnie had complained about having to make so many bathroom stops. She'd been so tempted to tell him her suspicions, but it was too soon. Her period was only a week late. But she'd known even then. It wasn't just the heaviness in her breasts or the fact that her bladder seemed to have shrunk to the size of a grape. She knew without a doubt that a new and wonderful being was growing inside her, and had commandeered her body and her emotions.

A silver van passed them on the left, cutting in so closely Vinnie had to jerk the wheel to the right.

Foxy grabbed the door handle, sucking in her breath. Vehicles filled in the void, leaving them no way to get back into the lane of traffic. "Aw, jeez! You gonna drive on the shoulder, then?"

Vinnie started laughing. "Does everyone in Minnesota talk like they did in *Fargo?*"

Foxy gave him a caustic look. "You do know Fargo's in North Dakota, don't you?"

"You betcha."

"Just watch the road and get back where you belong," she said, heading him off before he went through his whole stupid repertoire of Ole and Lena jokes.

When they were finally headed north on 35E, traffic lessened enough they could relax. Molly Pat, who'd been looking out the window from her perch on Foxy's lap, made her way to the back seat where she curled up on her blanket. For the most part, Vinnie kept his eyes ahead and said little. Foxy was grateful for the silence.

Ever since moving back to Minnesota, she'd driven this stretch alone except for Molly Pat. Maybe it was because she didn't have to concentrate on driving that she found her mind flooded with this jumble of memories. She pictured the first time she and Vinnie had driven up from the airport to visit her folks. She relived it now to the extent that her stomach was churning as it had then. Vinnie had looked a little green around the gills too, as she recalled. Her apprehension had been deserved. They'd barely gotten their coats off when her father had pounced on Vinnie, asking things like whether or not he was a churchgoer. When Vinnie answered he was raised Catholic, her father had said, "That's not what I asked. Do you two worship together?"

"Of course we do," Foxy had lied.

After 35E and 35W merged, Foxy instructed Vinnie to take the North Branch exit to grab a quick breakfast at Joe's on Main Street and see if the outlet stores there had real winter boots for him. At Joe's, they covered Molly Pat with another blanket while they went inside. Foxy ordered oatmeal. Vinnie ordered eggs, hash browns, and bacon. They ate hurriedly, neither one finishing what was on their plates. When she pointed out she'd seen him eat three times that much in the old days, he just shrugged and said, "A lot of things aren't what they used to be."

Back in the car, Vinnie held out the strip of bacon he'd reserved for the dog and Molly Pat daintily removed it from his fingers. Before putting the car in gear, he checked his rearview mirror as he'd done off and on throughout their drive.

"Are you still afraid someone's following us?" she asked.

"Haven't seen anyone yet." He thrummed his fingers on the wheel as they made a loop past the outlet store fronts. They circled again, but neither of them saw a place that sold the kind of boots Foxy wanted him to get.

Foxy said, "Let's just hang a left up at the road. There's a Fleet Farm only a few miles away in Cambridge."

"A farm store?"

"It's a lot more than that."

Driving into the Fleet Farm parking lot, Vinnie shook his head. "You're kidding, right? You expect me to buy clothes in a big orange silo?"

"Ya, I do." It wasn't exactly Foxy's haberdashery of choice, and it certainly wasn't Vinnie's either. "Sorry, no alligator shoes," she said to him as they walked in.

Vinnie was surprised at the scope of goods, and although they didn't have what he wanted in terms of style, they had exactly what he needed, a pair of sturdy black boots with wool felt liners. He paid for the boots and some Smartwool socks with a Visa card. Hanging onto Foxy's shoulder, he put the boots on and wore them out of the store.

Catching sight of his pointy-toed alligator shoes peeking from the top of the orange Fleet Farm bag, she laughed out loud. The only boots she'd ever seen him wear were cowboy boots. "If you're not careful, people might think you're a Minnesotan," she said.

Linking arms, they walked to the car, but before getting in, they scanned the parking lot for black SUVs amongst the pickup trucks. "His had duct tape on the side view mirror," he said, eliminating all four in the lot.

"I'll drive," Foxy said, in the hope she could control the flood of memories by concentrating on the road.

Vinnie handed her the keys. "Remember when I had to sleep in your brother's bedroom because we weren't married yet?" he said almost as soon as they were buckled in.

"Where did that come from?"

"I don't know. Just thinking about that first visit."

She sighed. "Mm-hmm." Actually, the part she remembered was him sneaking into her room, and the delicious, prohibited love-making in the bed where her teen-aged self had only fantasized about such things. She swallowed hard. "Long time ago, Vin."

He fell silent again, and she noticed he was no longer checking the mirror for suspicious vehicles.

As they got closer to places from her childhood, more memories popped up, unbidden. She steered onto the freeway exit. Soon she saw the road leading to a park where several families used to share picnic lunches in the summer after church. She remembered the pastor's son, Peter, who was a few years younger than she was. He'd turned out to be a handsome and accomplished man. The last time she'd seen Peter, he was tall, with an elegant bearing and a charming manner, but her mental image of him was that of a freckle-faced, round-bodied kid with an overbite and a penchant for crawling under the picnic tables to look under girls' skirts. The girls said he was a pervert, but to all appearances, he'd outgrown his preoccupation with seeing girls' underwear.

She couldn't recall being involved in more than a handful of activities that didn't have to do with the church. Church had been a huge influence—their whole lives, actually. Robin and Grace were members of a church in Minneapolis that sounded innocuous compared to the church of her childhood. Even though both were branches of the Lutheran church, which was so prevalent in Minnesota, the differences were immeasurable. There had been so many strictures and judgments in Pine Glen Lutheran that she believed well into high school, her only hope of salvation was to repent of anything she'd ever enjoyed or could possibly imagine enjoying at a future date.

When she was little, it had been oddly comforting to know exactly which activities were sanctioned and which would condemn her to eternal damnation. As long as she'd done this and not that, she'd been safe. That was when she still believed her parents and the church would keep her from all harm and that God's love meant she had special protection from the evil that would befall unbelievers. But soon she'd learned that was just an illusion. Bad things happened to good and bad people alike, and they happened even in sleepy little Pine Glen—Pastor Paul and his wife losing an infant daughter to meningitis, for instance. Foxy couldn't imagine they'd gotten through that without a crisis of faith.

Her own crisis of faith had begun in earnest when Mr. Linna, her fifth grade Sunday school teacher had placed his rough hands on her budding breasts one day and told her he loved her. He'd had tears in his eyes, and in her confusion, she'd felt sorry for him, even as she batted his arms away. Backing off, his lips curling, he'd said.

"You must pray, Frances. Satan takes many forms. He's using you to seduce me."

By the time she was in high school, right and wrong had gotten so muddied for Foxy, the idea of being protected seemed ridiculous. It wasn't as if Mr. Linna's behavior had been the one cataclysmic event that made her shun her church teachings and doubt the wisdom of her parents. It was more like slowly peeling away the whitewash to reveal something crumbling and decaying underneath. By the time she was in high school, listening to Pastor Paul thunder from the pulpit, it felt more like theater than theology.

To this day she believed moving away from Pine Glen had been the right decision, despite all that followed. Moving to Sin City, she'd embraced what had been forbidden. She'd taken up drinking and smoking. She'd worn skimpy clothing and paraded on stage. She'd fallen in love with an unbeliever, moving in with Vinnie before they were married, and no lightning bolts had fallen from the heavens. For a while, her life had been charmed.

Rebellion for the sake of rebellion lost its allure after a while, and without planning to, she slowly began to reclaim a few of the values she'd been taught. She'd begun to yearn for a helpmate, someone she could have children with. She knew women were supposed to entrust their husbands with their well-being and happiness, and when she and Vinnie had gotten married, she'd never doubted that love would keep them together, just like the Captain and Tenille song Vinnie used to sing to her.

In the beginning she'd believed whatever Vinnie said, but it didn't take long for her to discover he was a liar. When faced with his gambling, she'd prayed for God to deliver him from his addiction and trusted him when he promised to quit. When that didn't work, she resorted to scolding and begging and bargaining. She took on his inability to quit as her own failure.

By the time she and Vinnie divorced, she'd run out of trust. The mistrust didn't prevent her dating a few guys in Colorado and a few more in Minnesota, but ultimately, none of them had worked out. Her fortress of suspicion had caused more than one man to call her "cold." So far, Bill Harley had never said that of her, and she'd begun to trust again. Bill would've done anything to protect her—at least until yesterday. Now, he had every reason to think, along with all the others, that she had ice water running through her veins.

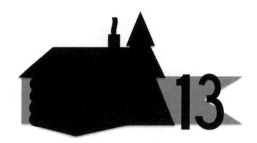

D on't we turn soon?" Vinnie asked, interrupting her thoughts. She glanced out the side windows to get her bearings. "It's still a few miles. We have to cross the creek first." Some people called it Brown Trout Creek, but most people called it "the swimming hole." This was where her father had taught her and Matt to swim. Just around the bend from there was where she'd had her first kiss with a boy. His braces had nicked her lip.

Crossing the creek, Vinnie gave her a quick look, and she knew he was remembering, too, the night they'd spread a blanket right next to the running water and had lain there for hours looking at the stars and planning their glorious future together. Vinnie's ideas had been more grandiose than Foxy's. He wanted to own a classy spa outside of the city that would attract a world-class chef, and where visiting celebrities and local performers could be pampered and renewed. She wanted to dance for a few more years and spend the rest of her life with this handsome, funny man who claimed to be crazy about her.

Foxy blinked rapidly, trying to keep her tears from spilling over. After a few more minutes she pointed to the road on their left. "That's the back way to town now. Pine Glen isn't the way you remember it. The population hasn't changed much, but most of the people I knew moved away. The little school is gone and now the kids are bused fifteen miles away. The church is gone too," she said. "My mother's nursing home is up there, just past the gas station."

Within minutes, they were getting out of the car in front of Senior Care Suites, which everyone referred to as Pine Glen Nursing Home, even though not one of those words was in the actual name. It was a simple, one-story clapboard structure with a wheelchair ramp and, when the snow was gone, a walkway that encircled the long building.

Foxy crossed the threshold and stopped to look the place over, as she did on each visit. They kept the facility way too warm, but at least it smelled good. That was important to her. When she and her brother Matt had checked out options for their mother's care, some of the places had smelled so foul they hadn't had the stomach to finish the tour. A couple facilities had the heavy pine scent of cleaners, and she and Matt had wondered just what smells they were trying to mask.

Vinnie hung back near the entryway, holding the tote full of Christmas presents Foxy had wrapped for his former mother-in-law. He hadn't seen her in years. Judging by the look on his face, Foxy knew her mother's deterioration took him by surprise.

Mary Tripp sat in a wing-backed chair in the common area. A handful of her housemates were scattered about the room. Some were watching television. Two men played a game of checkers, making up their own rules to allow teetering stacks of checkers to be moved around the board.

Although her mother's chair faced the television, she was gazing out the window. Her gray hair was unkempt, and her knobby fingers were knotted together in her lap.

Foxy approached her, saying, "Mother, it's me."

Her mother continued to stare out the window until Foxy put a hand on her shoulder. The older woman looked up, searching her face. Each time Foxy had visited her in the past year, recognition seemed to take a little longer. "Foxy," she said at last. Reaching for an embrace, her arms shook.

Foxy thought she felt thinner than she had only a month earlier. Crouching next to her chair, she asked how she was feeling, and if she'd eaten today.

One of Mary's favorite aides, a man from Barbados, came over to greet them. "She's had trouble sleeping the last few nights, so we gave her something last night." He bent over to touch her shoulder. He smiled broadly, revealing gleaming white teeth. "You slept good, didn't you, Mary?"

Mrs. Tripp patted her hair nervously. "I slept good." She started to rock, forward and backward. Her tongue darted in and out between her lips.

Foxy took her mother's hands in her own, gently squeezing each finger from base to tip and then stroking the palms with her thumbs in a circular motion until her nervousness abated.

Mary Tripp looked past her daughter and, for the first time, noticed Vinnie standing on the other side of the room. She cocked her head and stared at him.

Foxy motioned for him to come over.

Her mother's eyes didn't leave him as he walked across the room and set his load down on the nearby table. If there was recognition on her face when he greeted her as "Mother," it didn't show.

She looked down at his feet. He wore his new winter boots. "Wrong shoes," she said with a frown.

He and Foxy exchanged a grin.

"What's wrong with your leg?" she asked.

His expression was one of bemusement. "It got broken pretty bad. It happened a long time ago." To Foxy, he said, "The old girl always was observant."

The "old girl" glared at him. "My hearing's pretty damn good too, and you have a smart mouth."

Vinnie tucked his chin back and raised his eyebrows. "When did you learn to swear?"

"They teach me," she said, pointing a crooked finger at the men playing checkers.

Vinnie laughed. As he and Foxy pulled up chairs to chat, Mary kept looking back and forth from her daughter to Vinnie.

Once again Foxy felt as if she'd been thrown back two decades. Vinnie had always had a way with her mother. He got by with flattery and teasing in a way she didn't put up with in others. Foxy used to think it was endearing and sometimes a little maddening, but today she found it disorienting. How had Vinnie managed to come back into not only her life, but her mother's as well without missing a beat?

At the game table, the checker towers toppled. The two men playing laughed. One of them swept his hand across the table and dumped the rest on the floor. The aide came over, hands on hips. "Game time's over," he said.

Foxy turned back to her mother, asking about the other residents by name. Mary Tripp was coherent with her answers. Sweet-faced Irma, who'd befuddled everyone when she suddenly reverted to speaking in her native German, had recently begun wandering at night. Floyd just turned eighty-five, and they'd had a party for him with balloons. Foxy looked around the room and made note of who was there. Today, all the usual suspects were in place, except for the residents who took afternoon naps. "Is Pastor Paul taking a nap?" Foxy asked, recalling how surprised she'd been to see him here and in such rough shape during her last visit, after not seeing him in years.

"Pastor Paul?" her mother echoed with a blank expression. It was visible on her face when the words connected. "Paul. No, he's gone. Gone. Amen, the end." her mother said, punctuating her words by tapping Foxy's wrist. Mary had never liked using certain words, Foxy knew, and "dead" was at the top of her list.

"You mean he died?" Vinnie asked.

She nodded. "I mean gone. Just like Ichabod."

Foxy explained to Vinnie that Ichabod was how her mother had referred to the retired teacher who'd lived in the room next to hers. Then one day, according to her mother, "Pneumonia took poor old Ichabod to the big classroom in the sky."

"Pastor Paul died of pneumonia?" Foxy asked.

She nodded again. "Pneumonia, the old man's friend."

Having seen for herself how frail and incapacitated her former pastor had become, Foxy could well believe it.

"They move in, they move out." Mary tipped her hand back and forth. "Aloha on the steel guitar."

Foxy and Vinnie shook their heads in unison. Vinnie leaned forward in his chair, with elbows on knees and hands folded to support his chin. After a period of silence, he sat up and said, "Enough of the obits. Let's open presents."

Mrs. Tripp eyed the wrapped packages on the table. "Are those all for me?" Her voice was that of a little girl.

They handed her one after another and watched as she carefully picked off the tape and folded the wrapping paper before examining her gifts. She tried to open the perfume bottle, but Foxy stopped her and showed her how to spray it. When her mother opened the CDs, Foxy suggested going to her room so she could load them into the player.

As they accompanied her down the hall, toting her new robe and slippers and other items, they noticed the kitchen staff was already preparing supper. Mary's bed was made and Foxy saw the gilt-edged pages of the bible were open to the Psalms. Mary sat in her comfy chair. Soon her eyelids began to droop.

Foxy leaned down and kissed her cheek. "We need to go now, Mother. I love you. She slid one of the CDs into the plastic player, and fitted the headphones over her mother's ears.

"I love you," Foxy mouthed to her again.

Mary grabbed her hand and then Vinnie's. Staring at his face, she said loudly, "Will you come again?"

He looked at Foxy and nodded.

* * *

THEY'D LEFT ST. PAUL just after daybreak, and already, only nine hours later, the sunlight was fading. Walking out into the cold, Vinnie said. "Is there any reason we have to head up to Matt's tonight? I'm bushed. It's been a long couple of days."

Foxy had been thinking the same thing. Visits with her mother always drained her, but the emotional strain she'd been under in a short period of time was catching up with her—the unsettling calls, then hearing about Sierra's death and finding out she'd been stalked too. And then there was Vinnie's bizarre arrival. What had he been thinking? It was not simply that he'd come unannounced. That would have been enough stress, but at least it would have been consistent with some of his other boneheaded decisions. But to break into the house and scare her witless! Well, that was just plain dumb, masquerading as creepy.

The other stressor, she had to admit, was how she'd handled things with Bill Harley. She'd done her damnedest to live her life in harmony and integrity. She liked her life. And then Vinnie had come along and hijacked it. At this moment, all she wanted was to fall into bed and sleep until the world, with all its inhabitants and all its complications, went away.

Vinnie turned on the engine, and while he used the scraper on the windshield, Foxy brushed the dusting of snow off the other windows.

"I saw a little motel back by the main road," Vinnie said, walking around to scrape the rear window.

Foxy cut him off. "The one on Finland Road? Near where I used to live?"

Vinnie nodded.

Years ago, her family had lived less than two miles from what was the current center of Pine Glen. Their house on Finland Road had been a tan clapboard two-story with dormer windows. She could lie on her chenille bedspread in her little upstairs bedroom with a sloping ceiling, and see into the rooms of both houses across the road. Because the occupants, a boy in each house, could see into her room also, her parents cautioned her incessantly to close the heavy curtains.

They got into the car and Vinnie headed in the direction of the motel.

Thinking about some of the people in her old neighborhood made her sad. In the house directly across from hers lived the boy whose family hastily moved away after the boy and a couple of non-church friends were discovered sleeping under the altar one morning, stinking drunk.

She remembered bringing Sierra here for Christmas all those years ago, and the memory made her heart ache. Lying together on her old double bed in her old bedroom, she'd told Sierra all about that boy and his family.

She also talked about the occupants of the house next to his and directly across the street from Foxy's, where the pastor and his family lived. Their house was a little larger than the Tripp house, and had a beautiful old-fashioned garden. Many nights, their son Peter, the same one who liked to look up girls' skirts at the picnics, could be seen sitting by the open window with the lights out, smoking a cigarette. He wasn't even a teenager yet when he began slipping out at night by climbing onto a place where the roof dipped down. From there he'd jump a couple of feet to the sturdy branch of an oak tree, and climb down. Usually he didn't come home for hours.

Peter was a handful. That's what everyone said. There had been plenty of pressure on him, and he'd returned the favor by putting his parents through the wringer, proving the maxim about preachers' kids. Still freckle-faced and with an overbite, he'd begun acting out in school and church, walking a very fine line between normal, youthful rebellion and criminal behavior. It had surprised everyone when he'd followed his father's footsteps into the ministry.

One of the times Sierra came to visit, Peter was home from seminary, and together they watched him standing by the window in his room to take off his shirt. Foxy didn't agree with Sierra that he knew they were watching. They'd commented on his muscular body and giggled like a couple of teenagers. The next day, Foxy looked out the window to see Sierra outside with Peter, flipping her dark mane of hair in her seductive way as she talked. Sierra had been a handful too.

There was almost nothing left of the town she'd been so desperate to leave. When Pastor Niemi and his wife moved away from Pine Glen, his little congregation scattered. Foxy's parents moved to an apartment.

It turned out to be a good move for Pastor Paul Niemi. Moving to the Twin Cities, he led a flock that had tripled in size during his time there. Then, as senior pastor of a big, successful church, he'd been offered an administrative job in the synod, and his son Peter stepped right into the pulpit he'd vacated.

Looking at the sorry little motel, the only building on the block where she grew up, Foxy felt as desperate to leave Pine Glen as she had when she was a teenager. She said to Vinnie, "I don't want to stay here. Let's get back on the freeway and head north."

"Or we could backtrack. There's a big hotel in Hinckley."

She avoided looking at him. "No. There'll be something on the way to Cloquet." Of all the places to take a recovering gambler, she would never choose the hotel attached to the Grand Casino in Hinckley. That kind of backtracking was not an option.

S logging through the crowds at the Mall of America, Cate wondered what had possessed her to come here with her mother. Herds of teens walked four and five abreast, making it nearly impossible for people to pass them. They talked loudly and with broad arm movements. Bawling babies, darting toddlers, and scolding mothers added to the mayhem. Once Cate tuned into the din, she couldn't tune it out again.

Oblivious, her mother chattered happily, pointing out things in kiosks and wondering out loud what to get for Cate's brother and sister-in-law, Ricky and Bunny, who were going to stay at Cate's, along with her nephew, his wife and their son. And if that weren't enough, Erik's parents were coming too. She was suddenly overwhelmed at the commitment she'd made to have them all there, not just for a meal, but as houseguests. She hoped they'd all had "plays well with others" marked on their report cards.

Her mother was talking now about her friends at her senior apartment building, and Cate was truly interested in them. She and Robin had gotten to know so many of them when they'd been drawn into a missing persons case last year. The residents of Meadowpoint Manor had become very dear to the whole book club. She strained to hear over the crushing noise.

Wanda waved one hand in the air as she talked. "After the sing-along, Daisy invited us back to her apartment to see her snow globe collection. They were all lined up on her bookshelves. Some were from her travels, and some . . ."

Her mother's voice faded, crowded out by Cate's thoughts. Glass, snow, being trapped, red hair, spinning . . . she tried all the connections she could think of. What was she missing about the snow globe dream? She hated the way messages came to her sometimes. She'd get just enough information to worry, but not enough to act on.

Her mother tugged on her coat sleeve, bringing her along as she ducked through the foot traffic. "Let's look in here," she said.

Cate wondered what had caught her mother's eye. Wanda sometimes dressed younger than her years would indicate, and often had no regard for the weather conditions in Minnesota. She'd lived down south long enough to consider herself a Floridian, and Cate had been working to purge her mother's closet of strappy sandals and tank tops ever since she'd returned to Minnesota. Glancing around the racks of sweatshirts and sweaters, Cate was surprised her mom had chosen this, of all the stores in the mall, to do her shopping.

"Do you know Ricky's size?" her mother asked, holding up a sweater.

Cate stood back, trying not to show her reaction on her face. "Large, probably, but extra-long," she answered, wondering how to break it to her mother that she could not, in a million years, picture her nearly sixty-year-old brother in a sweater depicting gingerbread men standing on a diving board above a pool of milk.

"Oh, look, I could get them for the whole family!" She held up two sweaters, identical to the first except for the size.

"Um, Mom," Cate began haltingly.

Her mother threw back her head and cackled. "Just seeing if you're paying attention."

Cate pressed a hand to her forehead, feeling the beginnings of a headache. She pictured the bunch of them sitting around in identically silly sweaters. "Good grief!" she said, and started laughing. But in a few minutes, she was back to chasing butterflies of worry about Foxy. "Mom, I think we need to quit," she said.

Wanda gave her a questioning look.

"I feel a need to go to Foxy's apartment."

Soon they were wandering through the parking lot, trying to figure out where Cate had left her vehicle. When they found it, Cate got in and checked her cell phone for messages. "I hope Brad and Foxy are okay," she said to her mother.

"You mean Brad and Robin, don't you?" Wanda said, shaking her head. "Honestly, I worry about my memory sometimes, but at least I know Brad is married to Robin."

Cate chuckled. "And that's how rumors start." She explained that Robin's husband, Brad, and Foxy were both on the road today, but separately. Brad was heading to Colorado to pick up their daughter who was stranded in Denver, and Foxy—what exactly was Foxy up to? She decided to give Foxy's last official destination, saying she was visiting her brother in Ely.

Driving down the ramp at the Mall of America, Cate had to make a choice whether to go east or west on 494. "Do you mind if I drop by Foxy's house and check on the pets before I take you home?" she asked. "We can stop at my house, too. I have a bunch of cookies for you to take home with you."

"I don't need a lot of cookies."

"Then you can share them. I've seen those ladies fall on a plate of cookies like a pack of hyenas."

"What a lovely image," her mother said, "and very apt."

Traffic was heavy all the way into St. Paul. Cate found a place to park across the street from Foxy's apartment. Her mother opted to stay in the car, so she left the engine running. Mounting the stairs, she could feel the arthritis in her knees after a morning of walking the mall. Using the spare key, she let herself in. The cats were happy to see her, as always, and quickly gobbled down their canned turkey.

Everything looked to be in order. No weird animal energy, no signs of anything out of place, and yet Cate felt uneasy. She wandered through the apartment. Everything was nice and tidy the way Foxy always kept it. "Ha!" she exclaimed when she saw two, slightly damp bath towels hanging in the bathroom. "I knew Bill was here."

Foxy had adapted the small corner room for her massage therapy business. She'd been attentive to each detail, the silk scarves on the walls, hanging and standing plants, a rice paper screen and soft colors. Besides the massage table and stool, she had a long tray-topped bench that held her lotions, oils and candles, all nestled on a jumble of polished river rocks. It was Cate's favorite room in the apartment.

If she hadn't left her mother in the car, she might be tempted to cue up some mood music, stretch out on the table and escape from all thought of entertaining a house full of relatives. Regretfully, she shut off the light and closed the door to this little piece of serenity.

But she couldn't bring herself to leave, not yet. Wandering through the rooms again, she settled on the loveseat. She closed her eyes. The only image that came to her was of their book club luncheon at Robin's only two days ago, when they'd all raised their glasses and toasted to the spirit of Christmas yet to come. But even as they'd talked about the future, Cate remembered, she'd swirled her wine in her glass and stared into the red liquid. A phrase had popped into her mind that day. Don't forget the spirits past.

Now as she thought about that phrase, she took the time to brainstorm its meaning. Not spirit but spirits. Whose spirits? There were plenty that came to mind. At the top of the list was the spirit of Sierra, only recently passed on. And what about the man murdered on the streets of Las Vegas? Was Foxy being haunted by his spirit? Foxy had said the six witnesses to the murder had gone their own separate ways after that. Had they all forgotten the spirit of friendship? Or, what about the way Foxy just walked away from her past? What haunted her to the extent she never talked about her marriage? What or who else was she trying to forget?

A persistent sound made her open her eyes. She searched until she saw the source. Elvis pawed at a box tucked into the corner by the bookshelf. She hadn't noticed it before, but now it demanded her attention. It was a standard wine box. Foxy didn't usually have boxes lying around, and certainly not wine boxes. Of course people packed a lot of things in boxes from the liquor store. Cate walked into the kitchen and saw the wine rack with enough empty spaces to hold twelve more bottles of wine.

Elvis purred loudly and nudged her hand as she knelt on the floor to get a closer look. She was even more perplexed and intrigued when she saw the handwritten note taped to the side of the box. "Please make sure you give this to Frances Tripp," it said, and below that was Foxy's phone number and address.

The box had been opened and reclosed but not resealed. Cate wondered if it would violate Foxy's privacy if she had one little peek inside.

\* \* \*

"HOW LONG DOES IT TAKE to feed a couple of cats, for crying out loud?" Wanda said to herself, wishing she'd used the restroom at the mall. Her daughter was certainly taking her time. She leaned over and turned off the engine, pocketing the key.

Cate had parked close to the snowbank, and Wanda had to brace herself against the Land Rover to keep from slipping on the snow and ice. The car was filthy with dried road salt, and as she came around the back of Cate's vehicle, she paused to brush the white powder off her black coat. When she looked up, a man was getting out of a vehicle on the opposite side of the street. He was tall and wore a black dress coat and muffler. When he appeared to be heading to the same house as she was, she figured he must be Foxy's landlord. She found herself walking about twenty paces behind him, up a short stretch of sidewalk and then trailing him up the walk. It was a bit awkward.

He didn't acknowledge her until he reached the bottom step, and then turned around. "Are you following me?" he asked with a grin. He was attractive, with brown hair and a smattering of freckles.

Wanda laughed. "I guess I am. But no, I'm just checking on my daughter," she said. "She went up a while ago, and I got tired of waiting."

He seemed surprised. "Is your daughter, by any chance, Frances Tripp? I have an appointment with her."

For just a brief moment, she was uncomfortable talking to him, and wondered if that was how Cate got her premonitions about people. But then she relaxed. In her haste, Foxy must have missed canceling one of her appointments. "Oh, no, she's not here. That's why my daughter came over—"

"Does your daughter have a habit of visiting people when they're not home?" His grin was disarming.

Wanda enjoyed the banter. "Doesn't everybody? One learns so much about people that way." She laughed to let him know she was kidding. "My daughter is here to feed her pets, actually. Foxy had to leave suddenly. I'm sorry you didn't get her message," she told him.

"Ah, I see," he said in a reasonable tone. His brow furrowed and he said, "I hope she's all right. I don't suppose you know where Miss Tripp went, do you?"

She was taken aback by the question and decided to deflect it by using her flirtatious tone. "Sir, we just met! Surely you don't expect me to give out any such information so early in our relationship."

He looked sheepish. "Oh, dear, that was inappropriate. I only meant . . . They say the roads are getting bad, not so much here, but to the north and west and I was just concerned . . ." His voice trailed off.

She decided to let him off the hook. "I know, we're concerned, too. She's on her way to her brother's resort and it's way the heck up by the Canadian border."

He whistled. "The weather forecaster was saying—"

She held up her hand to stop him. "My friend Vivian calls them 'weather terrorists,' scaring us half to death with their dire predictions." She and the stranger shared a chuckle. By now she'd remembered why she'd come up to the house, and waiting any longer to find a bathroom would cause them both great embarrassment. "But, really, I do need to see what's keeping my daughter."

"Of course. Thank you for your help." He stepped aside and let her pass.

She looked at the box, trying to divine its contents. Hidden treasure, compromising photos, jewelry. The conversation she'd had with Robin popped into her mind. "Guess what, I've found the head of Jimmy Hoffa!" she said out loud, grinning as she imagined telling that to Robin.

By the time her curiosity compelled her to peel back the flaps, the last thing she expected to find in the wine box was wine. Twelve stupid bottles, nothing more.

She sat back on her heels, defeated. She'd been so sure.

The bell rang downstairs. She hung onto the bookcase to stand up. Making sure Elvis didn't shoot out the open door, she rushed down the stairs, slipping and almost falling on the last step. When she peeked through the fish eye, she saw her mother leering at her from the other side, her nose and one eye magnified as she tried to peer in.

"Bathroom!" Wanda said with some urgency as soon as Cate opened the door. She pushed past her.

"Careful, the stairs are steep."

Wanda was on a mission and didn't pause. Cate followed more slowly.

Back in the apartment, Cate felt a letdown. There was something tantalizing about that box, and in the couple of minutes it took to let her mother in, she'd convinced herself that Elvis, by pawing it, was telling her to open it. "I've read too many mysteries," she said to the cat, who walked up, circled the box, and sat in front of it.

Kneeling once more to close the box, she thought about a book the No Ordinary Women had considered reading when it first came out. She got a vivid image of the cover, picturing a sailboat on the rocky seas, and the title, *Message in a Bottle*. As soon as she'd pulled out the first two bottles, she knew she was onto something.

Her mother stepped out of the bathroom, took one look at her daughter and said, "What on earth are you doing?"

Four of the bottles were already standing in a line on the pass-through, and Cate was carrying two more to set beside them. The wine was an assortment from a California winery. Only last summer, Cate had discovered Big House wines when she was getting ready to host the book club at her house. That month, they'd been reading a book about Alcatraz, and she'd been elated to find the perfect wine to accompany it. The pinot noir was labeled Pinot Evil, and the chardonnay, The Great Escape. "I know there's a message on these bottles, Mom. Help me."

Wanda took the two from her hands and set them with the other four. "What am I looking for?" she asked, bending to peer intently at the labels.

Cate stopped. "I have no idea.

"But you're sure she chose this way to leave you a message? It seems a little obscure. Why not say it directly?"

"I don't know, Mom. I haven't a clue what we're looking for. Maybe someone wrote on the label or maybe when we line all the bottles all up in a certain order, they'll spell out a clue."

"Catherine," she said, using her given name, "what are you getting us into? I get the feeling you're leading us down that primrose path again."

"What?" Cate bent down, picked up the half-empty box.

"You know what I mean. Are we tracking down another murder?"

Cate stopped in her tracks. "You know, I think that's exactly what we're doing."

"Goody!" her mother said.

What a strange response to murder! Cate shook her head, and yet, to be fair, she'd never felt so alive as when she and her friends had been in pursuit of a murderer. Sure, they'd put themselves in danger, but it had all turned out okay. Hadn't it? "Goody!" she responded. "And damn the consequences. Whoever died from reading a wine label, anyway?" After setting the box on the counter near the sink, Cate extracted a bottle and turned it in her hands. Sliding her reading glasses down from where they were perched on the top of her head, she read the fine print.

They were still laughing when her mother reached into the box, pulled out a bottle, and said, "Oh! Oh my!" She held it up for Cate to see. It was a red wine named The Usual Suspect.

Cate went around the counter to take the bottle from her mother. Although it appeared to be full of wine, it was light in her hands, and when she tilted it back and forth, it didn't slosh. It was a screw-top, and she put her fingernail into the crease of the seal. It was already broken.

"Do it! Open it," Her mother urged.

"I always was an obedient child," Cate said.

"You were not!"

It was screwed on tightly, but Cate got the top off, and squinted inside. She turned it upside down and banged on the bottom. Then flipping on the overhead light, she held the bottle at various angles and stuck her finger into the opening.

Wanda leaned close, trying to get a look. "There is something in there, isn't there?"

"It looks like rolled up paper, but it's wider than the neck of the bottle. I can't figure out how to get it out."

"Here, let me have a crack at it." Wanda held out a hand.

Cate passed the bottle back to her and watched as her mother raised it and brought it down with a crack on the center divider of the double sink.

"Oh, my," her mother said again, picking up a large chunk of broken glass from the sink. "How clever! It looks like someone swirled red paint in the bottle to make it look full."

Cate reached past her to snatch up the contents. She set the tube of paper on the counter and tried to unroll it. It snapped back. "Help me, Mom."

Together, they flattened the sheets of paper, holding the corners so they could read what was written. Cate's mouth fell open. She stared at her mother and said, "I need to call Foxy."

Her hands shook as the pulled her cell phone out of her purse and pressed the numbers.

She turned her head when she picked up a faint ringing somewhere in the apartment. Pulling the phone from her ear, she handed it to her mother and went in search of the ringing phone. It stopped. "Redial it," she said.

She finally found it in the pocket of Foxy's wool jacket. It was not like Foxy to leave without her phone, but maybe she really needed to get away from it all. Flicking through Foxy's lists of contacts, she found Bill's number. Even though she hated to interrupt his time with Foxy, this felt too important to ignore.

Sheriff Harley answered, sounding tired, maybe even a couple sheets to the winds. "Yes?" he said with obvious annoyance.

"Hi, it's me, Cate Running Wolf."

"Okay?" It was not a friendly response.

When she explained Foxy had left her phone at home and that she needed to talk to her, Bill sounded confused and then aggravated. "What makes you think she's here?"

"I . . . I just thought . . ." she stammered.

"I get it. She took off, and you thought she was with me. Well, welcome to the club. I thought she was with me, too."

She apologized and hung up. "That was awkward," she said to her mother. "I've really stepped in it now."

On a hunch, she scrolled down and found Tina's number.

Waiting for Tina to answer, Cate recalled something she and Robin had talked about. They'd joked about a tontine, with each surviving investor accruing more and more money upon the death of one of them. *What am I doing, calling the one person with a motive to kill Foxy?* she thought, and quickly hung up.

Next she found Matt's number and called it. A message said the number was no longer in service. "Can you believe this?" she said to her mother as she pulled out her own phone and dialed Robin.

* * *

THE MOTEL SAID NO PETS ALLOWED. They had no trouble smuggling Molly Pat in. As soon as they checked in and got the dog settled, they walked to the restaurant just across the parking lot and ordered the spaghetti with meatballs special. While they waited for their food, Foxy checked her coat pockets and then her purse. "Damn it!"

"What are you looking for?"

"My phone. It must be in the car."

"I didn't see it."

"Well, it must be, Vinnie. I never go anywhere without my phone."

"Where did you last see it?"

She faced him with a sardonic look. "Well, if I knew that, would I be digging around for it? Oh, damn!" she swore again as she remembered. Just before they'd left her apartment, she'd decided to take a warmer coat, one with down filling and a hood, leaving her wool coat at home. "I left it in my other coat pocket."

He chuckled in a patronizing way that annoyed her. "We're good. If you really need to call someone, you can use my phone or make a call from the room."

She didn't want to think about their room right now, with its two double-beds. "I was just going to call Cate."

"What for?"

"Or Robin. Just to touch base, I guess." How could she explain that ever since she'd gotten the call about Sierra, she'd felt like she'd taken a tumble down the rabbit hole? After her initial shock at Vinnie's unannounced visit, his presence had been oddly comforting. But she'd barely had a moment to assimilate those two pieces of her past, Sierra and Vinnie, when she found herself fleeing to Pine Glen, where even more distant memories emerged. She'd kept her worlds separate for so long, and now they were colliding.

Suddenly, she was homesick for the life she'd made for herself in the Twin Cities, including her friends in the book club, who supported each other in ways she couldn't have imagined when she'd moved to Minnesota years ago, alone, mistrustful and apprehensive about her future.

So why, she wondered, was it so hard to tell the No Ordinary Women about her life? As hard as it was to explain her complicated feelings about Bill Harley, the past was an even messier quagmire. What would they say about Vinnie Romano, when she herself didn't know what to think of him? He was both loving and clueless, kind of a benign doofus.

Years ago, she'd imagined what it would look like if she were to chart the years she and Vinnie had been together. It would look like the graph made by a cardiac monitor, spiking and dipping in a predictable way over several years, and then going into arrhythmia before flatlining. But was it really dead?

When they were finished with their meal, they went back to their room. With Vinnie hovering nearby, it would be awkward talking to Bill, but she called him from the phone in the room anyway, but only after Vinnie promised not to clear his throat, cough, or make any other noises.

Bill didn't sound like himself, and his clipped responses didn't encourage a lot of conversation. Foxy apologized, explaining to him she'd felt the need to get away to think, and heard an edge of sarcasm in his voice when he politely thanked her for letting him know. "I care about you, you know," she said before they hung up, and he muttered that he cared about her too.

Sitting in the chair next to the window, Vinnie watched her with frank interest. "Sorry if my presence is a problem," he said.

She felt like she was teetering on the edge of a high wall that separated past and present. She could choose to fall on either side, but if she did nothing, the choice would be out of her hands, and she would fall or be pushed anyway. The muscles of her shoulders were giant knots of tension, and she made a concerted effort to breathe deeply and let herself relax. Suddenly she was overwhelmed with exhaustion. All she was capable of doing was to fall into bed.

He patted the mattress of the bed he'd claimed. "Want to sleep together?"

Even though he'd behaved himself at her house, she felt the need to remind the benign doofus there was to be no hanky panky. She claimed the bed by the window.

"Not even panky?"

She laughed. "No hanky. No panky."

"No problem," he said with a lazy grin, throwing back the bed-spread of the other bed. "I'm exhausted."

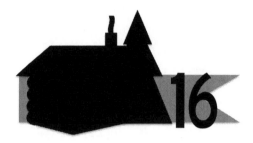

Sitting in front of the television, Robin worked on the last rows of the scarf of soft, hand-dyed merino wool she was knitting for Brad. She found herself pondering what Cate and her mother had told her about the message in the bottle. It was a bit theatrical leaving personal letters and the results of a paternity test behind, Robin thought, but then Sierra had been in a theatrical business.

It was more than that, though. She had no doubt Sierra had meant the contents of the wine bottle to be found only in the event of her death. But why? She was still young, at least too young to be contemplating her own death by natural means, unless, of course, she'd just found out she had a fatal illness. In that case, Robin might believe she'd taken her own life, but that theory didn't take into account the fact that she'd believed someone was following her.

If she hadn't died at her own hand, then whoever was stalking her would be the natural suspect. Fearing someone might kill her, Sierra may have felt compelled to hide papers that would be understood only by the recipient. Since she'd made sure the box wound up in Foxy's hands, it was safe to conclude Foxy would be able to interpret the contents of the bottle. Foxy was convinced the stalker was connected to the murder they'd all witnessed years ago, but the time lapse alone made that improbable—unless something else happened that Foxy either didn't know about or wasn't telling.

Foxy had referred to Sierra as "colorful." Was that a way of saying she took risks, had messy relationships, lived on the wrong side of the law? It was possible. Until the book club lunch, none of them had heard anything about Sierra. How important could she have been in Foxy's life if she'd never even mentioned her? And why had Sierra reached out to Foxy?

But now, Foxy was gone without discovering the message meant only for her. In her absence, Sierra's message from beyond the grave had fallen into the hands of strangers. "She's reaching out to us," Cate had said. Well, what on earth did Sierra expect them to do about it? If she'd only needed to confess an indiscretion, a lousy choice she'd made, it would be nobody's business but her own.

"You worry too much about everyone else," Brad had told her more than once, a polite way of telling her to mind her own business. "You don't need to get involved in every little intrigue, every unsolved mystery that comes along." Maybe in this instance Brad was right. Who was she to insert herself into the life—and death—of someone she'd never even heard about until three days ago?

Cutting the yarn, she buried the loose end by threading it along the finished side. Holding up the deep crimson scarf, she was pleased with its look and feel. She carried it to the basement where she wrapped it in decorative tissue paper and placed it in a cabinet with the other packages wrapped and ready for Christmas morning. There was nothing more for her to do before Christmas, which was still a week away.

In the living room, she felt a draft coming from one of the windows and when she went to close the shades, she looked across the street and down a rise to Lake Harriet. All day long the lake had been happily populated by skaters, people walking with dogs, or building snowmen and other snow sculptures, but tonight it felt desolate despite the lights lining the far shore. It was like her house—cheerless, even with all the trappings of Christmas.

All her home needed was her family. For years, making Christmas happen had been a team effort. She and Brad and the girls and her mother had baked and decorated and had taken in a holiday-themed show. Then the girls had gone off to school, one to each coast, and although they'd carved out a little family time over the holidays, life with Mom and Dad increasingly took a lower priority. Even her mother had her own plans putting on a Christmas party at her senior apartment complex, Meadowpoint Manor.

Maya, who typically holed up in her room writing some paper or another, would be home only for a few days of her Christmas break, and Cass, who hadn't planned to come home at all, was now stranded in Colorado, waiting to be rescued by her father.

She sat again in front of the TV and turned up the volume. The weather forecasts varied depending on the channel, yet all ended with the caveat that a slight deviation in the winds could change the path of the storm. With a drop of only two or three degrees, they all agreed, rain could turn to ice, snow, sleet, or some combination thereof. Watching the storm coverage, Robin remembered a favorite Dr. Seuss book, *Bartholomew and the Oobleck*, and imagined the climatologists all atwitter if sticky, green globs of oobleck were to fall from the sky.

Snow and blowing snow were not daunting to most lifelong Minnesotans. After all, if they stayed home every time a flake or two fell, they'd all be hermits for six or seven months out of every year.

She flipped off the TV and went to the bookshelf to pick a new book. Scanning the titles, she realized she wasn't in the mood to read, a rare occurrence. Sierra's death was still on her mind, but the one she was most concerned about was Foxy. She sorted through not so much what Cate had said, but how she'd said it. Clearly Cate had been troubled, as in her sixth-sense kind of worried. It was bad enough Foxy had left her phone at home, but now it turned out she wasn't with Sheriff Harley after all. Last year the No Ordinary Women had read a thriller in which an ordinary man had been forced to "go dark," cutting off all communications with family and friends in order to save someone he loved. Had Foxy gone dark on purpose?

She grabbed her laptop from the kitchen niche where she kept it, and plopped down again in front of the television, now with the sound on the weather channel muted. As she opened her computer, she started to resurrect everything Foxy had ever said about her brother Matthew's resort. The name of it escaped her, but she was pretty sure Foxy had talked about canoeing and kayaking there . . . and snowmobiling. Foxy once bragged about how proficient she was driving a snowmobile. Matthew's resort, according to Foxy, was a series of log cabins not terribly far from town, which Robin presumed to be Ely. Looking over the search results, she found several resorts that fit what she was looking for.

She was ready to give up when she remembered Foxy telling about an incident outside of one of the cabins five or six years ago. Some woman staying at the resort had been mauled by a bear, after luring the ill-fated creature up to her cabin with a bag of marshmallows. Her husband was standing on the front step, camera at the ready, when the bear charged his wife. She'd escaped with a deep gash on her arm. The bear had not been so fortunate. After documenting his own stupidity and his wife's blind obedience, the man had showed the photos to neighbors. She—it turned out it was a female bear with two cubs—was labeled a "bad bear" that had to be dispatched. Foxy had been incensed. More like hopping mad. "They killed the wrong animal!" she'd said, ranting about the egocentric insensitivity of humans.

Robin searched the Internet for the story, and soon came upon it in the archives of the *Ely Echo*. There it was, with a sidebar of other bear attacks, and quotes from people who, like Foxy, blamed the bear's death on the foolishness of the man and his wife. The caption read, "Bear Dispatched at Twin Loons Cabins and Resort."

Typing in that name, Robin found the simple website. The photos were not professionally done, but showed a lovely little getaway with few amenities. This little slice of nature was like the northern resorts of her childhood with running water and electricity but not much else. She pored over the photos and kicked herself for not taking Foxy up on the invitation to join her for a little break before Christmas. As a plan started to take form, Robin punched in the number given on the website, and got a message saying it was no longer in service. "Check the number and try again," the automated voice suggested, and so she did, and with the same results.

Once more she looked at the photos and read the accompanying text. "Leave your worries behind. Dip your toes in the clear waters of unspoiled lakes and watch the flight of herons and eagles. Sit under the stars and watch the dance of the Northern Lights. Strap on a pair of snowshoes and enjoy a brisk walk in nature." Robin's eyes stung as she thought of cross-country skiing through the hushed wilderness, just as she had done at her own cabin in Wisconsin. She imagined sitting with Foxy and her brother, sharing a glass of wine in front of the fireplace as they looked out the window at softly falling snow. In her memory, she smelled the pine trees that surrounded the old hunting lodge at Spirit Falls, and remembered how she and her friends had sat around in their pajamas, lighthearted and relaxed, giggling and carefree as children.

Almost without thinking, she reached for the phone. Even as she hit speed dial, she thought about Erik's words to Cate last year. "You have to stop letting Robin get you into messes." Cate, ever the smart mouth, had said, "No problem. I'll be the one to get her in trouble." Erik had gone so far as to threaten to have her committed if she ever got into another scrape like she had last year, and the year before. Robin figured Erik and Brad had talked about how they were going to keep their wives from venturing into another debacle.

When Cate answered, Robin told her the plan.

Cate groaned, "I can't leave. Family commitments. You don't know how much I'd rather hop in the car with you, even if you're headed for trouble."

"Are you kidding? It's always more fun when we're headed for trouble."

Cate laughed. "Unless it's fatal."

Robin's laugh was cut short.

"Tomorrow I have to pick up my in-laws at the airport, and then I need to be on hand when Ricky and Bunny and my nephew and his wife and baby come."

"Are you sure they'll be able to get here? You might check airport closings."

"My in-laws are coming from the east, so that's no problem, and Ricky and his family are watching the weather, and will leave South Dakota tonight if they need to. Everyone's expected to arrive on schedule, so I really do have to be here."

Of course Robin had known that. With Erik gone for some speaking engagement in Chicago, he wouldn't be back until the day after his parents arrived from Massachusetts. Much as Cate might wish she could take off on yet another mission, her schedule was tight and non-negotiable.

There was no point in calling Louise. She and her partner, Dean, had taken off the morning after the book club lunch—Was that just four days ago?—to spend Christmas with relatives in Virginia. This was the first time in Robin's memory that Louise and Dean had taken a trip over the holidays and left their antique store in the hands of their able assistant.

That had left Grace, who was usually up for an adventure. She, Fred and the boys had a quiet holiday planned. No other family, no overnight guests, no parties—just a morning of cross-country skiing, followed by Christmas dinner. It sounded heavenly. But when Robin had called to talk to Grace last night, Fred had informed her that Grace was spending the night at a sleep clinic and wouldn't be home until mid-morning. Even if Grace could make the drive up to Ely with her, she'd need time to get things together.

Robin calculated there would be less than nine hours of daylight to drive in and it was at least a four-hour drive to Twin Loons Resort, under good road conditions. Looking again at the Twin Loons website, she mapped out her route and hit the PRINT button.

* * *

THE SLEEP CLINIC WAS a miniature version of her college dormitory. Grace was led past the waiting room to one of the four sleeping rooms. It was painted pale blue and had a twin bed, a nightstand, and room-darkening curtains. A comfy chair faced the wall-mounted television. Grace set her toiletries, book, glasses, and a bottle of water on the table next to the chair.

The technician was a pinch-faced young woman who, in a heavily nasal voice, explained the procedure just as the nurse had at her appointment that morning. As she described how electrodes would transmit all the information they needed to discern any sleep abnormalities, Grace tried to figure out who Trudy reminded her of.

"Is that where you hide the camera?" Grace asked, pointing to the glass panel high on the wall at the foot of her bed.

"It is. We tape the session so we can observe the amount of tossing and turning. It's helpful for your diagnosis."

Grace rolled her eyes. If they thought she was going to fall asleep with them watching her—

"No worries," she said. "We just check in now and then. Our patients usually fall asleep with no trouble." After instructing her to get ready for bed, she stood, saying she was going to leave the room so Grace could change into her pajamas in privacy.

*As if there's anything private about all this! How does anyone manage to sleep in front of an audience?* Grace thought of every embarrassing thing that could happen to her. She thought about one of her more restless nights a couple of weeks ago, when she'd jerked and twitched so much trying to find a comfortable position that Fred had grabbed his pillow, saying it was like trying to sleep next to Joe Cocker with hives, and spent the rest of the night in the spare bedroom. How sexy was that?

In a while, the woman came back, tugging on a pair of latex gloves. "It's time to get you hooked up," she said in her nasal tone. That's when Grace realized who the woman looked like—Lily Tomlin as Ernestine, the switchboard operator.

After cleaning several spots on her head and chin, chest, and legs with alcohol wipes, she placed a sticky pad on each area. Opening a large drawer by the bed, she withdrew a swarm of cables and began snapping them onto the electrode pads. Once all the electrodes were plugged in, she taped down the leads and told Grace to finish getting ready for bed.

Walking with all the attached paraphernalia to the bathroom, Grace felt like a pre-strung Christmas tree waiting to be plugged in.

The technician was waiting in the bedroom for her with yet more fun. She bundled the whole tangle of leads and clipped them to a strap around her waist, then encircled her chest with another contraption to monitor her breathing. She showed Grace the CPAP machine they would use if warranted.

Swabbed, stuck, snapped, wired, taped, belted and clipped, Grace was allowed to read for a while or watch TV until she started to feel drowsy.

"You have got to be kidding me!" she said, with another eye roll.

"You'll be surprised how quickly you adjust," the sleep tech assured her.

Amazingly, after reading only two chapters of Louise Erdrich's latest book, Grace felt her eyelids droop, and summoned her nocturnal guide to tuck her in. When the sleep tech pulled out one more cord, Grace was afraid to ask where that one went, figuring she'd just about run out of body parts, and was relieved when Trudy slipped the pulse monitor over her finger.

"If you need me during the night, just talk out loud. The intercom will pick it up."

Grace lay still with her eyes closed for what seemed like hours. She couldn't stop thinking about people watching her, and told herself to think of it as performance art.

Finally, she slipped into a dream in which Foxy was trying to teach her to do the can-can. The problem was she couldn't pick up her feet. It was as if her legs were tied together and all she could do was wiggle her toes. The other dancers were doing high kicks while swirling their skirts. The tall dark-haired dancer pulled away and fixed her with the saddest look. "No dancing for you. You'll have to make yourself useful some other way."

With a jerk, she woke up to find herself in a cocoon of wires. "Help!" she called out.

The tech came in, disentangled her and reattached two of the leads. "You really got snarled up here," she said with a laugh.

"I was twirling," she said lamely.

"I can see that."

"No, I mean in my dream."

"This time, dream about lying still." It was supposed to be a joke, but Grace felt reprimanded for not sleeping properly. Worse yet, she'd somehow managed to flunk dreaming as well.

The next time she fell asleep, the technician woke her by strapping a contraption over her nose and mouth. At four in the morning when she woke again, she was told they'd gotten enough data and she was free to go home.

R obin popped the last bite of toast in her mouth and took her last swig of coffee. She'd made a full pot out of habit, even though Brad was long gone, and had managed to finish the whole thing, one cup at a time. Washing her plate and cup, she looked for something to keep her jangly nerves busy. Her suitcase was packed. Her car was gassed up, and the windshield wiper fluid topped off. It had all made perfect sense last night when Robin had fantasized about taking off with Cate to rescue the red-haired damsel in distress. Now it looked like the little jaunt wasn't going to happen after all.

It hadn't been unreasonable to expect, or at least hope, Cate might join her. They'd been partners in crime almost since the day they'd met at the University of Minnesota, when Robin had been the more cautious one, sensible and grounded, while Cate had taken more risks. But over the course of their friendship, she'd discovered caution didn't necessarily keep her safe, and Cate's recklessness hadn't led her to ruin, as had once seemed inevitable, and they'd grown a little more alike, feeling almost invincible in each other's company.

But of course they weren't invincible. Brad had been right to worry about them. She sighed and resigned herself to staying home. The roads were already getting a little dicey. All in all, it was a great day to stay home. Foxy would find out Sierra's secret as soon as the phones were working again at her brother's resort.

She hadn't realized she was standing almost catatonic in front of the kitchen sink, until her cats twined around her ankles to suggest to her she might as well drop more food into their dishes. Robin looked at them and said, "Oh, knock it off. I just fed you." Then, still talking out loud, she continued to process her dilemma. "Cate's out of the picture. It's a shame, with Brad gone, that we can't head out on a mission." Her eyes drifted to the suitcase by the door leading to the garage. She figured a recovering alcoholic must have a similar tug when seeing a bottle within easy reach.

Shaking herself as she went to the sunroom, she pulled her yoga mat from the wooden chest that served as a coffee table, and began her routine with the sun salutation. At the end of her routine, she lay on her mat to do relaxation stretches and meditation. Despite breathing deeply and rhythmically, she still felt fidgety.

Sitting up, the thought came to her that if Foxy could drive up there, possibly all by herself, so could she. It wasn't merely a desire to do something other than sit here alone. It was as if Sierra's spirit was nagging at her to get the message to Foxy. Was this how Cate felt when she got a premonition about something?

In the past, her friends had been keen on getting involved in such a venture, but maybe the rest of them had attained a level of sanity she hadn't. She experienced a pang, realizing how blithely she'd considered dragging her dearest friends into yet another mess.

* * *

CATE SLOWLY OPENED one eye a crack. Most people who knew her knew not to call before nine in the morning, yet the phone shrilled again. Grabbing it from the nightstand, she heard her mother's voice and said, "What's wrong? Are you okay?"

"I'm fine. Are you awake?" Wanda asked.

Although she was upright, no one could accuse her of being awake. "Oh, Mom, give me a minute. I'll call you right back." She went downstairs and stumbled into the kitchen, tripping over a rawhide bone on her way to the coffee pot. Rumpling her hair, she looked at the clock and saw it was six twenty-two in the flipping morning. She toyed with the idea of going back to bed, but her mother's feelings would get hurt if she didn't call back. Slumping down onto a stool, she saw Carleton and Mitsy standing near their dishes with similarly hopeful expressions, and she knew her morning had begun.

She waited until she'd drunk a full cup of coffee before making the call.

Wanda jumped right in. "I totally forgot to tell you what happened yesterday. After all the excitement over the wine bottle and all, I forgot all about the man I met."

Cate had seen her mother flirt with men, sometimes rather outrageously, but in the years since her dad died, her mother had never talked about anyone special. "Someone from Meadowpoint?"

"Of course not. They're all old."

Cate rolled her eyes. "I'm sure some of them are no—" She stopped herself.

Wanda snorted. "No older than me?"

"Um, I guess that's what I was going to say, but tell me all about the new man in your life. What did he do to sweep you off your feet?"

"Oh, stop it." Wanda sounded exasperated. "He's not from Meadowpoint. I happened to meet a man on the sidewalk outside of Foxy's house. He really was quite pleasant, but before you say it, he's not a love interest, so you can just put that thought right out of your head."

"Okay, okay."

"Although he was nice looking, I have to admit. He was going up the walk just ahead of me and we chatted for a bit. He said he was there for a massage, so I told him Foxy wasn't there."

"Mm hmm."

"He was nice enough. A real nice smile, you know?"

Cate's breathing quickened. "And?"

"Well, when he asked where Foxy was, I wasn't sure what to tell him. I'd only met the man. I had no idea what his relationship was with her, but—"

Cate listened with growing apprehension. "What did you say to him, Mom?"

"Well, I didn't tell him anything at first, but then . . . Oh, Cate, I might have made a huge blunder. He said he was concerned about Foxy—actually, he called her Frances—and he was concerned about her traveling with a storm coming, and I . . . well, I guess I got all caught up in worrying about her too."

Cate asked again, "What did you say to him?" She wanted to reach through the phone and shake her mother.

Her mother stammered, "I, I can't remember what I said, exactly. I mean, we were just chatting, and it didn't seem important at the time. I might have said she was heading up north to visit her brother. Yes, I did, because I remember saying it was way the heck up on the Canadian border. I don't know what else I said. Do you think . . . did I . . . ?"

"Mom, listen, I'm going to call up to the resort right now. Don't worry."

She hung up and immediately tried calling Matt's number from Foxy's phone. When she heard the recorded voice saying the number was out of service, she groaned. After pacing from living room to kitchen and back a few times, she stood with her hands on the counter and her head leaning against the cupboard, trying to calm her breath. This man her mother talked to had been no client of Foxy's. She'd bet her life on it.

She knew with equal certainty he must be Foxy's stalker, and her mother, her wonderfully gregarious and trusting mother, had led the predator directly to the prey. She didn't question how she knew this, she simply knew. The whole time her mother had been talking, Cate had felt danger as a tingling sensation in her hands, and heard it as a muffled howl.

\* \* \*

THE MINUTE SHE ANSWERED the phone, Robin knew from the pitch of Cate's voice that getting in touch with Foxy was suddenly urgent.

As they talked, two things were clear. First, Robin was in the best position to drive up there, and she'd have to go alone. Second, Cate could serve a valuable function staying home, where she could field calls and tend to pets at her own house, plus Foxy's and Robin's.

"Of course I'm worried about Foxy, but now I'm worried about you too. I hate to think of you tearing up there by yourself." Cate said, her voice tinged with alarm.

"Can you think of an alternative?" Robin asked as she stuffed granola bars and string cheese into a shopping bag. "Wait, let me see who's on the other line." She squinted at the name on her caller ID, but without her glasses, it was a blur. Because she never had figured out how to put someone on hold while she took another call, she promised to call Cate back. Pressing the button, she heard Grace's voice.

"I got home earlier than I thought, and Fred said you called. He said you might be going up to the resort with Foxy after all. Is that true?"

Robin explained to her that Foxy was already gone. She told her as briefly as she could about the message in the bottle. "Cate has a bad feeling about it. She thinks Foxy needs to know." After telling her about the man snooping around Foxy's apartment, she told Grace, "Cate and I think she might be walking right into trouble."

Grace laughed a throaty laugh. "Yeah, walking into trouble is usually our job."

"True. Not to mention driving or falling into it." The memory of their reconnoitering mission was still fresh in her mind. She could still picture how she and Grace had donned costumes to follow someone they thought was the prime suspect in the murder of a young woman. Grace had howled with laughter at Robin when she'd fallen into a Dumpster while trying to get up high enough to see through his apartment window. Despite her mounting worry, she had to grin.

"You can't go by yourself!"

Why did everyone say that?

"I'm going with you."

"Grace, you can't—"

"Can too. Just try to keep me away. You know Decembers are slow for me. I'm working at home all month, and whatever paperwork I have to do can wait. Fred, on the other hand, is working out at the gym whenever he's not holed up in the den watching sports or making phone calls about the teacher negotiations. He'll never know I'm gone."

"We'd be gone overnight."

"I figured. Listen, Fred's without a car for a couple days. His got nailed yesterday by a school bus, of all things. I'll just have him use my car and drop me off at your place."

Robin quit objecting and suddenly the trip to Ely felt less like a ludicrous decision and more like an adventure.

They'd reached the long, mostly unpopulated stretch between Cloquet and Virginia, up in the Iron Range, when Vinnie tried Matt's number again to see if it had been reconnected. He tapped buttons, groaned and, with a shake of his head, slipped the phone back in his jacket pocket. "Shit," he said under his breath.

"What?" demanded Foxy.

"The damn phone hasn't been holding a charge very well. I really need to get a new battery, but they're so expensive I was trying to make it last a little longer." He shook his head again and stared out the side window. It was a bleak stretch of road with no houses and very few evergreens to break up the barren tree line.

Foxy felt her irritation rise. What kind of dope would save money by not replacing a phone battery? If a person didn't know Vinnie at all, they'd tell her she was overreacting, but what they wouldn't know was that this one oversight embodied all the past moronic decisions that were uniquely Vinnie-esque. "You tell me this now, when we can't do anything about it?" she said. What a doofus! He didn't even have the good grace to be embarrassed.

Instead, he shot back with, "Okay, then, let's just use your phone." He raised his hands theatrically, and after an equally theatrical pause, said, "Oh, wait, you left yours in your coat pocket at home!"

She felt her jaw tighten. "Yeah, you're right. I forgot the phone at home. You, on the other hand, remembered it, but chose to bring it with a dead battery."

"So we're even."

"Forgetting isn't on quite the same level as choice."

"Result's the same."

He was so clueless, it would be funny if—she didn't want to finish the sentence, even in her head, but she did anyway—It would be funny if she hadn't given him the best years of her life. There were no do-overs, no way to reclaim those years. No point in thinking of the more stable and sensible men she could have married, any one of whom would have known enough to replace the phone battery or buy a new goddamn phone.

But instead she chose to marry fun, sexy, enticing Vinnie, who'd given up gambling in casinos, but still got the gambler's rush on little things like seeing how long he could make his dying battery perform. She looked at his hands, clenched in his lap.

His face was a mask. His shoulders drooped in defeat. "I know I screwed up, but we'll be fine. The gas tank's only down a couple bars. There's nothing to worry about."

She slapped her hands against the steering wheel. "If there's nothing to worry about, what on earth are we running from?"

Shrugging, he said, "I'd tell you to chill, but, sweetheart, I'm guessing you're already cold enough. Look, you're frosting up the windows." He grunted and then tilted the seat back and closed his eyes. He looked relaxed except for the fisted hands in his lap.

Suddenly, she wanted to turn the car around and head back, not to her own apartment and whatever danger might be lurking there, but to Bill Harley's small but sturdy home in Wisconsin only half an hour from Robin's old place at Spirit Falls. She longed to be sitting on Bill's big masculine leather sofa in front of his wood-burning fireplace right now, her own Molly Pat and Bill's dog, Grover, at her side. Given a little encouragement, she would open up to Bill about why Sierra's death had frightened her so. If she told him about the money that had been serendipitously dropped at their feet, Bill might tell her she was stupid for not considering how taking money that was not theirs could be more of a curse than a blessing. She'd rather he think her stupid than immoral.

They'd split the money and the money had returned the favor and split them. It was that simple—that is, until Sierra's death. Now it appeared the consequences would keep on coming as long as even one of them was alive.

It was time to lay all her cards on the table, no matter what happened next. Secrecy had gotten her nowhere. Of course, once Bill found out how greedy and deceitful she'd been, it would be a miracle if he'd still want her in his life. Surely he would come to the same conclusion they all had—almost every man she'd known. In her twenties and thirties, even into her forties, men had described her as hot, in the sense she was sexy to look at, but most who got to know her concluded she was cold inside—heartless, even. If Bill could look her in the eyes after all she had to tell him and say he loved her, then, maybe, just maybe, she would try to believe she was worthy of that love.

Her sins of omission had begun when she'd moved to Minnesota and met warm and funny Cate, whose moral compass pointed to true north. Foxy had felt instantly at home with her and her book club friends. They'd clicked, and she knew she'd stumbled onto the community, the family, she'd always longed for. They were principled, she'd realized early on, without being moralistic—just the opposite of the way she'd grown up. Having dealt with tough situations hadn't hardened them. They were serious about learning and eager to help with various causes, but despite all that, they laughed whenever they got together. Every time!

In their presence she'd gotten good at slipping around questions about her former job, so good, that by the time she thought it might be safe to talk freely about her past with them, they'd stopped asking and there was no reason to rock the boat.

On Saturday they'd been interested and concerned about Sierra's death, and taken aback when she told them about seeing a man gunned down, but no one had judged her. But would they still feel so kindly when they discovered she hadn't told them the whole story?

Vinnie had his eyes shut and his fisted hands were now relaxed. Foxy assumed he was asleep. She'd always resented his ability to sleep, no matter how bad things were. She had worked a long time to overcome a lifetime problem with insomnia, which had only gotten worse with her showgirl's night owl schedule, but for him, sleep was effortless.

His voice startled her. "What happened to us?" Vinnie said, raising his seatback again and facing her. His dark eyes looked sad.

"What?"

"What happened to us? We used to be dynamite together."

She sighed heavily. "Did you ever think that was the problem?"

Now it was his turn to say, "What?"

"Being dynamite together? Maybe that was the problem."

He laughed drily. "I get it. Ha ha. Good until someone lights the fuse. That's fitting." He pulled out a pack of Dentyne and offered her a piece before popping one in his mouth.

Foxy began to question herself, as she had for years since they'd divorced. "I guess at one point the good simply outweighed the bad."

"I suppose." He sighed. "You know, I had plenty of time in the hospital to think."

"I know. I was there." She was beginning to feel queasy.

"Yes, you were there, at least you were there in the flesh, but I could feel it, you know. I could tell you'd already left me in your heart."

She inhaled sharply. Slowly, she began to nod.

He cleared his throat and looked out the window, his jaws clenching on the chewing gum. He swiped the back of his hand under his nose and continued. "Lying there in a body cast, I decided I was done with gambling. I really did quit, you know." When she didn't say anything, he kept going. "I had one little lapse just before I left town, just to see if I could handle it, but all that did was prove to myself I had a real problem. I counsel enough people with addictions to know it's a pretty common reason to relapse." He paused and cleared his throat again. "I really believe we could've made a go of it. I was ready to do whatever I had to."

Foxy's eyes scanned the road, which was striped now with blowing snow. She felt him watching her, and felt the tears trickling down her cheek. Damn him, she thought, for drawing her into the Vinnie Vortex once again. She licked the corner of her mouth and tasted salt. The car drifted to the shoulder as she reached for a tissue. Over-correcting, she slipped across the center line and back again.

Up ahead on the right was a little bakery, which, as she remembered, was closed during the winter. As they approached it, she saw the small parking lot had not been plowed, but she managed to get her Saturn in far enough to ensure it wouldn't be clipped by a passing car.

"What're you doing?"

Shifting it to park, she turned to face her ex-husband. "It's not that simple to say we were good together. As it turns out, it just wasn't enough, Vin. Maybe we could've made it and maybe not. You and I were already rocky when we took that money, and it didn't change us for the better. But there's more to the story, Vinnie, and it's way past the time you knew it."

race was fussing with the zipper pull on her down coat when
Fred pulled up perpendicular to Robin's driveway, evidently in
too big a hurry to actually drive in. He was more edgy and irritated this morning than Grace had seen her husband in a long time,
and it was no wonder. The teachers' union in his school district was
threatening to strike over class size and achievement tests, and was calling for more special meetings. Buffeted on both sides by angry teachers
and angry taxpayers, he knew whatever his stance as school superin-
tendent, it would prove incendiary. Negotiations and hastily called
meetings had been gobbling up his time and his patience for days.

He rushed around to the back of the station wagon and easily
lifted her suitcase, setting it on the cleared patch of driveway. She
got out, grabbed her purse and her canvas tote and opened the back
door to get the rest of her things.

"You're not taking that, too, are you?" he said as she reached
in to pick up the sealed liquor store box.

"Yup, that too."

"You're taking a box of wine?"

She didn't have to justify taking a few bottles of wine to spend
a weekend with friends! "Yes," she snapped back, realizing she was
too tired to argue. When she'd first come home from the sleep study
early this morning, she'd been wide awake, and then, out of habit,

she'd poured three big mugs of coffee down her gullet, which jazzed her up even more. At this very moment, however, lethargy and brain fog were beginning to set in.

"Fine, I'll get it." With a dismissive shake of his head, he set the box down next to the suitcase and tote. Grace pulled two plastic grocery bags from the back seat and leaned in for a kiss. He brushed his lips across her cheek—about as intimate as if he were kissing his mother— and hustled back to slip behind the wheel. Rolling down the window, he called out, "Have fun. Drive carefully." Snow prevented him from squealing tires as he took off, but there was defiance in the way the car's rear end jerked back and forth all the way to the stop sign.

Abandoning her things, except for her purse, near the street, she went up the drive on foot, thinking how odd it was Robin had taken down the pretty wreath she'd had on the front door for their book club brunch. Since Saturday, she'd also managed to outline the porch in twinkly lights. Catching a blast of wind in her face, Grace's eyes watered, and she wrapped her muffler one more turn around her neck. Her glasses steamed up as she breathed into the wool scarf.

Ringing the bell, she waited, pounded, waited again and then tried the door. It was locked. She couldn't remember ever using the other door, but she made her way through the snow and around to the side near the garage. Thank God she'd worn her mukluks. This door was locked too. She peered through the small window, startled by the jumble of gargoyles and garden gnomes scattered just inside the door. They were so uncharacteristic of Robin's taste.

Trudging back to her pile of stuff on the driveway, Grace started to perch on the end of her suitcase and felt it tip. Her arms shot out and she caught herself before falling. It wasn't very graceful, and she hoped no one was peeping out their windows to see her ridiculous self, standing in the middle of her belongings like a refugee with no place to go.

By now her glasses had frosted up, and so she removed them, and then her mittens. The temperature had been hovering a few degrees below freezing, much warmer than the past week. It took someone born and raised in this climate to consider twenty-six degrees warm, but even a native Minnesotan got cold standing still in this weather. Pulling out her cell phone, she squinted, pressed Robin's number and listened to it ring. And ring. Looking back at the house, it occurred to her there were no lights on. "Keen observer," she said out loud.

She considered her options. Fred would not have his phone on since he'd still be driving, and he never talked on the phone when he drove. Besides, he would not be pleasant about turning back to fetch her. She really was in a pickle. It was too early to go knocking on doors throughout the neighborhood, and too damn cold to stand out here.

She called Robin a second time. Again, the disembodied voice at the other end told her that the person she was calling was unavailable, and instructed her to leave a message. "Hi, it's me," she said. "I knocked and you didn't answer. I'm standing here like a ninny at the end of your driveway with a full case of wine. Just look out your window."

She stood, put on her mittens again and placed her hands on her cheeks. The wind was icy. She flapped her arms at her sides and then over her head to stay warm. She paused when a car went past, then resumed her top-only jumping jacks. "Well, here's another fine mess you've gotten me into!" she said out loud.

When the phone in her pocket rang a few minutes later, the voice at the other end said, "Listen, honey, I'm thrilled that you're here, but I'm looking out my window and I don't see you."

"I'm right here." Grace said, her impatience growing. She turned to the house and waved.

"Well, then, bring the wine and come on up, but I have to say, I don't usually drink this early in the day."

"Um," Grace said, suddenly wondering if she was dreaming. None of it made sense.

"What are you doing in Philadelphia anyway?"

Philadelphia? What the heck? And then it sank in. She was talking to her old classmate, Rhonda, who'd moved out east a year ago. The second Grace realized she'd clicked the wrong name on her list of contacts—not Robin and Brad, but Rhonda and Bud—she guffawed into the phone. "Oh, my God, Rhonda, you will *not* believe this." She was laughing so hard, she could barely get the story out and when she finally disconnected, she wondered if Rhonda was telling her husband that Grace had finally lost her mind.

Before she could put her glasses on and call the correct number, the phone rang. This time it really was Robin who said, "Where are you? Are you okay?"

"I'm fine. Just look out front." She waved at the front window once more. It was too dark to see inside. "I'm right in front of your house. Where are you?" Grace retorted.

For a moment no one spoke. Grace waved again, and then looked more closely at the front door. Not only had the Bentleys removed the wreath and put up twinkly lights, they'd also repainted the door. For the second time that morning, she started laughing uncontrollably, and as soon as she could get out enough words for Robin to understand, Robin joined in.

In about three minutes, she saw Robin coming toward her from her own house exactly one block away. Still laughing, Grace hopped from one foot to the other, waving her arms over her head like a middle-aged cheerleader with pom-poms.

\* \* \*

FOXY'S VOICE WAS STEADY. Although she'd rehearsed the words in her mind so many times over the years, they didn't tumble out easily. Vinnie angled toward her in the passenger seat, searching her face for some clue.

She sucked in her breath and began. "It's convenient to say it all went wrong when we found the money and decided to keep it. We were naïve to think it wouldn't change us. Two-hundred thousand is a lot even by today's standards, but back then it meant everything to me—to us. But we were already floundering."

His eyes shifted to meet hers, and then slid away. The wariness she felt was echoed in his expression.

"We both knew I couldn't dance forever, Vin." Absent-mindedly, she rubbed her knee, which had begun to stiffen when she sat too long. "We talked about me quitting. I was coming up on forty years old, but I was bringing in more than you were."

"You think I don't know that?" He shook his head. "How do you think I felt when my own pop called me a *parassita?*"

"You weren't a parasite! I never thought of you that way. It was a fact of our lives, and I felt trapped by it. Do you think I wanted to work forever? I know it was a sore spot, but what was I supposed to do? Sierra was younger than I was and she'd already retired by then. It made me feel old, like I'd literally danced through my twenties and thirties and had nothing to show for it."

He grunted. "Yeah, the difference was, Sierra retired because she had a baby."

Biting the edge of her lip, she nodded slowly. "Yes, she did." She needed to tell the story her way, the way she'd rehearsed it. "We always said we wanted to have kids, but we never actually planned for them—like the cost of having a child without my income or where would be the best schools or neighborhoods for a kid or how we would raise a family without my salary—not even when we started talking about it in earnest."

"I remember when we decided to quit using protection."

"That's not exactly planning. We didn't have much in savings, and our house wasn't set up for kids. The hours we kept were atrocious."

His mouth twitched to the side and he sniffed. "Well, it doesn't matter. It never happened anyway. I kind of thought it might for a while, but then . . ."

"We didn't even throw away the birth control pills until I was almost thirty-five. I just assumed I'd get pregnant right away and retire from the show. I thought any month it might happen."

"Uh huh."

"But then a year went by and then two. Remember when I brought up the idea of taking a year off to see if I'd conceive?"

He shifted uneasily. "That never made a lot of sense to me. Even the doctor said it was safe to keep dancing if you got pregnant."

"Safety wasn't my concern. It was the way we lived. Maybe it was superstition, but by then, I'd started to think God was punishing me because of my lifestyle."

He raised his hands. "What was wrong with our lifestyle?"

"Not ours, mine. It was . . . decadent. I was causing men to lust." She knew the words coming from her mouth were planted there in her childhood. They were still inside her brain, no matter how hard she'd tried to eradicate them. "Some people assumed we were all prostitutes. It was degrading."

"We both knew you weren't doing anything wrong. We used to laugh about their narrow minds. Why can't you just let that stuff go?"

She groaned. "I thought I had, but do you know some idiots still think that's what it means to be a massage therapist? Back then my parents reminded me in every phone call and card that they, along with Pastor Paul, were praying for my soul."

"You don't believe that toxic crap anymore, do you?"

"Nnooo." She dragged out the word. "Not anymore, but I wrestled with it a lot when I was younger. Cripe, Vinnie, I heard stuff like that preached from the pulpit the whole time I was growing up—that vengeful, judgmental God thing, you know? And so month after month when I didn't get pregnant, the thought kept coming to me—why would God want to give a baby to someone who'd left the flock, especially someone who slept until noon, and then strutted around the stage in a bikini and ostrich plumes?"

"Jesus, Foxy, parenthood isn't based on merit. You know better. All you had to do was look around. Some people have kids, some don't. There are lousy parents with great kids and great parents with lousy kids, and everything in between. It's a crap shoot! Sierra was dancing when she got pregnant, and she and Wylie weren't even married. How does that fit your theory?"

She let her head fall back against the headrest. "I know, I know. The punishment thing doesn't hold up under scrutiny, but see, I wanted to quit anyway. I wanted things to change. It wasn't glamorous anymore—just a lot of crazy hours and aching feet. The longer we stayed in Vegas, the more tawdry and corrupt it felt, and the worse I felt about myself. I didn't want to go back to Pine Glen, but I did want something a little more . . . wholesome, I guess."

"Not everything in Las Vegas is unwholesome. There are plenty of real people with respectable lives who live there."

"You know what I mean, Vin. I didn't feel like *me* anymore. I'd gone out there when I was nineteen. I knew I had to break with my church and my family, and getting that job was my one big chance to get away. I was a good dancer, but it was never supposed to be a permanent thing."

"You were a damn good dancer."

She sighed, accepting the compliment. "But I never meant to pull away from them completely. I wanted to mend things with my family and be closer to them, especially Matt, and the more I thought about it, the more I wanted to get out of the desert and back to the woods and lakes."

"You never told me."

She sighed heavily. "I did, Vinnie, I did. You just never took me seriously. Vegas wasn't my home and this—" She spread her hands to encompass the wooded scenery around them. "This wasn't yours."

They sat in the car in silence for a while. Snow swirled and eddied around them. A deer, a large doe, stepped out of the trees, flicking her ears. Humans and deer stared at each other for a long time before the doe slipped back into the brush.

"Can you honestly picture living in Minnesota?" Foxy asked. "You and your alligator shoes?"

Their laughter broke the tension. For one tender minute, they looked at each other, and it all seemed right that they'd be sitting in a parked car in the middle of nowhere. Foxy savored the moment before wrecking their short-lived peace. "But then that last November we were together, I missed my period."

Sitting in a booth at a hotel restaurant near the airport, Cate sipped her third refill of coffee and read William Kent Krueger's latest in his mystery series. It was a pleasant enough way to pass the time until the plane was at the terminal, and she really didn't mind the wait, except that her in-laws refused to use the fancy new cell phone Erik had bought them. Both Chuck and Sally—they preferred to be called by their first names—thought cell phones were unnecessary, and Sally declared she couldn't figure out how to use one anyway.

Cate checked the time on her own phone and figured she had another fifteen minutes before heading out. The book was great. It would have been even better if she could have read it without listening to the idiotic Christmas music. There must be a speaker right over her head, and it pumped out enough volume to drown out all thought with the same endless loop that had been playing at every mall for a month. There were only so many times she could hear "Santa Baby" without wanting to throw herself under the sleigh.

Somehow, she got engrossed in the book and by the time she needed to leave, she'd read two chapters. She paid the bill and went out to find her car had accumulated almost an inch of fresh snow. As she swept the windows with a brush, she thought about how she missed the old days when she could park at the airport, sail past the ticket and baggage counters without anyone stopping her, maybe wander through the gift shops if the flight was delayed before meeting friends or family right at the gate. With the new system, timing was tricky. If she got there too early, she had to circle the airport until she spotted them at the curb. More than once, she'd been shooed away by airport cops who must have thought she looked like a terrorist. If she arrived too late, her father-in-law would give up on her and go back inside in search of a pay phone, where he'd call their home number because that was the one he'd memorized, and be in a pissy mood because nobody answered.

Traffic to the airport was especially heavy due to a combination of holiday air travel, weather and holiday shopping. Passing under the freeway into Minneapolis-St. Paul International, she saw a swirl of snow follow along the retaining wall like a ghost. She hoped Foxy was all right.

* * *

"WHAT?" VINNIE'S HEAD swung around and his grip on Foxy's thigh tightened. "Pregnant? When?"

She swallowed hard. "I suspected it that last time we came out here for Thanksgiving. Remember how grouchy you were when I kept asking you to stop at gas station bathrooms?"

His brow furrowed. "Oh, yeah. I thought you had the stomach flu or something. So that was . . ."

She watched his face and knew he was calculating how long ago it had been. They would have child in high school by now. His expression changed from bewilderment to shock to something akin to joy. "We have a child?"

The question stopped her like a bullet to the heart. "Oh, Vinnie, no. I never . . . I lost it." Lost was such innocuous word for what happened, she'd always thought. Lost was what happened to keys or glasses or games of poker.

"Ahh." His shoulders sagged with the exhalation. "When?" Emotion played across his features. "Why didn't you tell me?"

"Because—No, please let me tell it my way."

He knocked his knuckles together the way he did when he was impatient.

"As soon as we got home from Thanksgiving with my folks, I made an appointment and the doctor confirmed I really was pregnant. I was surprised and thrilled and scared. I was going to tell you, I swear, but I wanted to wait for the right time. With the crazy hours we both kept, you weren't easy to pin down."

His lips formed a thin line. "Are you saying it's my fault you didn't tell me?"

A picture flashed through her mind of the day, a few days after the doctor visit, when she'd begun to tell him. As excited as she'd been, it seemed Vinnie had been even more excited, interrupting her almost immediately to talk about how he'd won six-hundred dollars at the blackjack table. They'd wound up in a nasty fight, the result being she no longer had wanted to share her news with him. She reached for Vinnie's hand and said, "Things were running off the rails by then. We were fighting a lot, and you flat out told me you'd never quit gambling. I was already worried about what kind of parents we'd be anyway, but—"

He pulled his hand away. "I was a real asshole back then."

She didn't argue with him.

"But then things got better, or at least I fooled myself into thinking they were. You weren't going to the casinos so much and I even thought you'd figured out about the baby and had decided to grow up." She saw him flinch. "I mean, every day I saw how my body was changing, even that early, and I assumed everyone else could see the transformation."

Hanging his head, he mumbled, "I didn't have a clue about the . . . the pregnancy. If I was acting better, it was because I knew I needed to clean up my act or I was going to lose you." His voiced dropped. "Turns out, I lost you anyway."

For a while they both sat, staring ahead. The wind had picked up, driving the snow at an angle and shaking the car with the heavier gusts.

"So what happened? How did—? Were you pregnant that night, the night of Wylie's birthday?"

"I was. About six weeks."

Molly Pat startled them both by barking. Poking her nose between them, she rolled her eyes from one to the other.

"She needs to get out." Foxy opened the door and the dog leapt out, squatted, and when she was done, instead of heading back to the car, she took off toward the building, bounding through the snow and frolicking like a puppy.

Vinnie and Foxy pulled on their hats and mittens, buttoned up and got out of the car. They trudged through the fluffy snow past the bakery. Suddenly a pine tree appeared to swell and burst open as hundreds of small birds erupted from it. The chirping cloud flew over Molly Pat's head and disappeared over a rise. She tried to chase after them and barked long after they were out of sight.

"Keep going," Vinnie said when the dog's racket settled down. His words were clipped.

"That night is when it really sank in," Foxy said, "We were going to have a baby, and I couldn't figure out how to tell you I didn't want to raise a child in Las Vegas."

"I wish to God you had."

She nodded and they walked a little further. Along a wire fence, a trail had been worn in the snow. Foxy recognized it as an animal path used by several species—she recognized the upside-down heart shapes of white tailed deer prints. The other prints were probably raccoons, skunks, squirrels and weasels.

"The second that guy got murdered right in front of us, I knew we had to get out of Sin City," she said with a sideways glance. "And then we found out what was in the cooler bag." She spread her hands out, as if appealing to an unseen judge. "There was enough for all of us to get a fresh start. I was confused. Deep down, I knew it was wrong to keep it. If you remember, I argued that we needed to turn it in to the police."

"I remember."

"But, by the next day, I got it torqued around in my head to where I actually started to believe it was a sign, that God had given us that money to raise our kids someplace else. I just wanted a little time to figure things out so when I told you about the baby, I could have a plan in place for where we could go."

His face hardened as she spoke. "Is that what you think marriage is? You make a plan for both of us and tell me where I fit in?"

"No, it wasn't like that." But of course, that's exactly how it had been. He did things behind her back, and to protect herself, she discussed things with him if and when she deemed it wise. "The truth was I was scared about what you'd do with all that money."

"You never did trust me." He stopped and faced her, sucking in his breath for a counterattack, and then his face fell. "I didn't do much to instill faith, did I?"

She looked away.

Dropping a hand on her shoulder, he turned her to him. His eyes were wet with tears. For a while, they looked at each other. "What happened to our baby?" he asked at last.

"I told you, Vinnie, I lost it—him. It was a little boy." She tried to banish the memory of that day. The pain had begun as a dull ache in her low back with a tiny bit of spotting. By the time the pain was radiating to her belly, the blood started in earnest. There had been so much blood, so much pain, she expected to die. And when the doctor said miscarriage was inevitable, she actually hoped she would die.

His face crumpled. His eyes slid away from her and then back to meet hers. "Tell me."

She took another deep breath and puffed it out between pursed lips. "It happened after Christmas. The baby was perfect. He had no defects, and there was no reason they could give me, but I, I just miscarried. I was three months along, and—Vinnie, I swear I was going to tell you about the baby, but then so much happened, and when I lost him, I couldn't bring myself to tell you. I mean, you were lying in the hospital with tubes coming out of everywhere and in terrible pain. The timing—"

"That's when it happened? Wait, wait. Just let me take this in." He turned and retraced his steps through the snow.

She took deep breaths and waited for him to come back.

Coming to a stop in front of her, he had his hands plunged deep in his pockets. "Okay," he said. "Keep talking."

"From the beginning, the doctor had said the pregnancy was a little risky because of my age, but he also told me I was in great shape, and so I thought my age didn't matter. Women older than that had no complications and healthy babies. I'd already tried to tell you that one time, and since that didn't work, I decided it was best if I waited until I made it through the first trimester. See, if I managed to make it that far, the risk of miscarriage was less."

He frowned as she spoke, but didn't stop her.

"It was hard to keep it a secret. I'd just gone in for my three-month checkup and found out everything was coming along fine. I was thrilled. I could hardly wait to get home. On the way, I bought some flowers and a bottle of Chianti, and stopped at Siena Deli for sausage and peppers and pizzelles. I wanted to make a romantic dinner, and—" Her voice caught. "Vinnie, I was so excited to tell you."

Even with his head down, she could see him wince as he started to put together a timetable of events.

"When I put the gelato in the freezer, I moved the stuff in front so I could see our stash of money. It sounds stupid now, but I wanted to look at it and count it and think about how it would change our lives. I put the packets on the kitchen table and I thought they looked a little thinner. It took me a minute to see that they'd been opened and crimped down again. On one of them, the corner was crumbling and the money was wet."

He turned away from her, hands still jammed in his pockets. "Shit," he said and kicked his toe against a tree stump.

"Imagine me ripping the foil open and counting the money, and then counting it again, working myself into a panic. I could barely breathe. I knew you had to be the one who took it. And I knew what you'd done with it."

His head sunk lower, and he curled into himself as if her words were physical blows.

"You gambled it away, didn't you?" She spoke to his back now. "I went insane, Vinnie. I cried and I threw things, and then I went cold—shaking, shivering cold—and when I stopped shaking, I was numb. My only thoughts were how I could protect the baby, and so I packed up the rest of the money in a grocery bag and took it over to Sierra's. Vinnie, I couldn't let you gamble it away. I thought if I could just get the rest of money out of there, there would still be plenty. I was thinking you couldn't handle the temptation of having it in our house. Half of me was thinking if I could get you away from Vegas, you'd be the husband and father I needed, and the other half was thinking I'd better cut my losses and run."

His breathing changed. He spun around. When he spoke, his tone was menacing. "Did it ever occur to you I might have turned my life around sooner if I'd known I was going to be a father? Do you think I might have already known I was in trouble with my gambling? How about the possibility I might not have wound up in the hospital if you'd just said one God damn thing about our baby. Jesus, Foxy, didn't you ever ask yourself why those goons came and used me for a punching bag before they broke my leg like a dry twig?"

Molly Pat came to Foxy's side, nosing her mittened hand.

Foxy gaped at her ex-husband, and then she broke down. Tears spilled down her face and onto her scarf. Cupping her hand over her mouth, she moaned, knowing she'd brought all of this on herself. And on him. She could forgive him, but how could he ever grant her absolution?

He stood just inches away from her with his arms around his own chest, trying to hold in his rage.

There was no choice but to tell it all. With determination, she pulled herself together enough to continue with the narrative she'd held inside for all those years. "I didn't even think. I reacted. That money—it was like a miracle. Me getting pregnant after all that time was the first miracle. And then this money, this chance to raise our baby in a better place. All I was thinking was how to keep it out of your hands long enough to get away. When I ripped open all the packets and counted out the money, it was twenty thousand shy, and I did the math. In two months, you'd taken almost ten percent of our money. In less than two years it would be gone."

Vinnie said nothing, but she could feel the tension radiating from him. The air between them felt denser and charged with retribution. She gulped, but the lump in her throat stayed. "Sierra was the only one who knew I was pregnant. She had a child, and I thought she'd understand, and she did. Considering the off and on again relationship she and Wylie had, she'd talked to me about how she was going to support herself and Beau if and when Wylie took off for good."

Vinnie raised his dark eyebrows, but said nothing.

"I went straight to Sierra, and the more we talked, the clearer it was what I had to do. Beau woke up from his nap and I held him on my lap. I thought this was what it would be like when our baby was born, and I was overwhelmed with the responsibility of raising a child. I'd already picked out names and everything. I tried to picture us—you, me and the baby—but when I tried to picture us in our house there, I just couldn't see it. I thought about going it alone, maybe moving back in with my parents. But that felt all wrong too."

"That's when you decided to leave me."

"No, not then. It occurred to me even then that it might be the only way, but it wasn't what I wanted. What I wanted was to make it work with us." She pulled a tissue from her pocket and blew her nose. It was pointless to wipe away the tears because they kept coming.

The temper Vinnie had once been known for flared again. Slamming his fist into his hand, his voice rose, filling the air with angry noise. "You just had it all worked out, didn't you?" he yelled, punching the air to emphasize his words. He'd always spoken with his hands, and when they came too close to her face, she stepped back. "Tell me, did I have any say in anything? Moving to another state, having a baby? Christ, you just made plans and plugged me in however it suited you, and you never told me fucking anything!"

Molly Pat wedged herself between the two of them, making a low rumble in her throat.

Foxy let Vinnie go on, knowing she had to take the full brunt. "I had a right to know," he said more than once.

He'd had a right to know all of it, she'd known that all along, but seeing the mess she'd made of it, she understood more acutely. Fear had driven her to behave in ways she would never behave now. She couldn't go back and duplicate her flawed thought process, and even if she could, it wouldn't change a thing.

They barely looked up when a snowplow scraped its way down the road, sending a plume of snow that smacked into the rear of Foxy's car.

His anger spent, Vinnie hung his head and shook with silent sobs.

Foxy could handle the anger, but not the tears. It wouldn't do for them both to fall apart, and so she tried some of the techniques she used to deal with her panic attacks. She counted backwards from 100 by threes and breathed deeply. She tensed and released muscle groups, mentally naming them as she'd learned in her massage school's anatomy class. Soon she could feel her body absorbing the excess adrenaline. "Vinnie," she said with as much composure as she could muster. "Why did those guys beat you up?"

Vinnie was remembering that day as if it were unfolding now. Sometimes that's how it was, like the movie *Groundhog Day*. In the midst of a dreamlike memory he'd rouse enough to realize he'd lived every second of this day before. He was loath to keep reliving it, yet it would keep replaying until it reached the same sickening conclusion, and although his conscious mind recognized it as memory, the rest of him experienced all the same feelings, both exhilarating and excruciating, as if they were fresh.

In his recurring memory, he coasts up to the curb in front of the house he shares with Foxy. A white plastic chair tilts against the stucco wall. Their attempt at desert landscaping—prickly pear cactus and yucca plants—looks a little sad. It's a few minutes after noon and, assuming Foxy is still asleep, he slips off his shoes just before unlocking the front door. His movements are furtive, although he tries his best to convince himself he's merely being considerate so as not to wake her. She's been so tired lately.

From the kitchen, he can see the bedroom door is open a crack, and so he pads over and peers through the narrow space. The bed is made with those stupid gold-and-rust-colored pillows propped against the headboard. He hates those slippery pillows that have no function other than to clutter up the bed. He calls out to Foxy, but she's not there. Looking at the empty bed, he feels relief rather than curiosity about where she's gone.

No longer worried about making noise, he goes back to the kitchen, drinks some orange juice straight from the pitcher and then opens the freezer. Pushing aside bags of frozen peas and corn, he removes three paper-wrapped packages of meat, sets them on the table and reaches in for the now exposed foil packets of money. The first one he grabs sticks to the ice buildup. His first reaction is to be annoyed. Why can't Foxy defrost the freezer every now and then, he thinks as he tugs on another pack of money. His mother never let frost build up in her freezer, not even after she got rheumatoid arthritis so bad.

Now, seventeen years later, a more temperate Vinnie stood in the steadily falling snow and looked at the crusty ridge the snow plow had deposited between car and road. As his former wife reached into the trunk and held out a little trench shovel to him, her grin slid away almost as soon as it began.

He'd always loved all the ways she smiled—the little amused twitch at the corners of her mouth, the suggestive grin, the dazzling smile. People used to speak of her as vivacious. Today as he looked at her, the words that came to him were drained and edgy. Still, she was beautiful.

He cringed remembering the stupidity of his younger self and his irritation about his wife's aversion to defrosting the refrigerator. What kind of a dumb ass, he wondered now, would marry a woman like Foxy and then pick at her about such a trivial thing as that? But of course he knew now, the younger Vinnie had been angry at only one person—himself. In the years between Then and Now, he'd been through twelve-step programs, had a relapse or two, studied addiction and counseling, and had worked with scores of young men who took their own self-loathing out on those closest to them.

Slipping back into the endless-loop memory, he can almost feel the coolness of the money as he peels some hundred-dollar bills out of one packet and more from another. It doesn't look like much, so he digs for more, and then tucks the wad into the inside pocket of his leather jacket. After putting the remainder back in the freezer, just the way he'd found it so Foxy's eagle eyes would detect nothing out of place, he heads off in the direction of the Flamingo.

He drives fast, tapping the steering wheel nervously, bobbing his head as if he were listening to music, trying to calm the jitters. His most recent losing streak has left him depressed and agitated and he knows it has to be coming to an end. It's bad enough to have Foxy constantly on his case about playing cards or spinning the wheel, but then yesterday, Wylie decided to chew his butt about it, too. Like Wylie had never played games of chance! Wylie said to him, "Even if you don't care about losing your wife, you should at least think about yourself. Sooner or later, you're gonna find yourself in bed with the wrong people and they'll have your ass." That's what he said. It was like a prophecy, but one Vinnie wouldn't believe until after it had happened.

Well, screw Wylie and screw Foxy too. He knows Foxy has been trying to talk to him, but he's been avoiding her until he gets himself out of this hole he's dug for himself. Well, today, he's going to score big. That'll shut both of them up. The stars are aligned for a winning streak, and he's not about to pass up the opportunity. He can feel it coming like the cool front that moves in every fall to displace the scorching desert heat.

He's been gambling long enough to know when to hold 'em and when to fold 'em. As soon as he gets a win, he'll replace the ten-thousand he borrowed from the freezer, and hopefully have enough left over to take Foxy on a nice vacation. He feels bad he's been so irritated with her lately. She works so hard and lately her back has been hurting her. Maybe he'll take her to one of those Club Med places where she can just lie around and do nothing. She's earned that.

He doesn't even want to think about the other money he's taken from their stash. He's given a lot of thought to why he's had such a long losing streak. The problem, he's figured out, is the casinos themselves. It doesn't matter if you're playing black jack, roulette, or penny slots—the odds are stacked against the customer. It's all set up so you win just enough to think you might keep on winning. You fix a number or a goal in your head, like "I'll quit when I'm up seven-fifty," or "As soon as I double my money, I'm out of here." But the way it works for him, if he hits it big, maybe tripling his money, he says, "I'll just spend down to where it's double my original investment and then I'll quit," but then when he reaches that mark, he remembers how he feels coming from the bottom and is suddenly reaching out with both hands to pull all the chips toward him.

What makes him think his luck is changing was this. Yesterday, he and Wylie and Al were at the Flamingo playing nickel slots They bailed on him, but he was on a roll, and when he hit a four-thousand dollar jackpot, he moved over to the dollar slots. He expected to get another big hit each time the reels spun. Twice he got a win, fifty-two dollars on one and four-hundred sixty on the other, but he was going for the big win now. Again and again, he came up with nothing.

He was still sitting in front of the one-armed bandit with his head in his hands when the guy at the next machine introduced himself as John and said he looked like he could use a drink. Super nice guy, clean cut, genuine smile. Over at the bar, he and John threw back a couple scotch and sodas, and John picked up the tab and invited him to a private game of poker in his suite at the Flamingo.

A suite. He's stoked at the idea. He's always wanted to be one of those guys who's invited to play with the big boys.

And that's where he was headed with the ten-thousand dollars on the day he'd come to think of as The Day the Music Died. All these years later Vinnie can smell the smoke in John's suite, and can feel the slaps on his back as the other poker players welcome him. The memory is on him in full force.

He's disappointed to see that the suite is nothing all that special, but the guys John invited slap him on the back and hand him a drink. They're players—their clothes and jewelry say it all. They're rolling in it, and Vinnie means to relieve them of some of their wealth.

One guy smokes cigars, big fat ones, and cusses a lot. The others, except for John, smoke ordinary cigarettes. John fusses at the cigar smoker like a little old lady when he drops a chunk of ash on the table.

Vinnie takes to the setting and the card game like he's been born to it, like he's one of the favored. Even though the room is nothing compared to the glitz of Las Vegas and the guys are just regular guys, there's something lavish to it all. Maybe it's the way someone comes along and spills some damn fine scotch into his glass whenever it gets low.

For just a second as he stood looking out at all that snow, he remembered the taste of the scotch. Too quickly, it mingled with the taste of his own blood.

He's down a couple thou when he hits it big. He knows they're all watching him as his Adam's apple bobs up and down. He almost quits. It's right on the tip of his tongue to say he has to leave. What difference does it make it they think he's a pussy?

That's how he remembered it, anyway, but his sponsor told him years ago he was kidding himself, that no respectable addict would have quit when he was ahead. Still, in his memory, he liked to believe he was about to cash out and take his sorry self home.

Maybe they'd seen it in his eyes, but John, if that was really his name, took that moment to say he was looking for someone like Vinnie to manage his new sideline business. John didn't say what the business was, exactly, just kind of dangled the idea that it might be the key to Vinnie's future. "You got a real gift for dealing with people," John had said, and then hinted that the job Vinnie would be perfect for involved working with celebrities.

All the time John is talking, he's dealing the cards, and Vinnie is sliding a stack of chips into the middle of the table as if he's been taken over by some force outside of himself. He loses the next hand and the next, and still John is spinning some amazing future for him. John has a fatherly smile that gives Vinnie the false impression they're just playing for fun, and with a playful punch to his shoulder, he offers to stake him for the next round.

Vinnie had known better. It would have been obvious, if only he hadn't been so besotted with being invited to the table. It had felt fifty times better than the first time he was invited to sit at the grownup table at Thanksgiving dinner. It also didn't help that he'd been drinking—how much, he didn't know. Stories abounded about guys like him, guys who borrowed money to stay in the game. In the midst of Vinnie's undoing, Wylie's warning never even popped into his mind.

At almost 5:00 a.m., he's stumbling down the carpeted hall at the Flamingo accompanied by two of the poker players. They're both broad-shouldered and rock-hard. Their muscles ripple under their shirts. One has a pinkie ring on his meaty hand, a black stone surrounded by diamonds. The other one has a small scar at the corner of his right eye not quite concealed by his tinted glasses. Their jovial expressions remain, but the menacing undertone is unmistakable.

Vinnie has been thinking John and his friends might be playing him, but he's certain of it now that he's being escorted to his car. He promises to deliver the twenty-six thousand he owes them in cash, and is excruciatingly aware of his colossal lapse in judgment. All he wants is to get out of here without his face getting rearranged. The goons gave him until ten o'clock that night.

He looks back and forth between his poker-buddies-turned-captors, and dreads coming back here in the next few hours. The booze hits him hard, and his knees buckle. Tipping and slamming his shoulder against the wall, he bends over and throws up on his own shoes. Tinted Glasses hands him a hanky and tells him to keep it.

Down in the lot, the two goons shut the door of his car and watch him drive off. Pinky Ring grins and does a little toodle-oo wave through the driver's window.

Turning north on the Las Vegas Freeway, he looks in his rearview mirror. He doesn't think anyone is following him, but can't be sure. He wracks his brain trying to remember if he told anyone where he lives.

There's more than enough money in the freezer to cover his debt. He has to focus on that saving fact. On the sixteen-minute drive home, he cries and prays to a God and a few saints he's ignored for a while. He promises he's done gambling. Surely God will forgive him the sin of lying to his wife if it means he's giving up gambling, won't he?

He begins to work out the cover up. After bringing them the cash, he decides, he'll tell Foxy they've been robbed. There's a good chance she won't believe him, but she'll never be able to prove it. Besides, it's all he can come up with.

As the wrought iron fence of their house comes into view, he has the thought that he might just come clean and tell her the truth. The talk—no, it would be more of an ugly confrontation—takes shape in his mind. He doesn't know if he can bear the look on her face. But it's possible, he thinks as he steps through the door, to tell her the mess he's made of things. He'll throw himself at her mercy, and then he'll drive to the bridge at the Hoover Dam, climb over the wall and jump. Either way, he's done gambling.

He's still debating what he'll tell her when he opens the bedroom door and sees Foxy sleeping on her stomach with one arm draped over the side of the bed. As he watches from the hall, she groans and rolls so he can see her face. Her forehead wrinkles as if she's in pain, and still asleep, she groans again and turns away from him.

Closing the door quietly, he goes into the kitchen to get the money, still debating how to explain it to his wife.

The gaping hole in the freezer looms in his memory, and along with it, the feeling he'd just had his heart ripped out of his chest.

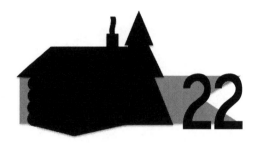

**M**innesota driving could be treacherous. Temperature extremes kept the state's Department of Transportation busy year round. Melting chemicals had to be poured onto icy roads, where melted ice then crept into fissures in the pavement to refreeze and swell, expanding the cracks. Robin was a skilled driver. She'd navigated over thirty-five years of whatever weather and road conditions Minnesota dished up, and that was saying a lot. For the first twenty miles, all they'd encountered were bone-rattling potholes, the kind that changed city streets into slalom courses.

"Someone called in to WCCO this morning to report she saw the face of Jesus in a pothole in front of her house," Grace said when Robin dodged a hole big enough to swallow a family of four. Inspired by the caller, Grace began searching for shapes in the road, like some people found shapes in clouds. She spotted the silhouette of Mona Lisa, a series of yeti footprints and the state of Montana. Robin managed not to sink her wheel in the Eye of Horus. When they reached Interstate 35, the roads were rutted in places, but overall traffic moved at a decent pace.

Today's winter storm warning promised "snow and blowing snow." The threat of whiteout conditions was relegated to the very southern part of the state.

By the time they were out of WCCO's range, Robin turned off the radio. "So, tell me what you found out at the sleep study."

"I snore. Fred was right. They told me I had . . . I don't know how many arousals per hour."

"Arousals?" Robin said.

"It doesn't mean what you think. It measures sleep disruptions." Grace scratched a place behind her ear and grimaced. "What on earth?" she said, extracting a gooey wad from her hair. "Oh, that's lovely. They left an electrode on my head. Yuck." She pulled a Kleenex out of the box on the console and wrapped it up. "I have to go back to the sleep doctor, and she'll probably put me on one of those machines. I just hope Fred follows through. I'm not going to be the designated snorer in our family."

Robin laughed. "It's more than just snoring, isn't it?"

"Yeah, it's a health risk, I guess," Grace admitted. "Now, tell me all about this mysterious message in a bottle."

Robin was, in fact, dying to talk about Sierra's papers Cate and her mother had found in Foxy's apartment.

Grace sat wide-eyed as the story unfolded, interrupting when she got to the part about breaking the bottle. "Wanda actually said, 'Let me have a crack at it?'"

Robin chuckled. "Her exact words."

"Okay, so they broke the bottle open. What was in it?"

"They found papers that prove Wylie, the guy Sierra was living with off and on, was not the father of her son. I don't think Foxy even suspected, because she referred to Wiley as Beau's father."

"Hmm." Grace ran her fingers through her hair, checking for more electrodes. She didn't find any, but her hair felt disgusting. "Do you think the real father knows?"

Robin twisted her mouth to one side. "Mm-hmm, I do. And I think he didn't want anyone else to know."

"You said there were other papers in the bottle."

"Yup, there was a handwritten note from the father acknowledging he'd received the results of the paternity test, and agreeing to help with costs. But only as long as she kept her mouth shut."

Grace turned in her seat and shook Robin's shoulder. "Well, for God's sake, aren't you going to tell me who the real father is?"

Robin shook her head. "You don't think he signed it, do you? There was a veiled threat in his message. I can't remember the exact wording, but here's what Cate thinks, and I have to agree. Sierra threatened to make it public, and he killed her."

Grace sat back, her eyes blinking rapidly. "Wow, how do we keep getting ourselves in the middle of murder cases? I can't figure out whether we merely track down trouble or attract it."

Robin shrugged. "Good question."

"There's a third possibility. Do you suppose it's possible we invent trouble?"

"Bad question." Robin's laugh was nervous. "Are you suggesting we should ignore this?"

Grace blew air from her cheeks. "I was only partly kidding. It just doesn't seem possible that we keep getting into these messes. But no, I'm not saying we should ignore it, but . . . well, help me understand. We're rushing up to the Canadian border—in the middle of a snowstorm—to tell Foxy we don't know who the father of her dead friend's son is, but that—with nothing other than a hunch to go on, mind you—we think he probably killed Sierra. Not only that, but if Foxy figures out who the father is, she could be next in line to be dead."

Robin pursed her lips. "Well, when you put it that way . . ."

"I know! It's nuts, right? Why do you think it has to do with Beau's father? What about the whole Las Vegas connection, you know, the murder they witnessed? Is there a connection or is that just Foxy's paranoia?"

"I have no idea. We don't know any of the people in Foxy's past other than Foxy. Maybe it was the shooting victim who was the father. No, that doesn't make sense. They saw him get murdered, so if he managed to murder Sierra seventeen years later, that would be some trick." She laughed nervously again.

Grace said, "What about the other guys? There was the one Foxy called Big Al, but he died a long time ago too, so he's out. That just leaves . . ." She widened her eyes for effect. "Foxy's husband."

"Vinnie? Why would he care who found out? What about Foxy's brother? Sierra spent time with him before Beau was born. Why couldn't he be the father?"

"But why would he care if someone found out? And what are you saying anyway, that he's just been pretending to be gay?"

A laugh erupted from Robin. "Of course not."

They sat in silence, and then Grace said, "It's not that I don't want to hang out with Foxy and her brother for a couple days, but really, besides that, why are we doing this?"

Robin said, "I've been questioning the sanity of all this, but look, Cate had an intuition about the papers she found and she's convinced they somehow place Foxy's in danger. I can't ignore that." Only then did she remember Cate was going to send her something. "Open my purse. My phone's in the inside pocket." She gave Grace the password to get into her e-mails. "Look for a message from Cate. She was going to take pictures of the notes and e-mail them to me."

"Why didn't you say so?" Grace reached into the back seat, snatched Robin's purse and grabbed the phone. Pressing the mail icon she scrolled down until she found Cate's message. Opening the first attached photo, she spread her fingers on the screen to enlarge the picture. "DNA test report," she read. "This must be the paternity test results."

"Right."

The report bore a case number and a date that would have been within Beau's first year of life. There were three columns of numbers, one marked "mother," one "child" and one "alleged father." No names were given, except for Sierra's, as the recipient of the letter, and the doctor who signed the report. Some of the numbers were circled in different colors. At the bottom was some kind of aggregate score and the words stating that the alleged father couldn't be excluded. The probability of paternity was 99.99 percent.

Grace thought about it and said, "The father isn't named. Why couldn't it be what's-his-name, the guy she was living with?"

"Wylie? I asked Cate the same thing. Maybe it's in the other papers. Did she send anything else?" Just then, a strong gust buffeted the car. "The wind's really picking up." Robin tightened her grip on the wheel. "We're coming up on the Hinckley exit. How about stopping for breakfast?"

\* \* \*

VINNIE'S ANGER HAD PASSED, replaced by a dull ache in his gut. He offered to drive the next stretch, and Foxy was grateful. As soon as they'd shoveled an opening in the packed snow, she fell into the car, exhausted. Turning the key in the ignition he backed up, then stopped. Maybe it was too late to save their relationship, but if he'd learned nothing else in his addiction programs, it was that it's never too late to do the right thing.

"The break-in and the beating . . . that wasn't a random crime," he said. "I owed those guys money." A glance at her told him Foxy wasn't as surprised as he'd expected. It was his last confession to her, and he wasn't going to hold back anything. Sitting in the car with the engine running, he told her about the night of high-stakes poker that had begun with such ridiculous hope and ended the next morning with his discovery that all the money he and Foxy had was gone. He told her about how later that night, after Foxy had left for work, the beefy guy with a scar over his eye pushed his way through the front door of their little house and slammed him into the wall. "Payback time," he'd snarled, with a knee to Vinnie's crotch.

He didn't feel compelled to tell Foxy every detail about how he'd cowered and pled for more time to come up with the cash, and how the guy had backed off, and for a second, Vinnie had actually thought he was going to relent. That's when the other one, the one with the pinky ring, had come up from behind, spun him around with one meaty hand and delivered an upward jab under his ribcage with the other.

He'd stayed conscious as they pulverized his face and kicked the ribs that were probably already broken. When one goon picked him up and held him, the other one grabbed hold of his legs. Vinnie told her about kicking and squirming as they held him down on the kitchen table with his legs sticking out over the edge. "I thought about the carving knife in the block by the stove, and was sure they were going to slice me open," he told Foxy and saw the pain in her features. He went on to tell her how Pinky Ring had put one giant paw on his knee and the other on his ankle and, using the edge of the table as a fulcrum, pressed down with all his weight. The sound of his leg breaking was sickening, even in his memory.

They'd left him screaming. He must have fallen to the floor when he lost consciousness, because that's where Foxy had found him.

In the hospital the police had grilled him about the attack as soon as he was out of surgery and conscious. For that first week he hadn't been able to remember much of anything, and so he'd told what he thought was the truth, that he didn't know who his assailants were, and didn't know how he'd wound up on the kitchen floor, near death from shock. But gradually, as his memory began to return, he'd never recanted his initial story to the police. Instead, he'd dug himself in deeper, insisting with increasing vehemence to the authorities and to Foxy that he'd been an innocent victim.

He turned to look Foxy squarely in the eyes for the first time since he'd begun to tell her the last shameful part of it.

"I always knew there had to be more to the story," she said quietly through her tears. "And I guessed it had to be something like that, but what I could never figure out is why they let you live."

He took a deep breath. "Pinky Ring came to the house the second day I was home from the hospital. They gave me twenty-four hours to come up with the money."

"Where did you get it?" Her voice was suddenly icy.

"Remember the break-in at my folks' business?" he began. Shame almost paralyzed him as he thought again about all the hard years his parents had invested in their thriving furrier business.

He could see it on his ex-wife's face as understanding came to her in spasms. "Oh, my God, Vinnie! Those monsters were the ones who stole all those fur coats?"

He lowered his head, shaking it back and forth.

Her eyes widened. "You did it? *You* stole all those furs?"

"I did. I robbed my own parents to pay off those sadists."

Her hand flew to her mouth. She faced the window rather than look at his face. For a long minute he thought she might bolt and run just to get away from him. Finally she spoke. "I'm glad you told me." She said it like she meant it.

He was still shaky from all their revelations when he finally pulled out onto the road. Although he was grateful to be given permission to put it all in the past, he knew it couldn't be that easy. He'd spent years examining how he'd allowed his addiction to wreck their marriage. It had taken a lot of counseling, but he'd finally come to terms with it. She was right—he was a better person now. He'd vowed more than once if he were ever to get another chance with Foxy, he'd make it right. And now, here he was with her, just the two of them, and he couldn't see any way to put it behind them.

Foxy's news of the miscarriage loomed again—a son he'd never known about because he'd never been born. How was he to put that behind him? He went over it in his mind.

It had happened four days after she'd found him unconscious, Foxy had informed him. She'd stayed at his side in his hospital room, catching bits of sleep whenever she could, curled up in a chair. He knew at the time she'd been sick with worry and disappointment, and on top of that, she'd found it almost impossible to sleep with all the staff coming in at all hours, not to mention how uncomfortable that chair must have been as a bed.

She'd lost the baby because of him. He'd always blamed himself and his gambling for the fact they'd never had kids. Foxy had put up with his antics for years—his weird hours and his wildly fluctuating moods that followed his roller coaster wins and losses—waiting for him to grow up. Then, when she couldn't wait any longer, she'd gone off the pill. But nothing had happened. Month after month, she'd failed to get pregnant and she said they'd waited too long. After he'd gotten his head on straight, he'd accepted the blame for them not having a family. That, unfortunately was still the case. This new information changed nothing but the details.

The roads were more rutted, and Vinnie slowed his speed. Wisps of snow blew from the top of high snowbanks on the left of the road, laying shifting stripes of white in their path and making him feel disoriented. As if everything else about this trip wasn't disorienting!

Foxy clasped and unclasped her hands in her lap. He could tell she was steeling herself to say something, and he steeled himself to listen. It didn't seem possible, after they'd just unburdened themselves in such a huge way, that there was anything left to say. His life had twisted in so many directions in the past week, he couldn't imagine anything surprising him now. In the old days, he would have done just about anything to avoid any more emotion, but today, he waited. He tilted his head back and forth to keep from bunching his shoulder muscles.

Whatever she said, whatever happened next, felt preordained. It was like spinning the roulette wheel or throwing the dice. As soon as it left your hands, your fate was already decided.

"I need to tell you the rest of the story, Vin. You have a right to know."

He felt dead calm.

"I took the money that day. I took it all and hid it at Tina's place."

He kept his eyes on the road. Bile rose in his throat. All those years ago, he'd accused Foxy of stealing it and she'd denied it. "I see."

"We took it out of the foil and crammed it inside that big green hassock of hers for safekeeping. It was a stupid place to put it. It was worn and the stuffing was already coming out, so we just pulled out some more stuffing, put the money in there and slapped duct tape over the bottom."

"You had the money all along! Jesus, Foxy, I believed you!"

She stared straight ahead, saying nothing.

"You took all our money and left me."

She dropped her head. "No, Vinnie, it's gone. I never got any of it either. The same day you came home from the hospital, Al tripped over the hassock and pitched a fit. He picked it up and said it was a piece of crap and was hauling it out to the trash can. Tina went after him and tried to pull it away. They tussled over it and the bottom mesh caught on something and tore enough that some of the money fell out."

If Al weren't already dead, at that moment Vinnie might have wanted to help him get dead.

"Al demanded to know where the money came from and Tina had no choice but to tell him it was ours. He was gone the next day, and so was all the money."

He smacked the steering wheel with both hands. "I always knew Big Al was the thief. That sneaky lowlife bastard!"

She tilted her head back, rolling it back and forth against the headrest in a headshake. "Not always, Vin. You accused me of stealing it, and I told you the truth when I said I didn't. At least it wasn't my intent to steal it. I just meant to hide it from you until—well, the truth is, I thought once we were away from the casinos, you'd change."

"Stop," Vinnie said. The car jerked on an icy patch. "We have to stop beating ourselves up. Haven't we suffered enough? Seventeen years! God!" He let his hand drop to rest on top of hers, and he gave it a squeeze. "We've already spent too much of our lives regretting what we can't change. It's water over the bridge."

"Dam."

He tensed.

"I think you mean water over the dam, or under the bridge, not over the bridge. It's a mixed metaphor."

He threw back his head and laughed.

They settled into a booth at Tobie's restaurant in Hinckley. Both of Grace's parents had family in Duluth, and so they'd traveled this stretch of road often, usually stopping at Tobie's, a convenient halfway point for a bathroom stop and a cinnamon or caramel roll.

As soon as they ordered, Grace handed Robin's phone back to her.

"Oh, that's not gonna happen," Robin said, squinting at the cramped handwriting in the second attachment. She muttered to herself as she dug in her purse. Pretty soon the table was littered with detritus from her large bag. She plopped a toothbrush on the pile of receipts, pens, and tubes of lipstick, and kept digging. "Oh, for crying out loud! I had my prescription glasses when we left this morning, and I always have a pair of cheaters in my purse."

Grace grinned at her. "Maybe you could try either pair up there." She pointed above Robin's head.

Robin's hand shot up, patting the two pairs of glasses perched on top of her head. She burst out laughing.

Grace joined in. Through her laughter, she said, "And I thought I was squirrelly after getting three hours of sleep."

Wiping her eyes, Robin chose her good glasses and put them on. Once more, she squinted at the small screen. The scanned letter wasn't perfect. The dark parts were too dark and the faint parts too faint, as if the pen had skipped as he wrote.

"Read it out loud," said Grace.

"He didn't sign it. Cate already told me that when she read it to me last night." Robin frowned, trying to make sense of the odd hand-writing. Each line began with a long tail that swooped up to the first letter, and some of the letters looked like they'd been gone over more than once. "He starts off with just the letter S." She read through the first couple of lines to herself and the pattern started to make sense to her, the way he closed some letters and left others open.

"He writes, 'I wonder why you assume I'm the father. After all, I'm not the only man in your life, and it does bring up the question of character. I'm sorry, but you have to understand I can't simply ac-cept your word on something so—.' He crosses off the word damag-ing and writes weighty," Robin said.

The waitress came with two coffees and two enormous pecan caramel rolls.

"The guy's a real peach!" Grace said, cutting off a chunk of the roll and sticking it in her mouth.

"No kidding." Robin picked up her phone again. And then he says, 'If it proves to be mine, I will bear part of the responsibility. You will think it unfair, but I want proof before I commit to helping with the financial burden. If I have indeed fathered an illegitimate child, I will do the right thing. After all, the fault does not lie with the child. Regardless whose it is, it deserves love and protection.'" Robin shook her head.

"How thoughtful!" Grace said. "What a standup guy!"

"Oh, wait," Robin said. "It gets better." She opened the next attachment. This note was typewritten. "There's no signature on this one either." She read aloud.

I hope you destroyed the other note as I instructed. I reflect on how this all has come to pass, and am deeply saddened. What began in love has turned to suspicion. I may have betrayed others in this whole affair, but I never betrayed you and do not want to do so now. I was all too willing in succumbing to your beauty and sensuality, but what I did, I did out of love. Yes, I loved you, more than I had any right to.

You complain to me that it's unfair to have to raise a child alone. Do you think I'm not aware you deceived me about birth control? Deceit comes easily to you, as evidenced by your willingness to allow your young man to believe he is the father. Where is the unfairness now?

I told you I'll send money as I can for the boy's care, and I'll honor my commitment, but only if you tell no one who Beau's father is. No one! You must understand I can't and won't jeopardize my family or my position. Think it through. If I were to lose my employment, how could I help support him? I need to know you will be discreet. Promise me you really did burn everything I've written to you. Burn this too.

If I find out you have talked to anyone, my withdrawal of financial support is only the first repercussion. I promise you, you do not want to provoke me.

"Wow!" Grace said.

Robin set the phone down. They stared at each other. "Does that sound like blackmail to you?"

Grace's brows pulled together in thought. "Maybe, maybe not. I mean, if he got her pregnant, doesn't she have the right to ask him for support?"

"It's a fine line, isn't it? But it's the kind of thing that happens all the time. Someone gets pregnant and the guy has reasons to keep it quiet, like a wife or—"

"Or a political career. Like John Edwards."

Robin said, "He, I mean John Edwards, tried his damnedest to keep his baby a secret, but he didn't murder anyone, and he had everything to lose. But this guy was threatening Sierra from the beginning. 'You don't want to provoke me,'" she quoted.

Grace shook her head. "I know. But don't you think if she'd blackmailed him back then, she'd have been dead a lot sooner?"

"Hmm, I see your point. Why didn't he just get rid of her back then? Obviously she was inconvenient to him, and so was Beau. Sooner or later, secrets have a way of getting out."

The server came and refilled their coffee cups.

"Does it make any more sense that she'd wait until now to blackmail him? Beau's almost an adult," Grace said.

"Maybe the father's suddenly got enough money to make it worth her while. Or maybe it went from child support to blackmail. Or maybe poor Wylie finally did the math and found out he couldn't have been the father and stirred things up," Robin suggested, only half serious.

* * *

ERIK'S PARENTS STRIPPED OFF their coats for Cate to hang up. Sally had never been comfortable with pets, and so every critter in the house was shut away for the time being. Cate offered coffee, which they refused, and tea, which they wanted only if it was Darjeeling. Soon they were sitting with steaming mugs in front of the television, watching the lines and colors move in accelerated time on the big weather map.

"It looks like we got here just in time," Chuck said to his wife. He picked up the remote, assuming only men could handle such complicated electronics, and started flipping through the channels. They listened as some meteorologists smugly said they'd properly warned people of a dangerous winter storm, while others admitted they'd been caught off guard by the weather system's rapid movement.

"Where's the real weather channel, the national one?" said her father-in-law as he clicked through the channels one by one.

Cate hoped her smile looked genuine. "You mean the first one I put on?"

"Perhaps. What channel was it."

She told him and he returned to it. The storm's track had not only shifted north, but had accelerated.

Cate heard a phone ring. It took her a moment to realize it was coming from the phone on the kitchen counter. Foxy's phone.

As soon as she said hello, the caller said, "It's me, Wylie."

Cate ducked into the laundry room and quickly told him she wasn't Foxy, and explained why she was in possession of her phone.

"Do you know how I can reach her?" There was an urgency to the way he asked.

Cate said she didn't. She wasn't about to give out information until she got some from him.

"Do you know where she and Vinnie are headed?" he said. "I really need to get hold of them."

Cate's head dropped. Even though Bill had said Foxy wasn't with him, she'd continued to hope she'd done the right thing and sought out safety at the sheriff's house. "Vinnie? Her ex-husband?" It all started to make sense.

"Hello? Are you there?"

"Still here," Cate answered. "Listen, you have to tell me what's going on."

Briefly, Wylie said he'd just talked to Sierra's parents. A man claiming to be an old friend of Sierra's had called them just a couple of days after her death. He said he wanted to hold a memorial for her and asked for names and addresses of her old friends from Las Vegas. "Mrs. Brady gave him my phone number and Foxy's address, and said we could help him."

Cate got chills. "He never called you, did he?"

"Hell no! He's tracking us down. Vinnie thinks so too."

"You think he killed Sierra, don't you?"

"The guy who called? Absolutely, and I need to warn Foxy before—"

"Wylie!" she said, interrupting him. "I need to tell you something. Sierra left Foxy a message."

That stopped him. She told him in as few words as possible about the paternity test and intimidating letters.

If he was surprised at finding out he wasn't Beau's biological father, he didn't show it. Instead, he asked, "Are they still going up to her brother's place?"

Cate made an instant decision she hoped she wouldn't regret. "Yes."

"I'm on my way up there but can't remember the name of the joint."

Luckily Robin had told her. "It's Twin Loons up by Ely."

He whooped and before she could ask anything else, he hung up.

Stunned, she stared at the phone in her hand for a moment and then called Robin, who was about to leave Hinckley. She did her best to recreate the alarming call from Wylie.

When she was done, Robin, sounding a little breathless said, "And he's on his way up to the resort?"

Cate could hear Robin relaying the information to Grace, and heard Grace's remark. "I hope Wylie's one of the good guys," she said.

Cate hoped so too. She didn't tell Robin she'd had the snow globe dream again last night, only this time Foxy was spread out on the snow like a snow angel, lying perfectly still. And there was a dark-haired man standing over her wearing a neck brace. It was too bizarre. "Please be careful," she said.

Robin assured her the roads weren't that bad.

With one eye on the Doppler radar, Cate gave her the latest update.

"What?" Robin said. "I'm getting a lot of static. Can you hear me okay?"

"It's a little crackly."

"What are they showing between Hinckley and Ely?"

"Not a lot of new snow, but the winds are gusting up to forty or fifty miles an hour just this side of Hinckley. The weather model says it's going faster than they expected, but it looks like you'll beat the worst of it if you leave now."

"We'll do that."

"Please exercise caution."

"I'll exercise caution, Mom," Robin answered, with emphasis on the word Mom.

"I'm serious. I don't want you and Grace risking your safety to help Foxy."

"What?"

Through the crackling connection, she repeated her words.

"Help Foxy," Robin echoed back. "And quit worrying. We're not scared of a little wind. Anyway, I did always want to visit Oz."

"Smart ass," Cate said. As she walked back to attend to her houseguests, she had the chilling thought that she didn't want those to be the last words she would say to Robin.

**D**o you remember the way Sierra threw herself at your brother?" Vinnie said.

Foxy put a hand to her forehead. "Well, you can blame me since I encouraged her. We didn't know about him being gay, and she couldn't figure out if he was just that innocent or really didn't find her attractive. It confused her."

"Poor Sierra."

"Poor Sierra," she agreed. "I've been thinking about it, Vin, and it just doesn't make sense her death is connected to the guy who got murdered in Las Vegas. If the killer didn't track us down while we lived there, why now?"

"I know. I've wondered about that too. I used to play with the idea that the guy's murder was somehow related to the clowns that put me in ICU."

"How so?"

"That's just it. I can't find a connection. The only thing I've ever come up with is that I said something at the casino. Maybe I was talking to Wylie or Al or maybe they said something to me—I can't remember. But I don't think it was a coincidence that John was sitting next to me at the slots when I ran out of money. It wouldn't be hard for a guy to scope out the clientele and find someone with a gambling problem who was willing to sell his car or pawn his watch just to stay in the game. I think John was looking for some chump like me who'd come into some money and was stupid enough to risk it all."

Foxy nodded. She took a long draw on the bottle of water they were sharing before offering him some.

He shook his head. "There are still some parts about that night I don't remember, but I do remember thinking John was like a father figure almost. I hit a losing streak. I was done, and he said he'd be willing to cover my bet if I had the money to repay him. I told him, and these were my exact words, that I had more than enough to cover it."

"Oh, Vinnie!"

"I keep trying to make those thugs fit into what's going on now, but I don't see the connection."

"They got what they wanted."

He grunted. "And then some."

"I think we're trying too hard to link Sierra's death to whatever it is we did back then. It was such a turning point for all of us, but maybe it has nothing to do with anything anymore."

Vinnie drummed his fingers on the steering wheel. "If I heard this from a client, I'd say they were still trying to work out their own shame."

"Mm. You think that's what we're doing?"

He snorted. "What do you think?"

"I think you've gotten smart in your old age."

"Yeah, too old smart, too young . . . how does that go?"

"Too soon old, too late smart."

"Right." He bobbed his head. "If Sierra's death had nothing to do with all of that, are you thinking she really did take her own life?"

"No." Foxy said quickly. "I don't."

A wind gust buffeted the Saturn, and Vinnie took his foot off the accelerator. "We don't have to keep driving, you know. We could spend the night in Virginia and drive up to Matt's in the morning."

In response, she punched the radio button and moved the dial until she got a good signal. When the classical piece—she thought it was Chopin—ended, the announcer, who had only a slight Iron Range accent, addressed the impending blizzard. What they were seeing, according to him, was nothing compared to what was coming. By evening, residents of Virginia and Hibbing, in fact all of Aitkin, Carlton and St. Louis counties would be under a blizzard warning.

Foxy rubbed her forehead and came up with a decision. "It's not even one o'clock. We'll get there well ahead of the big storm," she said.

Molly Pat slithered through the space between the seats and settled on Foxy's lap. She was shivering.

Vinnie shook his hands one at a time to get the tension out. "Sounds good. We can hole up at the main cabin and sit in front of the fireplace with a big bowl of popcorn and a glass of Chianti." He reached over and scratched the top of the dog's head. "You'd like that, wouldn't you, old girl?"

"You'd better be talking to Molly!" said Foxy.

Vinnie laughed his best old, carefree laugh.

Suddenly, that picture of domestic tranquility was all she wanted.

\* \* \*

ROBIN AND GRACE WERE almost to Cloquet when the car's Bluetooth ring startled them both. When Robin punched the TALK button, Brad's voice sounded like he had his head in a bucket.

"Hey," Robin greeted him. "How's it going?"

Brad sighed heavily. "Well, it's hard to tell. We were hashing it all out over breakfast this morning and Cass is already regretting her decision to have me come."

"Oh, great! What's your take on the whole situation?"

Brad explained they'd spent the night with Nick's parents, who graciously offered him a bed, knowing that it was late and motels were filled up. "I liked the parents, and we had a little chat before the kids were up. They might be a little snobbish but they like Cass. Nick's father even took me aside and said he thought his son was acting like a jackass."

"Wow. Where are you right now?"

"We went out to breakfast. Cass is outside talking to Nick on the phone. I don't know how it'll all shake out. I'll tell you more later. She's walking back into the restaurant right now, and it looks like she's crying."

Robin felt the miles between her and her daughter. "See if she wants to talk to me."

He asked her, and Cass declined. Brad said, "We're good. I've got it covered. You sound like you're in the car."

"I am. Grace and I are going to spend some time with Foxy," Robin told him.

"I'm missing some words. Maybe I shouldn't distract you while you're driving."

"Okay."

"I'll call you tomorrow if not sooner. Obviously we're not getting on the road until we sort this out."

"Wait," she said before he hung up. "How are the roads out there?"

"Nothing a Minnesotan can't handle. How about there?"

"Same answer."

After they'd said their good-byes and hung up, Grace started laughing out loud. "Spending some time with Foxy? Do you really think he's not gonna find out what we're up to?"

Robin sighed. "Eventually, but what's the point in getting him all worried now?"

Grace looked at her over the top of her glasses. "You mean, what's the point in telling him something that'll make him go ballistic. You don't think he's going to be just a wee bit pissed at you when you tell him after the fact?"

"I told him the truth. We are going to spend time with her."

Grace skewed her mouth to one side. "Yeah, I see no way that can backfire."

"Okay, smarty pants, what did you tell Fred?"

"That you and I were going to Foxy's cabin north of the Cities."

"Did you, by any chance, tell him it was four hours north, in good weather?"

"I did not."

\* \* \*

In Virginia, they stopped and got burgers and fries, the kind of thing Foxy rarely ate, but somehow being here with Vinnie had thrown her back a couple of decades. Sitting in the car to eat, the three of them, Foxy, Vinnie, and Molly Pat gobbled the fast food and got back on the road. Driving on Highway 169 was still fairly good, and the scenery as beautiful as ever.

As they drove, Foxy and Vinnie reminisced about Sierra's life the way people did in the hours and days after burying someone close to them. This social convention was, Foxy had always thought, a way of reaffirming life, claiming the stories of the deceased—the good, the bad and the questionable—as their own to tell.

Vinnie brought up the time Sierra forgot garlic bread in the oven and set off the fire alarm during a dinner party. Foxy remembered how she loved to sing along with the radio. "She was this gorgeous creature, until she opened her mouth to sing. I used to think she was trying to sound bad, but she was completely tone deaf."

"She was pretty awful," he agreed. "Luckily, she had other assets."

"Yes, and she wasn't afraid to flaunt them, either."

"Didn't she do something kind of outrageous when you brought her home one time?

"Not just one time. She pulled something every time I brought her there." Foxy sighed. "I'd forgotten how embarrassing she could be. She said there was something about small town narrow-mindedness that brought out the devil in her. I was just thinking about that the other day when we were driving into Pine Glen. She knew how repressive my upbringing had been, and she must have spent a lot of time coming up with ways to poke fun at the church. When Peter, the pastor's son was home from the seminary, she asked me all about him, and before I knew it, she was outside being all seductive with him."

"Didn't she go skinny dipping in the creek too?

Foxy covered her face. "She certainly did. I'd gotten out of the water and was trying to get a tan, so I slipped the straps off my shoulders. Next thing I know, she's throwing her bikini on the bank and telling me to let her know if anyone's coming. When I saw a car coming down the hill, I yelled 'Car!' thinking she'd hide over by the willow tree, but no, she steps out of the water and stands on the bank, posing like some sea nymph. You know who it was that drove up? Peter and his father."

Vinnie laughed out loud. "That's right! She had balls, that's for sure."

"Peter went back to seminary before the sun set, and Pastor Paul, in the process of praying for her wickedness, made it clear Sierra was not to have contact with his beloved son."

"He was a big boy. I'm sure he made his own decisions."

"Maybe so, but he grew almost as straight-laced as his father."

"So you don't think it's possible Sierra found a way to get in touch with Peter, or the other way around? They were adults, for God's sake."

Foxy frowned. Something tickled at the edges of that memory.

The sky behind them was dark and heavy. Vinnie turned on the headlights. Snow skirled across the road, obliterating the lines. "Poor Sierra," he said for the second time. "She was so spirited. Wherever she went, every man in the room stared at her. Frankly, I found her a little intimidating."

"I know. She was beautiful and charismatic, but none of it made her happy."

"No."

Foxy felt a deep sadness, thinking about her old friend. "The thing I never understood is that she could've been with anyone, so why do you think she kept coming back to Wylie? I'm not saying he was a terrible person, but those two always blew so hot and cold. She dated other guys who doted on her, but then she and Wylie would make up and she'd drop the other guy flat. She could have married someone kind and dependable."

"Maybe she didn't want kind and dependable."

Foxy looked at him, surprised at his wisdom. "You may be right."

"She always struck me as someone who liked to keep things stirred up. If things were going too smoothly, she'd do something impulsive, keep people off balance."

She thought about that. "She didn't always like to play by the rules, if that's what you mean."

He shook his head. "That too, but I'm talking about how every time they talked about getting married, she'd flirt with someone in front of Wylie and provoke him into a fight."

"You heard Wylie's side of it," Foxy said, "but she told me as soon as they got serious, he'd get crazy with jealousy if she so much as looked at a guy."

"Well, that's how codependency works, isn't it? They both had to agree to stay in that pattern. They finally cut the cord, but it took a long time. Do you remember when she ran away right after Wylie proposed that time?"

Foxy remembered the day Sierra had shown up at work, flaunting the carat-and-a-half diamond Wylie had given her. That same night after changing into her street clothes, Foxy had turned down the hall that led to the restrooms and had seen Sierra in what looked like a lover's embrace with their assistant manager. Sierra denied it being anything but a friendly hug. But then, two days later she'd up and disappeared for almost a week. The assistant manager was still at the hotel every day, so obviously Sierra hadn't run off with him.

When she came back, all Sierra said in explanation was that she'd needed to get away and think. She went back to Wylie and the two of them had stayed sequestered in their place for days. Foxy and Vinnie had thought they worked out their problems together, but when they emerged, the engagement was off. For the time being, anyway. They'd gotten engaged again. For a short time, it looked like Sierra and Wylie and baby Beau would be a real family at last, and then everything fell apart.

Foxy frowned. Again, there was that sense of something tickling at her mind.

Facing a stand of birch trees, Wylie heard the car's engine. It figured. He hadn't seen a car in the last half hour, but the minute he got out to take a leak, someone turned down the same side road. He zipped up and walked back to his truck as a black SUV came into view.

The driver must not have seen him stopped in the middle of the road until too late. He hit his brakes and skidded, barely missing Wylie's truck and burying his left front wheel in a snowbank. Revving the engine, he backed up onto the road and stopped. The sound of tire scraping on metal was unmistakable. He eased himself out of the driver's seat to assess the damage. Wearing a dress coat and aviator glasses, he looked out of place in the north woods. Wylie noticed he at least wore snow boots.

Wylie walked over. "I think the fender's bent," he said.

"Yes, it certainly is." The man adjusted the tilt of his aviator glasses, ducked his head and looked away.

Sketchy. It set Wylie's nerves jangling. Suddenly he was aware how isolated they were. He looked back to the main road and to the expanse ahead of him on the side road. There was no one in sight. He felt the guy looking at him and turned to face him.

Now the man had his muffler pulled up to cover part of his chin. "What the heck were you doing stopped in the middle of the road?" he said, his voice low.

Wylie's first thought was to wonder how many guys would be able to ask that question without a few choice expletives. His second thought was that it made his simple question more menacing.

"Are you going to stand there or are you going to give me a hand?" His hand gestures, when he spoke, gave Wylie the impression he was used to speaking to an audience. An actor, maybe. In any case, he looked like he wasn't used to getting his hands dirty.

Wylie bent down to see where the front right fender and tire were binding. He buckled the wrists of his Gore-Tex gloves so he wouldn't get snow up his sleeves, and went to work tugging on the fender. The metal barely budged. "I'm gonna get a crowbar from my truck," he said.

As soon as the crowbar was in his grip, he felt safer. Turning back to the other vehicle, he saw that the sketchy guy was removing his own crowbar from the back of his vehicle.

Fighting the urge to jump into his car and drive off, he took a couple of deep breaths, told himself he was letting his imagination take him to a crazy place, and went back to the Acura SUV. "I'll use both crowbars," Wylie said, hoping to relieve the guy of a potential weapon.

Reluctantly he handed it over and bent over to watch as Wylie got down on his knees and went to work. Soon he'd bent the fender back enough to keep it from ripping up the tire. "That'll hold you 'til you can get it to a shop," Wylie said, handing him his crowbar. And then as an afterthought, he said, "You gonna report this?"

The man looked at him. His glasses were steamed up. They stood face to face, each holding a crowbar, and Wylie wondered again if the guy might be an actor. He even looked a little like a young Burt Lancaster. Ever the smartass, Wylie said, "Were you in the movie *Gunfight at the O.K. Corral?*"

His cheek twitched and then he smiled.

Wylie smiled back. "No, really, you look familiar. Are you an actor?"

He laughed. It was a nice laugh. "Nope. Just up here for a meeting."

Wylie spread his arms to encompass the wide expanse of white. "Who're you meeting with? Polar bears?"

The pleasant face hardened. "Thanks for the help," he said abruptly.

"It was the least I could do." Wylie looked at him closely before starting back to his truck. He'd gotten only a couple steps away when he realized why the man had looked so familiar. The smile, the little gap between his front teeth. He hadn't seen Sierra's son in months, but this guy—Shit! It was like looking at an older version of Beau. His feet stuttered.

He realized he hadn't heard the man's door shut yet. Clenching the crowbar he glanced over his shoulder.

The man nodded at him and waited for him to get into his truck.

Wylie laid the crowbar across the seat and took off, glancing in his rear view mirror until he was well away from the man he now knew had to be Beau's father. What a bizarre coincidence, he thought. It took only a couple of seconds to realize it was no coincidence at all.

When the road came to a T, he took a left, realized it was a dead end and doubled back. The snow was coming down in earnest now, and blowing hard enough he had to concentrate to stay on the road and not drift off on the shoulder.

His mind was following a maze of clues. Of course he'd known from the beginning that Beau was not his son. Sierra had had a lot of faults, but she'd been straight with him about that. She never had revealed who'd fathered her child, but said it was "not a sustainable relationship." He assumed it'd been a one-night stand. At first he'd thought he could accept their arrangement and raise Beau as his own. He was nuts about the kid, but he and Sierra were drifting apart.

They argued. They made up, only to argue again. She confessed to him that the real father had agreed to send child support on a regular basis, and in return she'd agreed to keep his identity a secret. He remembered how crazy he'd gotten then, snooping through every pocket of every item of clothing and every handbag, looking for some clue to the man's identity. He invoked the help of a friend who worked in billing for Sun Country airlines to see if Sierra had flown somewhere when she'd gone AWOL. The friend had hesitated, then said, "It's my job on the line if I tell you, man. Yeah, I remember about the time she went missing, I saw her name on the passenger list for a flight to Minneapolis."

He'd been able to piece this much together. Sierra's lover was from Minnesota, and since she'd stayed in Foxy's home town more than once, he figured it was someone she'd met in the little town of Pine Glen. But before he could enact his fantasy of going to Pine Glen and interviewing every male resident over thirteen, Sierra had packed up everything, including Beau, and moved to California.

So here, finally, was the Minnesota connection he'd been seeking, this man who looked a little like Burt Lancaster and a lot like Beau Brady. In the next few minutes other things fell into place. Beau's father had somehow figured out where Foxy and Vinnie were headed. He felt like he might throw up.

He was concentrating on the road that meandered around small lakes. The sound of another car on the quiet road startled him. He gripped the wheel. In his rear view mirror, he saw the black Acura SUV bearing down on him, trying to pass him. He edged as far to the right as he dared. Up ahead, it looked like the road narrowed, but he couldn't slow down without fishtailing on the ice. He was about to cross a bridge.

Metal screeched against metal as the right side of his truck hit the guardrail. He struggled to keep his wheels on the road. It felt like an explosion when the SUV slammed into him from the left rear. The rail provided little resistance. He tore through it, and his car plummeted twenty-five feet to the ice below. He didn't even have time to scream.

\* \* \*

THE CAR RADIO WAS TUNED to WELY, and the announcer kept telling people to "hunker down." In his lilting accent, he said, "I hope you all got stocked up on groceries and other provisions at Zup's, because they're closing at two-thirty." Then he went through a long list of cancelled activities, including a meeting at St. Mary's Episcopal Church, which he pronounced Epis-COP-al. Vinnie and Foxy both burst into laughter.

"I've missed this place," Foxy said, and meant it.

"Is this where I turn?" Vinnie asked.

"Yes. No wait. I think it's the next one." They'd just turned off Highway 1, and would be at Twin Loons before long. "No worries," Foxy assured him when he reminded her the grocery store would be closed. "Matt will have the place stocked." Despite the earlier drama, the closer they got, the more she relaxed. The snow fell heavier now, and the car rocked with each wind gust, but it felt oddly comforting to her to have the snow wrap around her like a soft, fluffy cocoon.

Vinnie said, "Bet you didn't think you and I would ever get snowbound together."

"That doesn't sound all bad, in fact, not bad at all. No one gets out, but no one gets in either. A glass of wine, another log on the fire, and I won't care about anything." She was about to take his hand when she heard the siren behind them. "Slow down, Vin."

The car began to fishtail. "I'm trying to," he said, sounding irritated. "You think they're going to nail me for speeding?"

Vinnie moved to the side and had almost come to a stop when the police car passed them, followed by more lights and sirens. An ambulance passed them too. Vinnie was shaken, and they sat at the side of the road for a few minutes before he put the car in drive.

The road was icier where it twisted and rose above a couple of small lakes. They saw where the emergency vehicles had stopped. There was a rupture in the guard rail, and when the policeman directed them to pass, Foxy looked below. "There's a truck down there on its side. I can't imagine anyone surviving that," she said.

"People who drive trucks get cocky and think they can drive faster than the rest of us."

The comment annoyed her. "If we hadn't seen all the flashing lights, we could've wound up going off the bridge too."

A few miles later, they drove down the road to the resort. Ahead, they saw two cabins. Near the edge of the lake, Vinnie pointed out a large sign buried so deeply in a snowdrift that it simply read, "DON'T." It made Foxy laugh out loud.

Pulling up in the main parking lot, Matt, bundled up in a parka and pouring gasoline into the tank of a snowmobile, looked up. His face broke into a broad grin.

Matt looked more like Foxy now than they had as kids. Both had prominent cheekbones and pointed chins. Looking into his big blue eyes, Foxy thought, not for the first time, was like looking in the mirror.

Striding over to them, he pulled Foxy's door open and practically lifted her out to hug her. "I've been listening to the weather reports," he said. "With the phones out, I couldn't even call you and tell you not to come. Christ, I'm glad you're here." Foxy thought he seemed more lonesome than she'd ever seen him.

Molly Pat didn't miss her chance to leap out, run a few circles, and then throw herself into a deep spot of snow, where she writhed around with a sappy, tongue-hanging-out expression.

Vinnie came around the car, holding out his hand to his former brother-in-law. Instead of taking his hand, Matt clapped him on the shoulder, and then wrapped him in a bear hug, saying, "It's good to see you, man. Really." He looked back and forth between Vinnie and his sister, and his smile took on an impish look. "Together."

"We're not—" Foxy began, but the words died before she uttered them. Maybe they were together again. Last week, she thought with a stab of guilt, Bill Harley was the man in her life. Just four days ago she couldn't have imagined Vinnie coming back into her life, but her life, suddenly, felt utterly out of her control.

**M**att had closed the small cabins until after Christmas, but there were two guest rooms besides his quarters in the main building. Calling it a lodge made it sound grander than it was. The main floor had a two-story lounge with fireplace and cozy seating, plus a small but efficient kitchen and the owner suite. Above that were two bedrooms and a single bath. Simple and practical.

Foxy put dog food in a dish and filled a water bowl for the dog while Matt and Vinnie brought in their things.

"What's with your phone not working?" Foxy wanted to know as soon as Matt had set their bags down.

Matt made a face. "Yeah, sorry about that. I forgot to pay the bill. It got crazy busy here after . . . in the fall, and I let some of that business stuff slip through the cracks."

"Jeez, Matt," Foxy said.

"I know, I know." He hung his head.

Foxy had said her brother was depressed after Patrick left, and Vinnie could well remember the feeling. He thumped Matt on the shoulder. "C'mon, I'll help you finish gassing the snowmobiles. Trotting after his former brother-in-law, Vinnie felt like a kid. "I've never even ridden one before. Are they hard to drive?"

Matt gave him a questioning look. "I thought you went out with us once, the time you and Foxy came with Sierra and Wylie and that other couple, remember?"

"Tina and Al." Vinnie remembered that trip. "Yup, I was here, but I said I wasn't feeling good and while you all were snowmobiling, I drove to some little casino south of here."

"In Tower?"

"Sounds right. I spent a couple hours playing bingo, of all the idiotic ways for a guy from Las Vegas to spend his vacation."

He laughed. "I guess I don't remember." Matt handed him a gas can from the garage. "So, what's going on with you two?"

Vinnie threw his hands up. "Damned if I know."

"Ya, she's a puzzle." There were four machines in a row. After unscrewing all the caps and checking the oil, he told Vinnie he needed to start the engines to make sure they were running right. He sat down on one and turned the ignition, and then motioned for Vinnie to do the same.

Vinnie straddled one and felt a rush of excitement when the engine growled. When they'd run all four for a minute or two, he was reluctant to get off.

Matt watched him with a curious expression. "Wanna take it out for a spin?"

Vinnie nodded, eager, despite the worsening weather. Or maybe because of it. Foxy used to tell him he was an excitement junkie, and in his recovery program, he realized she'd been right. Once a junkie, always a junkie, they said.

"Just leave the keys in the ignition. I need to do a few things in the lodge, so I'll ask my sister to give you a quick lesson. You up for that?"

"Hell, yes. I feel like I'm sixteen years old and my dad just offered me the keys to his Camaro Z-28. "

Matt laughed. "Hey, if you two are really back together, you're gonna have to know these things. Let's top off the car, too while we're at it." He picked up a full gas can and walked over to the Saturn.

Vinnie popped the cover to the gas tank. "I wish I knew what's up with her and me. We've always had our ups and downs, you know."

"The only question is, do you want to be with her?"

Vinnie already knew the answer to that, but it wasn't a simple one. "If we could be together without hurting each other and playing mind games, I'd be a happy man. I'm not sure that's possible, though. If I met her now, y'know, without the messy history . . ."

"Can't you put it behind you?"

Vinnie didn't know what all Foxy had told him. "I'm trying, but it's like she's closed a part of herself, like she's afraid to love or let herself be loved. I don't know what it is, but even when things were good with us I used to think that."

They walked back to the garage, where Matt slammed the empty gas can on the work bench. He pulled the main door closed and they both stood inside, away from the icy sting of blowing snow. "Unfortunately, I have a pretty good idea what it's about. We got a load of brainwashing growing up. Dear old Pastor Paul," he said with a sneer, "did a number on every kid in that church, including his own son."

"Did he touch you?" Vinnie had asked Foxy the same question years ago.

"No. He never touched us. It wasn't like that." Matt's answer was the same as his sister's had been. "What he did was to teach us love was treacherous. He didn't say it in those exact words, but there was all that judgment and crap about how God might love you in spite of your unworthiness, but if you broke certain rules, he'd see that you wound up in hell. And you had to be suspicious of anyone saying they love you, because the Tempter could take any shape, even that of the person you loved."

He was right about one thing, Vinnie thought. Love could be treacherous.

"For a while I thought I was more virtuous than the other guys because I didn't talk about girls the way they did. There was a girl two grades ahead of me. Her name was Betty. Everyone called her Betty Boobs after she let a bunch of us take a look at 'em. We had to pay her fifty cents apiece, and I couldn't figure out why anyone would waste their money on that. It took me a while to figure out it wasn't virtue on my part."

"Must've been rough growing up gay, especially in that town."

His laugh was hard-edged. "Especially when your minister tells you God doesn't hate you. He just hates everything you are. Figure that out."

Vinnie grunted. "How long did it take you to figure out it was a load of crap?"

"Still working on it." Matt slapped him on the back. "When Patrick moved out in September I had to work through the shame all over again."

"I thought Foxy said he had to move for a business opportunity. You guys broke up?"

Matt shrugged. "Ya, he got fed up with me. He wanted to turn this place into a big fancy resort, and I'm content to keep it the way it is, you know, casual, just making enough money to pay the bills and have a little down time for myself. So he took off. Left me with all the bills to pay and all the cabins to maintain. That's how I wound up letting the phone get shut off."

Exiting through the side door, they walked the twenty yards to the lodge. Snow swirled at their feet and wind rattled the siding of the garage. Vinnie felt fingers of ice blow down the neck of his partially open jacket.

Matt was yelling over the wind now. "In another hour or so, this is gonna get nasty, so you better go now. And don't stay out long, just a couple turns around the lake. It's way too easy to get turned around when the snow is coming down and the wind is blowing away your tracks. Foxy knows what she's doing, so follow her lead and don't take risks."

"I don't mind a little risk-taking."

Matt punched him in the arm. "I just spent the last few hours worrying about you two on the road. I'm not kidding, okay?"

He nodded, already resenting Matt's attitude. He figured his brother-in-law knew about his gambling addiction. Now he wondered what else Foxy had told him that made him go on and on about safety rules. He could drive a car and a motorcycle and a speedboat. How different could this be?

Inside, they found Foxy with her legs flung over the arm of a big leather chair. Sitting on the cedar plank coffee table nearby was a package of Oreos and a bag of dill pickle potato chips, both open. Her hand stopped midair, and a look of guilt froze her features. "What?' she said, popping a cookie in her mouth.

The two men raised their eyebrows at each other, "Didn't take you long to find my stash," Matt teased.

"You gonna report her to the health food police?" Vinnie asked.

She threw an Oreo at them, which Molly Pat deftly intercepted.

"How'd she do that? She was clear on the other side of the room," Vinnie said.

Foxy laughed. "She's sneaky that way."

Matt explained to her about Vinnie wanting to drive a snowmobile. "I told him you'd teach him."

"Right now?" She looked at the fireplace, the cozy pine paneling, and then at her slippered feet.

"Not for very long. If we get snowed in, those machines'll be the only transportation we'll have for a while. I'd feel better knowing we can all operate a snowmobile if we have to get somewhere."

With great reluctance, she gave up her junk food and the fireplace and led Vinnie to the closet where her brother stored the gear. By the time they were suited up, there was another half-inch of snow on the ground, and it was still coming, not so much down as sideways. Looking like giant insects, one orange and black, the other black and white, they clomped out the door, with Matt warning them to stay on the trails.

\* \* \*

THEY WERE NEARING the town of Tower when Robin's gas gauge began showing orange. She glanced over at her companion, whose head had fallen back against the headrest with her mouth open. She was snoring loudly. "Gracie!" she said, more sharply than she'd intended.

Grace sat up, startled, and wiped the corner of her mouth. "Sorry, I guess I nodded off for a minute."

"Could you keep an eye out for a filling station?"

She seemed confused. "How long was I asleep? It's dark outside."

"You were asleep only about ten or fifteen minutes. It's dark because the storm's getting worse." She fought the temptation to fixate on the moving patches and diagonal strips of white, which were not only distracting, but disorienting. "I'm having trouble driving and watching for signs at the same time."

"You want me to look for a sign?" Grace was waking up now. "If God sends us a sign, it'll probably be something like, "Don't do it!'"

"Don't do what?"

"Anything you're thinking of. Just don't."

"I'm getting low on gas. Help me look for a station, okay?" she asked again.

"You bet." Grace stared ahead trying to read the few road signs, but every one of them was plastered with snow. She leaned to look at the gas gauge. "How far can you drive once the light goes on?"

Robin sighed heavily. "I'm not sure. I've never run out of gas. If we don't do something stupid, like missing our turn, we should make it okay, but with this headwind we've been gobbling up gas."

They passed the Soudan mine without sighting a place to stop. Looking at the small map on her phone, Grace said they'd be in the next town in minutes. "How about if I try calling Matt's number again." She poked buttons and came up with the same result they'd gotten all day. "Nope. Still down."

They drove through Tower, and still there was no place to stop for gas. They passed only five vehicles in the next few miles, and three of them were in the ditch. The snow came straight at them now, a vortex of white. Adding to the hypnotic effect, the windshield wipers whooshed back and forth rhythmically. Robin tried the headlights on normal and high beam, but rather than make her vision better, all it did was blind her as the light reflected back from the falling snow. If for no other reason, she needed to warn oncoming cars of their presence, and so she settled on fog lights.

"Um, maybe we should slow down."

Robin would have guessed her speed to be at least forty miles an hour, yet the speedometer hung between fifteen and twenty. She knew it was an illusion, but she couldn't convince herself she wasn't speeding. They could have been sitting at a dead stop and still would have had the sense of motion. She bit down on her lip. "Make sure my phone is charged in case we need to call for help," she instructed Grace.

She nodded and complied. Filling her cheeks up with air, Grace exhaled like she was blowing out birthday candles. "I'm glad you're driving. This is getting bad, isn't it?"

"Yup." Robin tried not to think of Brad's reaction if he discovered she wasn't over at Foxy's apartment for a relaxing visit. She'd been kicking herself for last hour. Not only had she told a half-lie to

Brad, but she was risking her safety and Grace's, and for what? To tell Foxy about Sierra's secret? That whoever killed Sierra might be after Foxy? Well, if he was out to get Foxy, he'd have to be driving through this mess too. Fat chance.

After a while they hit a stretch where the snow let up a little and they were able to pick up speed—all the way up to thirty-two miles an hour. Finally, with Grace following their route on her phone, she said, "In a mile or so we're going to turn left. I'll watch for the road. Whoa, slow down, there's something happening up ahead." Something large came toward them with flashing red lights.

As the tow truck passed them, Grace saw its cargo and said, "Oh, that did not look good. Whoever was driving that pickup truck must be in pretty bad shape."

**M**atthew had always enjoyed cooking, but without Patrick there to appreciate it, he'd reverted to bachelor mode— grabbing a burger in town or throwing a frozen pizza in the oven. But as soon as Foxy said she and Vinnie were coming, he'd had fun stocking up on food she would enjoy. Over the years, she'd gone from eating just about anything to various fad diets. When she moved to Colorado, she went completely vegan, but had soon re- laxed her regimen to eating mostly organic, which did not, he was pretty sure, include dill pickle chips and Oreos. The food she pre- ferred wasn't always easy to find in the stores up here. Luckily, he had plenty of fish and venison in the freezer, and the new organic market and bistro in Ely provided what he couldn't find at Zup's.

In the refrigerator were two packages of venison steaks, thawed. His plan was to fry them in butter at the last minute and serve them on heated plates with a red wine sauce and baby portabella mush- rooms. He got out onions, a couple cloves of garlic and a knob of ginger for his favorite sweet potato bisque. He'd always hummed when he was happy, and he hummed now.

Pausing with his chef's knife poised over the onion, he cocked his head and listened, thinking he'd heard an engine, but it was too early for Foxy and Vinnie to be back. He looked out the window that faced the garage. Their snowmobiles were still gone. A drift had piled up between Foxy's Saturn and the garage. He went back to work chopping the onion. He jumped, nicking his knuckle with the blade when the front door buzzer sounded. Dropping the knife on the cutting board, he hastily wrapped his thumb in a kitchen towel.

In the brief time it took for him to bind up his hand, walk to the door and open it, he figured some wayfarer had gotten stuck in the storm and was looking for refuge. Opening the door, he said, "Come on in," before he realized the person standing in front of him was no stranger. Even though the man's muffler covered the lower part of his face, Matt knew this man, and he was about the last person he expected to see.

The man held out his hand and greeted him by name.

Stepping aside to let him in, Matt declined the proffered hand. "What brings you here?" He couldn't make himself say the name. He'd long ago dropped the names Pastor Paul and Pastor Peter when talking to either the father or the son. It implied more warmth than he felt.

"I'm sorry to drop in on you like this without calling. Did you know your phone is on the fritz?"

"I'm aware." Matt swallowed hard and blinked. "What brings you here?" He already regretted having let this man into his home.

"I need a place to stay. They're closing some of the roads south of here."

It had been four or five years since Matt had run into him, and he'd aged, even though his hair showed no signs of gray. Matt had been in kindergarten when Paul Niemi came to them, fresh-faced from the University in Duluth and ready to lead his small flock in the ways of the Lord. He'd begun as a lay preacher, which was what their small community could afford, and not unusual in this offshoot sect of Lutheranism. Long before he was ordained, he'd told the congregation to call him Pastor Paul.

Matt couldn't help but stare at this man who for years had evoked in him self-hatred and fear. It had taken time and persistence to grow beyond Paul Niemi's sphere of influence, but he'd managed. And now, right in front of him stood this bogeyman of his youth looking strong and healthy. *Christ*, Matt thought, *he has to be in his late sixties.*

"The driving is getting hazardous and I remembered you had a resort around here. I've just been in Ely, visiting an old parishioner of mine."

"Oh, yeah? Who'd you visit?" Matt asked. It was a direct challenge. He knew of no one from Pine Glen living in Ely.

Pastor Niemi wrinkled his brow and said, "Now, Matthew, you know that kind of information is confidential, but you wouldn't know him anyway. He was a member of my church in Minneapolis. My son Peter is the lead pastor at West Church now, you know." From the way his chin tilted, Matt could see his pride in his son, Peter.

"I heard." When Paul Niemi had left the pulpit in Pine Glen, his son was finishing his last year in seminary. Everyone had assumed Peter would take over their little church, but instead, he'd accepted a position as pastor to two rural churches in southern Minnesota, where he shuttled back and forth until he negotiated a merger of the two struggling churches. With that achievement on his resume, he'd moved on to take over when his father left the pulpit as senior pastor at West Lutheran, a thriving church in the west suburbs of Minneapolis.

Matt gestured to the chairs by the fireplace. Niemi took off his gloves and hung his coat and muffler on a peg by the door. Selecting a straight-backed chair, he sat.

"I would've thought you'd have retired by now."

Niemi lowered his head and studied his hands. "What would I do with all my time, now that Anna's gone?"

Matt shrugged. He remembered now that Anna Niemi had suffered from some fatal autoimmune disorder. "So they kicked you upstairs, huh? I heard you're working for the synod now."

He nodded. "For almost six years now."

"Where's your car?" Matt asked, realizing he hadn't seen another vehicle.

"Oh, I parked by the building over there." He pointed in the direction of the closest cabin, which was hidden from view in a stand of pines. "Are there other guests here? I saw a car by the garage."

"Which is where normal people park," Matt muttered under his breath. To his unwelcome visitor, he said, "It's my sister's. She's up here for a few days."

Niemi smiled. "Frances? What a wonderful surprise." It was that same disarming smile Matt remembered from childhood, when the young pastor had taught three bible classes each week, one for toddlers through grade school, one for the upper grades and one for adults. "It'll be a reunion, then. Where is she?"

"Snowmobiling." He felt nervous. "She'll be back soon."

"I know I'm imposing, but might you have another room for me?"

There's no room in the inn, Matt was tempted to tell him. Instead, he looked him over and reminded himself he no longer had reason to fear the larger-than-life Pastor Paul. "There's one room upstairs. Can you manage stairs?"

"Yes, I suppose I can now. If you'd asked me a month ago, I'd have had to say no. I had a hip replacement not that long ago, and honestly, after that first week or so, I've been getting along quite well. I think I'm doing well, don't you?"

Matt agreed that he was.

"It's remarkable what they do to get you mobile right away. They had me doing physical therapy and stairs as soon as possible when I was in rehab at the, well, now that I think of it, it's the nursing home where your mother lives now. I had a choice of where I could do rehab and I suppose it was nostalgia that made me choose the place in Pine Glen. I had some nice chats with your mother while I was there."

Matt raised his eyebrows.

"Oh, I suppose she didn't tell you. Her memory isn't what it used to be, is it?"

Matt shook his head.

The older man asked Matt to get his valise from where he set it on the floor under the coat pegs. "My friend gave me a bottle of wine as a thank you for driving all the way up to visit him—in a blizzard, as it turns out. Would you like to have a glass?"

Actually, I think I'll have the whole bottle, Matt thought. "I didn't realize you drink alcohol."

He faced his palms upward, shrugging his shoulders. "I'm not that rigid anymore. I know in the old days I preached against drink, and I believed that was what God wanted, but my views softened. My Minneapolis church was . . . is more liberal than our sect was."

He handed him the valise. "Oh, ya, I forgot. You had a sect change." Matt laughed drily.

Surprisingly, Pastor Niemi laughed too. "Very good. I'll have to share that one with the bishop. But seriously, I discovered I could relax my views and still be faithful. After all, Jesus didn't turn water into chamomile tea now, did he?"

For a few seconds, Matt was speechless, caught between rage at this man who couldn't practice what he preached, and a dark sense of victory that his former pastor was now willing to drink with someone he'd once referred to as a sodomite.

Matt took the bottle into the kitchen to open. He returned with two round goblets of red wine, handing one to Niemi and setting the other one on the cedar plank coffee table.

"Before you sit, could I trouble you for a glass of water? I need to take my pills."

"Not a problem." Matt turned back to the kitchen.

"And a couple crackers if you have them?" he called out.

When Matt held out the little plate of crackers and cheese to him, he said, "Don't you have to bless these before you take communion?"

For the second time, Pastor Paul surprised him by laughing heartily.

\* \* \*

GRACE LEANED FORWARD, her eyes following along the right side of the road as far ahead as she could see, which wasn't far at all. Robin's eyes darted back and forth, covering the narrow swath of what she hoped was the road ahead. Wind drove snow straight at the windshield, blinding, yet mesmerizing.

Robin's hands ached from gripping the wheel, and yet she knew stopping was more perilous than forging ahead. If another driver were foolish enough to be out in this weather, they wouldn't see each other until they collided. She'd heard of snowplow drivers unknowingly burying stalled cars with occupants still inside under tons of snow—a chilling thought in all respects. Besides, pulling off the road meant knowing where the edges of the road were, which she didn't, and so she crept along, trying to ignore the fact that Grace kept her phone in her hands, ready to call for help the second they ran into a ditch or hit another car.

It was not yet night, but dark nevertheless. Driving could only get worse when the last of the sunlight was gone, and that was coming soon enough.

"The resort's only five miles now." Grace said. Glancing at the speedometer, she said, "I'm too tired to do the math, but I think it'll be another half hour at this rate."

There was no point listening to the radio, which would only caution them to stay home and remind them that emergency vehicles were the only ones that had any business being on the road. Come to think of it, the tow truck was the last vehicle they'd seen.

28

Removing her helmet, Foxy let her reddish curls spill out. She glowered at Vinnie as he pulled his machine up next to hers by the garage.

Hopping off his snowmobile, he hit the quick release on his helmet. "Aw, c'mon Foxy. Don't be mad."

She hated the way he did his sheepish look as if it righted all wrongs. "You were supposed to follow my lead and you took off on your own." She bent into the wind to make her way to the lodge. The idea of being snowbound with Vinnie for days hadn't seemed like such a bad idea when they were getting along. "Come on. Let's not keep Matt waiting any longer."

Vinnie caught up with her.

As soon as she opened the door, she felt something was wrong. There were no wonderful aromas of food when they stepped in, no happy humming from the kitchen. Outside, the storm was moaning, but inside it was eerily quiet.

"Now I know what that sign meant," Vinnie intoned and quoted a line from a horror movie they'd seen together. "Don't go in the basement."

"Shut up!" she hissed and jabbed him with her elbow. Her voice shook when she called out, "Matt? We're back." She waited. They set their mitts and helmets on the long bench by the door.

"Matt? Molly Pat?" Vinnie shouted, walking into the great room. More silence.

Following him, Foxy's breathing was shallow.

"He's over here," Vinnie said in a loud whisper, and sure enough, Matt was napping in his favorite chair with his head tilted back. An empty wine glass sat on the side table next to him.

Foxy had seen Matt drunk on exactly two occasions, and they'd both been years ago. She'd seen her share of mean drunks, but Matt was more of a sloppy drunk. All he did was get boisterous and silly. He had never, to her knowledge, drunk enough that he'd lost consciousness, and she'd never had a reason to think he had a problem with alcohol. She watched as Vinnie put a hand on his shoulder and shook him gently.

Matt groaned. His head rolled, settling closer to his chest. He began to snore.

"Frances, Vincent!" The voice came from the stairway and echoed in the high-ceilinged room.

They both jumped. Foxy gasped at the unexpected sound. Looking for the source of the voice, Foxy felt her chest spasm painfully when her eyes landed on someone who looked exactly like Pastor Paul leaning with an arm on the railing at the top of the stairs, beaming down at them like they were long lost relatives. She knew it was just a hallucination. Pastor Paul was dead. Her mother had just told them so.

She and Vinnie stood, as if in a freeze frame. Then Vinnie reached out and clasped her hand.

The apparition began to descend the stairs, still wearing that ridiculous smile. A scream caught in her throat, emerging only as a squeak. Thoughts collided in her brain. Her heartbeat pounded in her ears.

"Is that—? Jesus Christ, I thought he was dead," Vinnie said in a rush of exhaled air.

She found her voice. "Mom said he died of pneumonia."

He reached the bottom of the stairs and headed in their direction, not floating as she expected, but taking normal, human steps. This was not a ghostly image she could see through, but what appeared to be a flesh-and-blood man in robust health.

"It must be Peter," Vinnie said out of the corner of his mouth.

The two looked similar, but that booming voice could belong to only one person.

"Is it the father or the son?" Vinnie asked. He laughed nervously and added, "Or the holy ghost?"

Foxy didn't laugh. Unless Peter had grown several inches, this was definitely his father. "It's the father, Pastor Paul."

Vinnie blinked, starting to regain his composure. "Obviously, your mother was confused." He squeezed her hand. "You okay?"

"No." Even in the event her mother had gotten it wrong about his death, which was a real possibility, Foxy had seen her old pastor at the nursing home just over a month ago. He'd been in a wheelchair, sagging to one side and totally out of it. Certainly he hadn't appeared to be physically or mentally capable of walking down a flight of stairs. How, in God's name, she asked herself, could he be here now, in this place?

She and Vinnie stood utterly immobile as he neared them, holding out his arms like a father calling his small children to him. "Oh, dear, I frightened you. I'm terribly sorry. Didn't Matthew tell you I was coming?"

Matt not mentioning this little detail seemed as implausible to Foxy as Pastor Niemi's miraculous recovery. Matt had not been a big fan of this man, even before he'd tried to pray him straight. Why would he allow him to come to his resort? And even if, for some reason, Matt had known he was coming, he would have been anxious enough about it to mention it to his own sister, wouldn't he? "No," she said emphatically. "He never said a word." None of this was making any sense.

Paul reached out and placed his hands on her arms in an awkward greeting. "Frances, it's a pleasure seeing you again." He turned to Vinnie and shook his hand. "And you too. What a delightful surprise! I didn't realize you were back together."

Vinnie said nothing. His face was a mask.

Foxy's skin crawled under his touch. She extracted herself from Niemi's grip, taking a step to put herself between him and Matt. "What's wrong with my brother?"

Paul's avuncular expression was new to Foxy. He threw a fond glance in Matt's direction. "Matthew is drunk, I'm afraid."

Everything she saw supported that conclusion, but she still couldn't believe it. She looked around. "Where's my dog?"

"That little terrier? Asleep on the bed." He pointed to the room at the top of the stairs. The door stood open, just as she'd left it.

"Molly Pat," she called. "Come here, girl." She heard the jangling of her tags and then a furry muzzle appeared between the slats of the railing upstairs. Molly gave a yip and yawned. With a little more coaxing, she reluctantly came down the stairs, and immediately stretched out in front of the fireplace.

"I didn't see your car," Vinnie said.

"I parked over there," he said, jerking his thumb toward the west. "I assumed Matthew was going to put me up in the same cabin he did before."

Before? Although the cabin on that side was only a few yards from the lodge, it was almost completely hidden from view. She had to admit it was plausible. Seeing her dog acting unafraid of Paul, she began to relax, and even felt a little foolish for being in such a panic seeing this man who'd been so prominent in her youth. He was nowhere near as imposing as he'd been in those days. His face was wrinkled now, and the enlarged knuckles on his hands told her he suffered from arthritis. Her practiced eye as a healer told her he was favoring his hip.

"Well, don't just stand there," Pastor Paul said. "You two must be freezing. Come, there's a nice fire."

Foxy crouched next to Molly Pat and ran a hand from the top of her head to her tail. She seemed perfectly fine, although tired. When Vinnie suggested the dog may have gotten into the wine too, Foxy chuckled. "She was tearing all over the place when we first got here. She always has to check out every room and sniff every smell until she wears herself out." The dog yawned again and closed her eyes.

Outside, the wind blew and gusted. Icy pellets clicked against the windowpanes like the keys of an old typewriter.

"Before he passed out, your brother told me you two had decided to go out snowmobiling in this blizzard. Not very smart." He wagged his finger in a teasing way.

Foxy didn't budge. Her head turned toward Matt, whose chest continued to rise and fall with his snoring.

"It looks like he's out for the count," Paul said, following her gaze. "Let me make you some cocoa. I'll gladly take my turn as host until he's back on his feet." When they didn't answer, he turned and walked into the kitchen.

"Could this be any weirder?" she whispered to Vinnie.

He shook his head in disbelief. "I can't imagine how."

"Take your wet clothes off and make yourselves comfortable," called the voice from the kitchen. "I'll take care of everything." When Vinnie reached up to unzip his suit the rest of the way, Foxy shook her head vigorously and he let his hand drop.

Still in their bulky suits, they perched on the edge of the leather sofa, side by side, and listened to sounds of Paul searching in cupboards and drawers. Niemi poked his head out and again urged them to relax. Vinnie started talking loudly, babbling actually, about the weather and the exhilaration of driving a snowmobile for the first time. It was the way he coped with a case of nerves. All the time, his eyes stayed on hers, communicating something beneath the small talk—puzzlement, and also a warning.

Matt's light snoring was interrupted by a loud snort. His head jerked, and then settled back.

Foxy went to him, taking his face in her hands, trying to ease his head into a more comfortable position. His eyes opened to slits. He smiled crookedly and muttered something incoherent before falling back to sleep. She found a small pillow and placed it where it would cradle his neck. "Do you think I should call for help? Should we be worried about alcohol poisoning?" she whispered to Vinnie.

Vinnie hovered over him. "Did you see this?" He picked up Matt's hand so she could see the blood oozing through and around a Band-Aid on his thumb.

"He's fine." Paul said. He stood, framed in the archway between kitchen and great room. "When I arrived, he'd just cut himself with a kitchen knife. It's nothing serious, I can assure you. I bandaged it myself."

Evidently it could get weirder!

"It happens all the time," Paul said, appearing at her side with a paper towel to blot the seepage. Handing Foxy a fresh Band-Aid, he removed the sodden one and wrapped it in the paper towel. "People have a glass of wine or two while they prepare dinner, and without giving it a second's though, they pick up the cutlery." He patted Matt on the hand. "Were you aware of his drinking problem?"

Foxy shook her head.

"I'm sorry to be the one to tell you, but I think you should know this isn't the first time I've seen him overindulge. Last year when I came up here, well, I'm afraid he got drunk then, too."

Foxy wanted to say, *Maybe drinking is the only way he can be in the same room with a man who thought of him as an abomination!*

"I suppose I should have paid more attention to how much he was drinking. I suspect he started long before I got here. Addicts can be very creative in hiding their behaviors."

Foxy felt Vinnie's nervousness.

"The next day he was quite embarrassed about it, so I think it best if we don't make a fuss. Let him keep his dignity." His eyes passed over Matt in a way that Foxy thought might be compassion. Maybe the old fire-and-brimstone preacher had mellowed in his later years.

Still, there was something very wrong with this scene.

**F**oxy stared at her former pastor, still not able to understand why he set her nerves on edge. "I didn't realize you and my brother were on such a friendly basis."

His eyes narrowed almost imperceptibly. "I hope you're not insinuating anything untoward in our relationship."

"What? Of course not!"

"Just to be clear, I care about him more as his pastor than as a friend, even though he's fallen away from the church. Once his pastor, always his pastor, you know." Then his smile returned and he said, "I come up here because it's a chance to be out in nature and away from the demands of my work. Clergy are always on call, you know. We live life in a fishbowl. It's necessary to take a break from that. My job at the synod is quite demanding, and Peter's church expects a great deal from him. When we get a chance to get away from all of that, this is one of our favorite places to come."

"Peter's here too?"

"Heavens no! It's Advent." He went back to the kitchen.

"Freak!" Vinnie whispered close to her ear.

To the uninitiated, this reference would have made little sense, but Foxy knew a minister's life was ruled by the liturgical calendar. Advent, the weeks leading up to Christmas, and Lent, the forty days culminating in Easter, were especially demanding on a minister. "So, how did you manage to get away?" She spoke loudly so he could hear her in the kitchen.

He poked his head around the corner. "I'm an administrator at the synod offices now. This isn't a particularly busy time for us, and so I took some time off."

Improbable, all of it, but it was remotely possible he was telling the truth about coming here on a regular basis. She and Matt didn't talk as frequently as they should, and they rarely shared confidences, so perhaps the subject just hadn't come up, but why? Why would he keep it to himself that Paul and Peter frequented the resort?

Pastor Paul came back with two large mugs, which he set on the coffee table in front of them. The pattern on hers was a lake scene. Vinnie's bore the silhouette of a howling wolf. "I put a little cinnamon on top. I hope it tastes all right. I couldn't find an expiration date on the box of cocoa."

"Freak!" Vinnie said again without moving his lips.

"I'll be right back." As Paul turned back toward the kitchen, Foxy studied his walk. She'd worked on enough clients with joint replacements to recognize the limp. He must have noticed her noticing because when he came out with his own steaming mug, he said, "I had a hip replacement a few weeks ago. It was bone on bone, so it had to be done. I'll be back to work full time after the first of the year." He sat across from them again. Foxy recognized the mug he'd chosen for himself. She'd given it to Matt for his birthday one year. It said, "Think you can't walk on water? Try ice fishing."

Foxy reflected on her mother's hip replacement almost a decade ago. She and Matt had been worried about her bouncing back from such major surgery, and urged her to do rehab at the facility in Pine Glen. Her recovery had been impressive, and so when they were looking for a place for her to take up permanent residence when her memory issues became a problem, they were relieved and delighted to find out the place in Pine Glen had an opening.

Pastor Paul at the Pine Glen nursing home—of course! If her mother hadn't thrown her off by insisting he'd died, Foxy would have figured out right away that he'd been there to recuperate from surgery. What she'd assumed to be ill health and even senility when she'd seen him in November had been nothing more than exhaustion from major surgery. He was probably on some powerful opiates too. She pictured him slouched in a wheelchair with his head drooping on his chest, much the way Matt was right now—nothing like this man who was obviously still vital and still very much on top of his game.

Pastor Paul sipped from his mug and raised it like he was toasting them. "Drink up."

"I'll wait for it to cool off a bit," she said, planting her hand on top of Vinnie's and pressing hard before he could drink anything.

Paul shrugged and took another sip. He rested his elbows on the chair arms and tented his fingers, his dark eyes meeting hers. "I can't think of when I saw you last, Frances."

It sounded like an offhand remark, yet it put her instantly on guard. For some reason, Foxy didn't want to reveal she'd seen him at the nursing home, and it wasn't, as he'd used the phrase in reference to Matt, "to let him keep his dignity."

"I believe the last I saw you, you'd come home for a visit," he prompted. "How long ago was that? It was before I moved to Minneapolis, obviously. I seem to recall you had a friend with you."

She filled in the name. "Sierra."

"Yes, yes, I remembered it was an unusual name."

And suddenly she was flooded with memories of that trip. It had been both fun and disturbing. Sierra had pulled out all the stops, turning her charms on Peter as soon as she'd found out he was a seminary student. At the time, Foxy had gotten the impression that it wasn't so much that Sierra wanted to pursue Peter for who he was, but for what he represented. Over the course of a few days, she'd behaved as if it were a game to see if she could cause Peter to break his fundamentalist vows of chastity.

Luckily his father, Pastor Paul, had comprehended what was going on and decided to put a stop to the nonsense. Foxy had found her friend's behavior embarrassing. In discussing the whole matter on the plane ride home, Sierra had laughed and said Peter's father wouldn't even be interfering in his grown son's sex life if he were happy with his own. It was classic Sierra.

But Sierra hadn't quit there. She'd gone on to make some off-color remarks about Peter's father, and it had become clear to Foxy that her friend planned to keep things stirred up by flirting with both the father and the son. If Peter, the minister in training, had been a challenge, Foxy could only imagine Sierra's triumph if she managed to seduce the older man who wore not only a clerical collar, but a wedding ring as well. On the ride home, she'd told Sierra to stop playing with people's lives, and the younger woman had pouted and said Foxy couldn't take a joke.

Like a Chinese puzzle, these memories clicked into place. She searched Pastor Paul's face for any likeness to Sierra's son. He looked back at her with those dark eyes, so like Beau's. Why had she never noticed the resemblance before?

That memory and that resemblance unlocked another memory, this one more recent. When Foxy heard Sierra was living in Minnesota, she'd tried to arrange a meeting, but each time there was some complication or another. Their last conversation had begun as a lighthearted chat. Sierra couldn't seem to find time to get together yet again. She claimed she was preoccupied with getting her finances sorted out. Evidently their move had complicated several plans and had interfered with Beau meeting deadlines to apply for scholarships, which meant Sierra was scrambling to find a way to pay for his college education.

When Foxy had suggested it was time for Wylie to step in and help out, Sierra had been cagey and slow to answer. When she did, it was a vague statement about how he'd done all she could expect from him. Whatever that meant. Sierra explained she'd set up a small investment account years ago for Beau's education, but admitted she'd had to tap into his college fund over the years to pay for things like sports fees, hiking boots, a school-sponsored camping trip to Yosemite, a used car. At that point in the conversation, Foxy had said something about "robbing Peter to pay Paul," and that flippant comment had been met with utter silence. And then Sierra suddenly had ended the conversation. At the time, Foxy had thought it odd, even rude, but until now she'd seen nothing sinister in it.

"What ever happened to your friend? Sienna, was it?" Again, he was working too hard to sound casual.

"Sierra," she corrected him without answering his real question. She sensed Vinnie inhaling as he was about to say something, and decided to answer him before Vinnie could give away anything. "We lost touch a while back."

"Hmm," he said, running his finger around the lip of his mug. "That's too bad. When's the last time you talked to her?"

Again, she conjured the picture of Pastor Paul, crunched down in a wheelchair, asleep, but this time the rest of the memory came to her. Her mother had been lucid that day. She'd asked about Sierra, too. "What about the dark-haired one?" she'd asked. "Did she ever get married?" Because of her hearing problem, Mrs. Tripp either spoke too softly or too loudly. That day, Foxy remembered, the conversation had been conducted at high volume.

Foxy told her Sierra had never married, and then, because it was fresh on her mind, she talked about her frustration trying to get together with Sierra who'd moved to Minnesota. "I think she talks to Tina and Wylie more than she talks to me," she'd complained to her mother. It was the day after her most frustrating phone call to Sierra. "She's having big money problems because of her son, and she says she's going to have to resolve it one way or another. I told her she has to stop letting Wylie off the hook," she remembered saying to her mother. "I told her he needs to pay, but Sierra said not to worry because she had a plan to get money from Beau's father."

Shivers ran from her neck and down her back as if a door had opened to the cold. At the time she'd been talking to her mother, she'd never considered that her old pastor might be of sound mind, and could have roused from his medication-induced stupor to hear everything she said to Mrs. Tripp. She'd even quoted Sierra's last cryptic comment to her. "If I don't see you soon, I left something with my parents for you." It had meant nothing at the time, but now it all made sense. The wine! She was certain now that Sierra had had a premonition, and had left her some clue in that box of wine in case she wound up dead. If Foxy's hunch was right, in broadcasting this information at the nursing home, she'd played a pivotal role in Sierra's death.

"I hate to nag, but you really should drink that before it gets cold," said the man whose eyes so resembled Beau's.

"Oh, yes." Foxy's eyes fell on the mug. "I forgot all about it." She and Vinnie leaned forward at the same moment, reached out and slipped their fingers through the handles, and raised their drinks. Foxy's mug dipped suddenly. Cocoa sloshed on her hand and she joggled it the other way. As if they'd choreographed it, their mugs collided with enough force to crack one of them and splatter cocoa in every direction. "Damn it, I am such a klutz!" she said, brushing cocoa off her waterproof suit.

Paul was on his feet. He grabbed a basket of paper napkins from the coffee table and dumped it out on the biggest puddle. "You go ahead and clean it up and I'll make you some more cocoa."

"Oh, thank you," Foxy said effusively. "I'd love that."

She and Vinnie locked eyes. She jerked her head to where the helmets and chopper mitts dangled from pegs on the right side of the door. As one, they sprinted to the door, zipping their jackets and snatching their headgear and mitts on the way out.

"We need to draw him away from here. Then we can circle back and get help," she said as they ran.

"What?"

"I'll drive," Foxy screamed to Vinnie over the howling wind.

Together they raced to the machine she'd driven earlier. Vinnie jumped on first.

"I said I'm driving!"

"Fine!" He got off.

She looked behind her. The door to the lodge opened and then she saw Pastor Paul blow through it and head away from them to the other side of the cabin. Foxy hopped on the snowmobile. She couldn't get a good seal on her goggles, but it couldn't be helped now. Vinnie took an agonizing few seconds to get his helmet and goggles on right, then buckled the chin strap and cinched the wrists of his mitts before he hopped on behind her.

"He's getting his car! Hang on," she yelled and turned the key in the ignition. Vinnie clung to her as the snowmobile jolted forward, over a berm and onto the lake.

At times, Robin could see only a few yards ahead, and heavy snow blanketed signs and obscured side roads. Afraid of missing their turn, Grace did her best to follow their progress on her cell phone, not an easy task since phone reception cut in and out as they got nearer the resort. They were on the home stretch now. They craned their necks to see any sign of "rustic cabins, nestled among pines in this quiet lakeside setting," as it was described on the website. The white landscape went on for miles.

"Well, that's ominous," Grace said, pointing out her window.

"What?"

"That sign back there. All it said was, 'Don't.'"

Robin guffawed. "You were looking for a sign."

By the time they saw the main building, they were practically on top of it and knew they'd arrived at the right place when they saw Foxy's Saturn parked between two of the buildings. "There'd better be indoor plumbing. I've had to pee for the last hour," Grace said as she stepped out of the car and waded through a small snow-drift toward the lodge.

They reached the door at the same time. Grace rang the bell and Robin pounded on the door. Inside, Molly Pat barked frantically but no one came to let them in. Wind howled between the buildings, driving snow into their faces.

Grace, practically hopping up and down with urgency, suggested it might be unlocked.

Robin tried the handle and the door swung open, aided by a wind gust. Still barking, the dog shot out, circling them and leaping. "Did they leave you here all by yourself, girl?" Robin tried to pet the jumping dog, but Molly must have thought it was a game, because she nipped at her hands. It took some coaxing to get the dog back inside.

"You're acting very un-Molly-Pat-like," Grace said. "Where did Foxy go?"

The dog danced backwards yipping.

While Grace went in search of the bathroom, Robin shrugged off her coat and was about to hang it on a peg when she saw a pair of shoes on the footrest of a recliner. The shoes appeared to be filled with feet. "Hello," she called out, hearing the quaver in her voice.

No one answered. The feet on the recliner didn't even twitch. Everything had been off kilter since they'd arrived—Foxy was gone, the dog was agitated, and an unconscious man lay immovable in the chair. What more evidence did she need? The mentally sound part of her brain told her to run.

With a hand over her heart, she stepped cautiously to the still figure, whom she recognized as Foxy's brother. "Hello? Matt?" she called from two feet away. "Matt?"

He didn't budge. She pushed on his shoulder, gently at first and then with more force until his eyelids fluttered and he snorted loudly. Then her eyes fell on the wine bottle, and she was about to back away, embarrassed for disturbing him. She might have left him there, too, except that Molly Pat chose that moment to jump up with her paws on the footrest. Taking his pants leg in her teeth, she tugged.

"Holy shit!" Grace said, from behind Robin, startling her even more. "Is that Matt?" Before Robin could answer, Grace shook him by the shoulder and yelled at him to wake up. His head flopped with her movements, and his breathing came out in snorts and gasps. "Call 9-1-1," she yelled at Robin. "That is not normal snoring."

* * *

THE TRAIL ON THE DIRT ROAD had been groomed earlier, but shifting and blowing snow obliterated it in places. Foxy took the first few snow-drifts like a pro, initially accelerating and then reducing the throttle pressure. Vinnie's arms were tight around her waist, and when she pulled herself into a semi-standing position, they rose in unison.

On one hard-packed patch, the skis started to slip and she ap-plied the brake perfectly, but when she slowed for a turn, they got bogged down, coming to a complete stop, and they had to get off and use their hands to dig snow out from under the front of the skis.

That's when she heard the engine of the SUV. They turned to see Paul's vehicle farther back on the rutted road, but coming fast enough to be on them in no time.

Vinnie wasn't about to wait for him to mow them down. He jumped onto the snowmobile. When Foxy pushed his shoulder and yelled at him to let her drive, he shook his head. He tugged her sleeve and she got behind him, with no time to lose.

His first challenge was to take the turn at the right speed. Too fast, and he could flip the snowmobile, too slow and they'd get hung up again, where they'd be an easy target for the SUV.

He took off, satisfied that his years of motorcycles and dirt bikes and downhill skis had instilled in him an instinct for when to lean and when to shift his center of gravity forward to get better visibility or backward to get better traction. She moved with him as if they'd done this before.

Vinnie remembered the narrow opening where they could get snowmobile access to the lake. It was a calculated risk, and he was counting on it working. If Paul tried to follow them in his oversized vehicle, he could wind up wedging himself between trees. If they could ditch Paul, they'd be able to get back to Matt or stop for help at one of the houses across the lake before Paul got himself unstuck. If, however, Paul found another road to the lake, all bets were off. On a flat surface out in the open like that, the odds were even at best.

He slowed too much and felt the treads slipping. Leaning forward and giving it a shot of gas, the machine slewed to the left, catching at the last second and giving them just enough spin to make the tight turn.

"Woo hoo!" Foxy yelled in his ear. She'd plastered herself to his back and held on for dear life. They rocketed down the short stretch of trail. The snowdrift at the shoreline was bigger than he'd calculated, but all he could do was to gut it out. "Hang on!" he yelled. The instant the snowmobile was airborne, he felt the adrenaline rush and wanted it to last forever. They slammed down on the ice, still upright. He spun them around so they had a clear view of the lake's edge. There was no sign of Paul and his SUV.

Vinnie whooped and made a pumping motion with his fist. "I'm heading back to get Matt," he yelled.

"What?"

"Matt!"

She nodded and held on. He pointed them in the direction he thought they'd come from. They were closing in on the shore. Directly ahead of them, he saw what he thought was a branch sticking up from under the snow. He made a quick correction, and was almost jolted out of his seat by the force of their collision. The branch, he realized too late, was attached to something larger and more deadly. He gripped the handlebars and held on, even as he felt Foxy's grip loosen. She shrieked in his ear, and then slipped away altogether.

He felt the blood drain from his head. Their speed, he knew, had been insane for these conditions. He didn't have to be an expert snowmobiler to know the impact when she landed on ice was going to be brutal. He had to focus all his thoughts on getting back to her.

Squeezing the brake with his left hand, he started a controlled turn, leaning into it. At first all he saw was shifting snow. And then he saw a dark shape in the snow. As he got closer, he saw it was actually two shapes. Her head was attached to the larger of the pieces, and the other shape was part of a leg, he saw with growing horror. He gasped for breath. Nothing could have prepared him for the sight of her beautiful body torn in half like that.

Howling at the top of his lungs, he sped up to her. He didn't hear the car's engine behind him. The jolt, when the SUV clipped him, was powerful enough to send him and the snowmobile flying. He let go just before the machine rolled, sliding on its side in a slow arc. Momentum drove the SUV forward into the spinning snowmobile.

Vinnie smacked down hard and felt something snap inside him. As he was slipping into unconsciousness, he saw the two machines merge into one black mess. And that mess was skidding right toward where he'd seen Foxy.

Following the advice of the dispatcher, Robin and Grace, still in their coats and boots, maneuvered Matt off the recliner and onto the floor, where they rolled him onto his side, positioning his arms in front of him and a soft throw pillow behind him to keep him from rolling onto his back. His breathing immediately sounded less labored. It took them a moment to figure out what it meant to "tilt his chin up, while keeping his mouth in a downward position," in what the dispatcher had referred to as the "recovery position," designed to keep his airway unobstructed even if he threw up.

Waiting for an ambulance, Robin checked his pulse while Grace patted his hand and talked to him. Molly, who'd kept quiet while the humans talked on the cell phone, went to the door and barked until Grace got up and let her out.

The dog streaked past Foxy's car, sniffing out two sets of footprints which led directly to the three snowmobiles by the garage. Turning to look directly at Grace, who stood watching from the doorway, Molly Pat bayed at her.

"What on earth?" Robin said, standing to check out the racket. "I don't speak dog. Do you?"

"No, but I get the gist. She's telling us something about Foxy."

"Do you think we can leave Matt?" Robin asked, coming to the door. "The dispatcher said they'd be here any minute."

Molly bayed again, leaving them no doubt what they needed to do.

They both grabbed their mittens and hats and headed out the door. It took no great powers of deduction to see where a fourth snowmobile had been parked until very recently. The two sets of footprints ended, replaced by a corrugated swath in between the parallel lines of snowmobile skis, still visible in the falling snow.

"I'm assuming one set of footprints belongs to Foxy, and the other to her ex-husband," Grace said. Her hair slapped across her face and her eyes watered.

Robin's eyes were wide and she bit on her lower lip.

Molly's sharp bark told them there was no time to waste. The two women followed where she led them, around the far side of the garage to where the snowmobile tracks headed into the woods. Judging the path wide enough for their car, Grace grabbed Robin by the sleeve. "We can't wait for help. We have to get to Foxy before—" She didn't finish the sentence.

They ran back to their parked car. "Molly, come!" yelled Robin, throwing her door open. That was all the prompting Molly Pat needed. They set out by car, following the fresh trail of snowmobile tracks, which soon converged with the wider tire tracks of a heavy vehicle.

Grace leaned forward. "Someone's chasing her."

Robin instantly pictured the black SUV Cate's mother had seen in front of Foxy's apartment. Wanda had described the driver as "biggish," with broad shoulders and dark hair. He could be formidable even without being encased in three tons of steel, for which a snowmobile would be no match. For that matter, her car would lose that battle too.

"Go left!" Grace pointed ahead of them to where the crude road split. Nodding, Robin took the fork that followed above the lake's edge. Although it was manageable by car, at least so far, Robin knew one mistake could send them hurtling down the embankment.

Picturing them hitting a tree or slipping off the road into a ravine, Robin drove with some semblance of caution.

Perched with her hind feet on Grace's thighs and her forepaws on the dashboard, Molly Pat yipped and yelped steadily as if urging them to hurry. Suddenly, her ears perked up and she turned her muzzle to focus her attention on something ahead and to their left.

"What is it, Mol?" Robin said. "What is she looking at?"

Grace leaned forward and squinted in the general direction. "Snow and trees, and then more snow and more trees. That pretty much sums it up."

Robin couldn't see what had caught Molly's attention, but it had to be something on the lake below. When the dog tried to prop herself up on the steering wheel, Grace pulled her back and held her tightly. Molly's bark was getting shriller by the minute.

It was hard to see more than a few yards away, but every now and then Robin could glimpse the lake through the trees and driving snow. The drive from Virginia on had been harrowing enough, but this was insane. Hours of hunching over the steering wheel, straining to concentrate on driving, had caused her shoulder muscles to bunch up, but now the adrenaline had pushed the pain back.

"Whoa," Grace said, "Back up. I think I just saw a way down to the lake."

"Shouldn't we stay on Foxy's trail?"

"I know her tracks go straight, but Foxy must have gotten to the lake by now. That's where her dog is looking. And I think we just passed a little side road. God willing, it leads to the lake."

Ahead of them, the wide tracks of a heavy vehicle had ended. Dubious about the wisdom of leaving Foxy's trail to follow that of her pursuer, Robin hesitated, and then backed up. There indeed was a narrow path going to the lake, and someone had driven on it very recently.

Pointing the car downhill, Robin's heart beat wildly. The tracks they were following, she was certain, had been made by a black SUV driven by a large man with dark hair. What she couldn't figure out was why this man was so desperate to conceal the fact he was Beau's father. "Oh, Gracie, what are we getting ourselves into?" she moaned.

"Another fine mess," Grace answered, trying to make a joke of it, but failing to get a laugh from Robin.

They bumped their way down the hill. Robin let out a string of "damns" and "Oh, Lords" and Grace began laughing like a loon—a very nervous loon. By the time they were close enough to see the ridge of snow at the bottom of the hill, Grace's attempt at suppressing a scream resulted in a monotone "Ahhhh!" that didn't end until they'd ploughed through a drift and sailed through a narrow opening in the trees and onto the lake.

Almost immediately, her wheels skidded on the ice underneath the snow. Robin held her breath as they spun, and when the spinning stopped, she had to take a moment to reorient herself. Molly Pat whined and shuddered. In all directions, the landscape looked the same, just as Grace had said earlier. It was nothing but snow and trees.

But as she sat still, trying to figure out which direction to go, she started seeing something through the blowing snow, and knew they were not alone on this out-of-the-way lake in the middle of a blizzard. From one direction came a low moving shape with headlights, unmistakably a snowmobile. And then another, larger shape appeared from a different angle.

Grace pressed forward, pointing over the dashboard. "Snowmobile and car!" she intoned.

"Moose and squirrel!" Robin said in her best impression of Boris Badenoff. "Must catch moose and squirrel." Her eyes widened as she realized the two vehicles were on a collision course.

Grace's laugh was cut off. "Oh, God!" she and Robin said at the same moment.

In front of them on the lake, the two vehicles converged and caromed off each other. The crash was soundless to the two women in the car. They watched headlights spin madly in two directions, illuminating the snowflakes and creating infinite dancing specks of light—more like a ballet or a psychedelic light show than the violent demolition derby it actually was.

Robin tentatively depressed the accelerator. The wheels spun, then caught. It was hard to pick up speed, but they soon arrived at the scene. The snowmobile was on its side, and whoever had driven it was nowhere in sight. "It isn't even running," Robin said.

"Dead man switch," Grace answered. "When there isn't any weight on the seat, the engine stops. It's a safety feature."

Robin turned to look at her.

"I have sons." Grace opened the door. She'd barely gotten one boot on the ground when Molly Pat leapt over her outstretched arm and shot off into the vast whiteness. "Molly!" she yelled, but knew she had to let the dog go. She plodded through the snow to where the machine lay, illuminated by Robin's headlights. She bent to get a better look, walked to the other side, and then hurried back to the car. Tears were streaming down her face from the biting wind. "Nobody underneath," she said to Robin as she got in, "and I lost the dog. She went in that—oh, wait! I think something's over there."

Robin looked where she pointed, and steered the car in the direction of the large dark vehicle, which had come to rest about fifty yards from the overturned snowmobile. Before they got there, Robin saw something else and without thinking, slammed on the brakes. Again, the car lost traction and made at least two revolutions before she got it under control. Moving forward very slowly, she gasped at what she could plainly see straight ahead of her, caught in the headlights. Someone was crawling across the lake, keeping low, like the soldiers she'd seen in movies. Just then, the figure collapsed and lay still.

Grace pointed and squawked, "Foxy!"

Robin stopped the car only feet from the crawling person. "Please be Foxy," she said. Exiting the safety of the car, she and

Grace threw caution to the gale force winds and dashed over to rescue their friend.

Grace fell on her knees next to the person in the snowmobile suit. "Foxy?" she yelled.

Bending to put a hand on the shoulder of the collapsed figure, Robin echoed the name.

The person rolled and struggled, one-handed, to try to open the visor. Grace shucked off her mittens and worked the visor open. She saw immediately it was not Foxy.

The first to respond was a volunteer with the Ely Fire Department known as Flash, not only because he fought fires and had the reputation for being the first on the scene, but because his real name was Gordon. Arriving by snowmobile ahead of the other emergency responders, he found Matt unconscious, his lips taking on the bluish hue of cyanosis, and his breathing slow and ragged. Flash talked loudly to him, shook his shoulders and rubbed his knuckles across his sternum in an attempt to rouse him, but with no response. He noted the nearly empty wine glass on the table. As Flash checked vital signs, Matt gasped for breath once and then his breathing returned to slow and shallow.

Flash tried to remember exactly what the woman had said in the call he'd picked up on the police scanner. She clearly said someone at Twin Loons was unconscious. And she said his name, too. She might have said "Matt is drunk," but he could have sworn she'd said "drugged."

Matthew Tripp was no stranger to him. Theirs was a small, close-knit community of outdoor enthusiasts. Just last week he and Matt had gone snowshoeing with a group from Ely. Afterwards, they'd headed over to Silver Rapids Lodge for steaks and drinks. He and Matt had ordered one glass of wine apiece, and the other four shared a pitcher of beer. It wasn't a heavy drinking crowd.

Drug overdose was consistent with the symptoms. He couldn't wait any longer for the ambulance to get there. In fact, he could only hope he'd gotten there in time. Pulling a bottle of naloxone from his rescue kit, he drew up five milliliters into a syringe, attached an atomizer, and sprayed half of it into Matt's nostril. Opiate overdoses were becoming more and more common. Over the summer, Flash had been on the scene when a twelve-year-old honor student died from taking his mom's prescription painkillers. If Matt hadn't overdosed on heroin or OxyContin or morphine, the naloxone wouldn't harm him, but if he had, the opiate antagonist would buy him precious time.

* * *

LOOKING INTO THE STRANGER'S EYES inside the helmet, Grace shrieked when a strong hand gripped her wrist and hung on. A gravelly male voice said, "Go to Foxy."

"Who are you?"

He shoved her away from him. "Go!" he said, pointing in the direction he'd been crawling.

Grace and Robin stared into the whorl of snow. There was nothing but white, but then suddenly Robin saw the dark shape of a vehicle in the distance, and knew, without a doubt, they'd found the black SUV driven by a murderer. It sat, unmoving. As she stared, a blur of movement passed across her vision between them and the vehicle, racing in the direction the man in the snowmobile suit pointed. She thought she heard barking through the noise of the storm. "Molly Pat!" she yelled to Grace as she tore off after the dog.

Grace turned her attention to the man lying in front of her. "Let me help you to the car."

"No!"

"It's just a few feet. Can you walk?"

"Don't move me." He mumbled something else she couldn't hear.

She had no choice but to leave him. Grace stood awkwardly and immediately slipped on the ice. She scrambled on hands and knees to the open door. Hauling herself up, she reached into the back seat and grabbed Molly's blanket. She covered the injured man, pulled her cell phone from her pocket and hit the numbers 9-1-1. "Help is on the way," she hollered to him over the howling wind.

"Help Foxy," he said again.

Leaving the phone on, she shoved it into the palm of the man's mitt and ran, or rather, hobbled, after the fading silhouette of Robin. In Girl Scouts, she'd learned how to find her way in the wilderness by lining up at least two trees ahead of her to avoid walking in circles. She wondered, idly, if lining up Robin and Molly Pat counted. She pulled the hood of her coat over her hat, which meant she could only see straight ahead through the tunnel of fabric.

Swirling snow changed the landscape, building white hills and valleys that shifted by the minute. She'd lost sight of Molly Pat long ago, and now Robin's figure blanked out, only to reappear in a different place than she'd expected. The dark SUV loomed closer. She tried to ignore the danger it represented.

She stopped walking and closed her eyes against a strong gust of wind, and when she opened them, she saw a strange tableau only twenty feet away. Against the backdrop of a small snow-covered island, Robin knelt over an black-clad body that lay perfectly still, curled up as if to ward off a blow. A single black boot lay three feet away, giving the illusion she'd been cut in two. Red hair spilled from under the snowmobile helmet. The black-and-white terrier whined and yipped as she nosed the body in an attempt to revive her owner.

"Is she alive?" Grace yelled to Robin, coming up behind her.

At the exact moment Robin's face turned toward Grace, the SUV's engine came to life. They watched in horror as the vehicle picked up speed, heading right toward them. And then suddenly, the SUV became a giant spinning top. As it spun, it created a flume of snow in an arc around it. There was no chance of getting out of its way. Robin and Cate shrieked as it bore down on them, circling ever closer.

As it spun past them, the side-view mirror grazed Grace's back and knocked her onto Robin, who fell onto Foxy's outstretched arm. Robin and Grace, the top two layers on this heap of humanity, flinched when they heard a loud thud. Peeling herself off Robin, Grace knelt and helped her to her knees. They looked up to see the SUV sitting lopsided next to the rocky outcropping at the point of an island.

As they considered the situation, the driver's door opened and a hulking figure stepped out. Grace watched in horror as he lumbered toward them.

"We can take him," Robin said in a tough voice that sounded nothing like her.

All Grace could think was *If he's armed, we're all dead.*

"Hey!" he yelled. His voice was deep and sonorous. "Is she okay?"

"Help is on the way!" Grace yelled back, for the second time that day.

He walked with a distinct limp, even dragging one foot along the snow and ice. His head swung from them to where Grace assumed Matt's cabin must be and then to where Foxy lay.

He was only a couple of body lengths from them now. His dark hair was mostly concealed by his stocking cap, but nothing could conceal the fanatical gleam of his eyes. "Leave her to me. I'll take it from here." The way he growled this order told Grace he expected to be obeyed.

He was close enough Grace could see his grim expression. She glanced quickly at Robin, who raised her eyebrows and nodded her head very slightly. It was a signal.

He was only two feet from Foxy. Looking at Robin, Grace braced herself. The stranger leaned down, his lips parted in a phony smile and then opened in a shout as Robin and Grace aimed their kicks at his injured leg. His foot slewed to the side and he went down hard. The crack of bone was audible and his wail mimicked the sound of the raging storm.

\* \* \*

VINNIE KNEW SOMETHING was broken, but he managed to drag himself to the car. Pain tore through his side. Propping one arm on the seat, he was able to press a button on the dash to turn on the flares. Then he leaned on the horn.

He was still honking the horn when the rescue worker drove up on his snowmobile. Although he was slipping in and out of consciousness, Vinnie managed to point in Foxy's direction and say, "My wife. I think she's hurt bad. Her leg's ripped off."

But the man shook his head and said, "Don't worry. We've got someone on the way." And sure enough, Vinnie saw a pair of headlights heading toward where he knew Foxy had been thrown off the snowmobile.

The guy who introduced himself as Flash asked him a bunch of questions and then helped him onto a toboggan he towed behind him. "I've got an ambulance waiting on shore. We don't have to go far."

Vinnie's pain, once he was covered with a blanket and strapped into the toboggan, lessened enough so he could close his eyes and let himself drift into oblivion.

\* \* \*

FOXY WAS ALIVE. She'd roused enough to say her abdomen hurt and she was cold . . . so cold. In light of the fact they couldn't find any visible injury, those words made ice water run through Robin's veins. Internal injuries could be fatal.

The man lying just feet from her groaned. "What about me?" he yelled.

"Yeah, what about you?" Robin said with exaggerated calm.

"I'm a pastor, goddamit! Don't I get any consideration here?"

Foxy mumbled something and Robin and Grace leaned to hear, asking her to repeat when necessary. Her voice was faint and getting fainter, but she managed to pack a lot of information into a few words.

Turning to the man Foxy had just identified, Robin said, "Foxy just said you can go to hell."

"I was just trying to help you!" he bellowed.

Grace set her jaw and stood. Looming over him, hands on hips, she said, "How were you helping, exactly? By killing Sierra and trying to kill Matt?"

"Who? You can't—" Like a cobra striking, his hand shot out and grabbed her around the ankle. Instead of falling backwards on the ice, she tilted forward to fall, and wound up planting all her weight on his midsection, knocking the air out of him.

He gasped and then screamed in pain.

Grace shoved herself into a standing position, put her hands on her hips again and said, "You're not going to try that again, are you?"

"I'm not a bad person," he said, and began to cry.

Robin screamed suddenly, jumping to her feet and waving her arms. "Here! We're over here!"

Through the snow and dim light, a pair of headlights appeared. A vehicle stopped within arm's length of her. Molly Pat didn't move from her owner's side, even when the person in a heavy parka and Steger mukluks got out of the four-wheeler.

It occurred to Robin she should be suspicious of yet another stranger who just happened to show up in the middle of the lake in a blizzard, but she had only so much energy, and she wasn't going to waste it on any emotion other than hope, or any thought other than saving her friend.

Leaning over Foxy, the latest arrival asked her, "Can you talk?"

Foxy answered in the affirmative. Molly licked her face.

"I'm a doctor," the young woman said. "Tell me where you hurt." She pressed her fingers to Foxy's throat. "I'm going to get you out of here."

"What about me?" The voice behind them boomed. "I broke my fucking hip!"

The doctor gave him a backward glance and said, "Someone's coming with another board. We'll get you to the hospital as soon as possible. Just hang in there."

"My balls are frozen to the ice," he moaned.

"That's what he worries about?" the doctor muttered as she got a bright yellow rescue board from her vehicle. "Oh, look!" she called back to the man Foxy had identified as her former pastor and father of Sierra's only child. "Help is here."

Together, Grace, Robin and the doctor lifted Foxy onto the board and got her secured for the ride. Molly Pat, not about to be left behind, jumped in and lay by her side.

Another snowmobile zoomed up, trailing a toboggan. Paul's rescuer wore the badge of the Ely Police Department.

**33**

The storm raged for another hour, and then, as night fell, the winds began to die down. The exhausted staff at Ely-Bloomenson Hospital was already overworked, what with downed power lines, a number of falls, and even more car accidents. In the summer, a lot of their patients came from out of town. They were the weekend warriors who appreciated the beauty of the wilderness but didn't understand nature's power or their own limitations. At this time of year, though, it was mostly locals.

This blizzard was going to break a few records, and everyone pitched in to help. Ignoring their normal work schedules, workers pulled double shifts or came in on their days off to help. Some of the staff said they'd gladly brave the storm, if need be, to rescue or treat people who couldn't make it to the hospital, offering up an assortment of winter vehicles, from heavy duty trucks to snowmobiles and four-wheelers. One doctor who bred sled dogs said she could hitch up a team if the roads were impassable. The camaraderie was phenomenal. Still, everyone was stretched pretty thin.

And then the real craziness began. It started with the guy whose truck had gone off the bridge at Eagles Nest Lake. They'd had to use the jaws of life to get him out of his truck, but he'd been dead on arrival. The sheriff intimated it might have been a hit and run, judging by the marks on the dead guy's left rear panel and bumper. His plates were from out of state.

One of the locals, Matthew Tripp, owner of Twin Loons Resort, came in with an overdose of painkillers. Lots of the staff knew him, and were shocked since he wasn't a known druggie. More than one person referred to his recent breakup as the reason for his suicide attempt.

But then Matt Tripp had begun coming around and claimed he'd been drugged—by the pastor from his hometown, of all people.

Then, just as the storm was beginning to abate, two snowmobile accidents came in at about the same time, a man and woman, both non-locals. The guy named Vincent referred to Frances as "Foxy" and said she was his wife, but Frances insisted they were not married. His injuries, a fractured fibula and broken ribs, weren't life threatening. The broken ribs would have to be left alone to heal on their own, and his fibula, broken just above the ankle, required only a brace and ample time to heal before he put weight on it. But he was in pain, and it wasn't just physical. He kept asking about his wife and finally he'd been sedated because of his anxiety.

His wife, or not his wife, depending on who you believed, was brought in by Dr. Warren, who ordered up three units of blood and whisked her right into surgery. Her injuries were more serious, three broken ribs located just over a ruptured spleen. Someone said she was Matt's sister, and more than a couple people said they could see the resemblance.

Somehow, in a bizarre turn of events, there had been one more person rescued from the frozen lake, yet another out-of-towner, this one with a dislocated artificial hip. The hip replacement had been recent, and the man was sputtering mad to have to go through the surgery and pain and recuperation all over again. He had a foul mouth on him for a pastor. A police officer who'd been part of the rescue, stuck around just on the other side of the curtain in the E.R.

The receptionist didn't know what to do with the little dog, a black-and-white thing that must have been some kind of terrier mix.

Doctor Warren had brought the dog in along with one of the snow-mobile accidents, and told the receptionist to be nice to it until the patient's friends arrived.

The friends turned out to be two women who were, to no one's surprise, not from Ely. But once they got there, they didn't leave, and so the dog stayed with the blonde one while the one with dark hair got blood-typed to be a donor for their friend who was headed for surgery.

Flash, the fireman who'd been first on the scene at Twin Loons, had also brought in the guy who'd crashed his snowmobile. He'd stuck around the hospital until Matt Tripp was stabilized. He came down-stairs, talked to the blonde who was sitting with the dog, and then he left with the dog in his arms. After that the two women took turns snooping around, roaming the halls, asking a lot of questions and making a bunch of phone calls. Another cop came in and ushered them into one of the vacant offices. They were there quite a while.

When Doctor Warren came out of surgery, she huddled with the two women in the corner, and they left that meeting looking, if not happy, at least a little relieved.

* * *

AFTER CALLING CATE one more time with the update, Robin realized how bone-achingly tired she was. The aching in her shoulders that had begun on the drive up came back, this time accompanied by a crushing headache. She'd arrived at Matt's resort exhausted by the harrowing drive, and had immediately been thrown into drama with a capital D. Now her worry about Foxy and her brother consumed the last of her inner resources.

Grace had fallen asleep in the waiting room chair with her head at an awkward angle. Robin shook her shoulder. "We need to get a

motel," she said. "We can't go back to Matt's lodge. The police are
protecting the crime scene."

"Crime scene," Grace blearily repeated and got up. They en-
quired at the desk about a where to stay, and the woman blew her
nose and rattled off a few names that were only a mile or so from the
hospital. When she suggested the Adventure Inn on Sheridan Avenue, Grace turned to Robin. "What do you think? Can we handle
any more adventure?"

"The real question," Robin answered without cracking a smile,
"is whether or not we can avoid it?"

In the end, they passed up the chance for more adventure and
stayed at the Super 8 just down the road. It was simple and more
than adequate as a place to lay their weary heads. Once in their
room, they sat at the little table by the windows for a while, talking
and watching the stars come out as the cloud cover disappeared. It
was amazing to see how many more stars were visible here than what
they could see in the Cities, and it was hard for Robin to pry herself
away from the reaffirming beauty of the heavens.

But tomorrow would be another big day, even without any new
curve balls thrown their way. Stripping down to underpants and a
turtleneck, she crawled into bed and fell asleep while Grace was still
talking to her.

By morning, sunlight glinted off the sculpted snow. It was beautiful and serene—eerily so. Aching all over, Robin heaved herself
out of bed and threw a packet of coffee in the room's coffeemaker.
Grace jerked and twitched in her sleep. Her snoring was downright
flamboyant. No wonder she'd been so tired lately, Robin thought as
she considered rolling her onto her side.

Grace roused enough to open one eye. Swinging her legs over
the side of the bed, she reached behind her to feel the sore spot just
below her shoulder blade where the SUV's side mirror had left a

colorful bruise. "Wow, I had some crazy dreams!" She wiped the corners of her mouth. "Did my snoring wake you up?"

Robin shook her head. "I'm just antsy to get to the hospital."

She took the Styrofoam cup from Robin's hands. "But was I snoring just now?"

"Just a little," Robin lied.

After downing the coffee and eating power bars from the emergency kit from Robin's car, they quickly dressed and drove to the hospital. None of the hospital staff from last night was in evidence. Grace asked at the main registration desk where Foxy's room was, and was told Frances Tripp could not have visitors yet.

"How about her brother, Matthew Tripp? Can we visit him?" asked Robin, and they were given a room number and directed to turn right at the nurses' station. Turning left instead, they saw a uniformed policeman halfway down the corridor, sitting on a chair outside one of the rooms. "Must be the pastor's room," Grace whispered. They smiled at him as they passed the closed door, and two rooms later, they saw a mass of auburn hair against the white linens, and ducked inside before anyone could stop them.

Foxy looked pale. A nasogastric tube came out of her nose and cords ran from different parts of her to beeping machines. Initially her eyes were closed, but as her friends whispered about whether or not to leave, she croaked, "I'm awake." She cracked her eyes open, and suddenly opened them wide. She seemed surprised to find herself in a hospital. When she spoke, her voice was scratchy. "Oh, God, I keep thinking if I go to sleep and wake up again, I'll find out it was all just a dream, but it really happened, didn't it? The snowmobile and Vinnie. And Pastor Paul. Did he really try to kill us all?" She looked from one face to another. "And my brother! Is he—?"

"He's down the hall," said a nurse as she came in and began checking the machines. "Your brother is gonna be just fine after a day or two. He's been asking about you too. Maybe we can bring him down here later for a visit."

Foxy managed a smile.

"Are you family?" the nurse asked as if she were seeing Grace and Robin for the first time.

"They're my sisters," Foxy answered, and asked her "sisters" where Molly Pat was.

"The guy who saved your brother's life offered to take her home for as long as you need. His name is Flash and everyone around here knows him. We couldn't bring the dog here today anyway. He can even take her when he goes to work at the lumber yard."

"He's a good man," the nurse said.

Foxy nodded, looking too drowsy to hold her head up. Her lips were parched. "My poor baby brother. What about the freak that drugged him? Did he get away?"

The nurse just shook her head, and typed something into the computer. "I hear you all had this place hopping last night."

"Someone said the doctor who operated on my pancreas was the woman who rescued me. Is that true?"

"Ya, and she's a fine doctor. You'll be back to normal in no time." She looked at the IV on the back of Foxy's hand and then inspected her surgical site, commenting how much quicker the recovery would be with those five small laparoscopic incisions instead of one big one.

After the nurse left, Foxy rolled her eyes from Robin to Cate and said, "I put a few things together, but not until . . ." Trying to pick up her water cup, she grimaced. "Can't twist." As soon as Grace refilled it with ice water and gave it to her, Foxy sipped through the straw. She handed it back and sighed. "Here's what I figured out. That creep, my old pastor, is Beau's father, and I'd bet anything he killed Sierra."

They both nodded for her to go on, and she did. "It's my fault," she said.

"What?" they said in unison.

She told them how, during that visit in November, she'd let it slip to her mother that her old friend Sierra was desperate for money and had some big scheme to get it from someone. She'd said it in Pastor Paul's presence, believing him to be semiconscious and too addled to understand anyway. "He looked like he was at death's door. It never occurred to me he was taking it all in. When my mom asked about my old friends, I went through the whole list—Vinnie, Tina, Wylie and Sierra." She winced and grabbed her belly.

When Grace asked if she should call the nurse, Foxy said, "It hurts when I try to sit up."

"They have a handy little contraption for that." Robin handed her the bed control.

"I actually know how to work a hospital bed. I just forgot I can't move right. I still think my body should work like it used to."

Grace snorted. "Me two."

"Me three," Robin chimed in.

With the bed raised, Foxy took another sip of water and continued. "My mom said he was dead. Well, she didn't actually use that word, but she used all her other euphemisms for dead. 'Aloha on the steel guitar' is what she actually said. And then, all of a sudden a month later he's at the lodge at Matt's resort walking down the stairs and talking to us like we're long lost friends. My God, I thought I was looking at a ghost. After I got over my shock, he said he'd been at my mom's nursing home recovering from a hip replacement, and that's when I remembered what I'd said. I put it together. I mean it all fell together in a big rush and I knew Pastor Paul was Beau's father and I knew he'd killed Sierra before she could blow his cover."

Robin was about to confirm some of her suspicions by telling her about the paternity papers in the wine bottle and the unsigned letters, when a ruckus erupted in the hallway.

"I'm his son," bellowed a deep voice.

The three women looked at each other wide-eyed.

"Go listen," Foxy instructed. "That sounds like Paul's son Peter."

Robin stared at her and then stepped into the hallway, pretending to make a call on her cell phone. The racket was coming from a dark-haired man outside of the pastor's room. He was hectoring the cop for not letting him see his own father. When the man unzipped his ski jacket, holding it open like a caricature of a flasher, Robin saw he wore a clerical collar.

He stood tall, puffing out his chest in a male display of power. "I have clergy privileges in hospitals."

The cop looked unperturbed. "Tell you what, why don't you cool your heels in the cafeteria and I'll check with my superior officer just as soon as he calls to tell me he's done at the crime scene."

Paul's son jerked his head back as if he'd been slapped. "Crime scene? What does that have to do with my father?"

They both ignored Robin as she talked quietly into the dead phone. She saw the moment of dawning realization on Peter's face. There was a hint of melodrama in the way he took a step back and put a hand to his chest. "I . . . I'll be downstairs."

She popped back into Foxy's room and reported the scene to her and Grace.

Foxy listened, her face grim. "Uh huh, that's Paul's son, Peter. He's a big wig in the church too. Do you suppose he knows how crazy his father is?"

Robin shrugged. "Do you suppose he's mixed up in this, somehow? What if he found out about his father having another son and didn't want competition for the family fortune, for instance?"

"I think," Grace said, "he's pretty shaken up right now and might be open to talking to a stranger over a cup of coffee. Why don't you see what you can find out."

"Do it!" Foxy grinned.

But Robin shook her head. "Not me. He's seen me. Besides, I know someone who's perfect for the job. What do you think, Gracie? Want to chat him up?"

Grace's eyes lit up. "Sure!"

"Before you go," Foxy said, "I want to know something. They said one of you donated blood for a transfusion, so I want to know whose blood they put in me."

Grace rolled up her sleeve, showing the bandage in the crook of her arm.

Foxy's eyes filled with tears. "I guess we're blood sisters now, huh?"

**34**

Grace, as Robin had said, had a gift for putting people at ease and getting them to talk. She was concerned though that Peter, as a man of the cloth, was trained to hold confidences, and would be naturally reticent to open up to a stranger. The idea hit her on her way to the cafeteria. She stopped in the bathroom and tucked her white turtleneck under so only an inch-wide band showed above her sweater.

Peter Niemi sat with his hands clasped in front of him on the table. His glasses lay off to the side. His eyes were downcast and it looked like it took too much effort for him to keep his head upright.

Grace grabbed a cup of coffee and a gooey cinnamon roll and headed for the small table next to his, sitting so they were almost facing each other. When he looked up, she smiled. He did a double-take, his eyes grabbing onto the white band around her neck that looked not too different from his own.

She grinned and he nodded back.

He sipped his tea.

Pointing to her plate, she said, "This roll is more than I should eat. Will you take half?" He looked like he was about to decline, and so she said, "Please. At least remove the temptation." She slid the plate over and he took a piece, setting it on a napkin in front of him.

"What's your trick getting in to see patients?" she asked. "I drove up from Virginia just to visit one of my people, and they won't let me see her. They must have a pretty strict policy."

He looked weary. "I just had the same experience. I came all the way from Minneapolis."

"That's tough." When he didn't answer, she said, "They must think clergy have a cushy job. You'd think people have figured out by now that it's not just an hour or two on Sunday morning."

His chuckle was void of humor. "It's not even one of my flock I came to see. It's my father!"

She frowned. "Good heavens! The hospital doesn't even allow family members? I've never run into that."

He hesitated, his eyes darting once more to her white collar. Sucking in his breath, he looked away. "It's not the hospital. It's the police."

She raised her eyebrows. "Oh! Well, that is a touchy situation. I won't ask, but I'm here if you want to unburden yourself or want me to pray with you."

Rolling his lower lip between thumb and forefinger, he said nothing.

"People just don't understand how stressful this calling can be."

He bobbed his head. "No quarrel there."

"My own son had a run-in with the law a couple years back, and I know the strain it put on me. My husband and I both got some counseling to deal with it."

He lifted his eyes to meet hers, making a decision. "I'm not under so much stress myself, but Dad is. He's ordained too. In fact, I took over the pulpit at his church in the Cities when he took a position at the synod. As stressful as it is to be in parish ministry—well, I don't need to tell you—he's been under tremendous pressure with this job. This last year has really taken a toll on him."

"Oh?" Grace used her silence to encourage him to keep talking.

He stared off in the distance and said, "He was always . . . demanding, a real stickler, but he's gotten more difficult lately. Something's really eating at him. In my opinion, the responsibility of overseeing the finances for the entire synod is way too much for one man to handle, and now they're gearing up for a big, comprehensive audit. The worry is getting to him. I've been urging him to retire, but there's no point in wasting my breath. He's the most obstinate . . ." He stopped and from the look on his face he knew he'd said too much.

And that little tidbit, Grace knew in her gut, was the missing piece they'd been searching for.

When she got up to leave, she saw Robin sitting at a table near the door, pretending not to know her. Figuring she had a good reason for her behavior, Grace walked past without acknowledging her. She sensed Robin get up to follow her out.

As soon as they were around the corner, Robin said she'd been "hanging around" between the front desk and the business office and overheard one of the staff asking her coworker if Wylie was spelled with an "ie" or an "ey" and if Stuart was with "u" or a "w." "I was about to ask for Wylie's room number when I picked up on the words "next of kin" and "morgue" so I hung around and one of them said, 'Wylie Stuart. Is that the guy whose truck went off the bridge?' Gracie, I'd bet anything that was the accident we saw."

Grace's mouth fell open. "Sierra's old boyfriend? How on earth—?"

Robin stared back at her. "Grace, are you wearing a clerical collar?"

\* \* \*

THAT AFTERNOON AFTER A SHORT NAP, Foxy stretched the definition of "family" to get her brother, her ex-husband and her two friends in for a brief visit. With very limited time to pull all their stories together, they got down to business, and as they each shared what they knew, the pieces started to form a complete picture.

When the nurse came along twenty minutes later and kicked everyone out, she told Matt and Vinnie they looked like they needed rest. Matt, Robin saw, looked a little green around the gills, as her mother liked to say, and Vinnie, sitting in a wheelchair with his left leg extended, was ashen and holding a hand over his broken ribs.

The nurse pulled the curtain around Foxy, shutting them out.

After watching the two men head off to their rooms, Grace and Robin stopped in front of the uniformed officer guarding Paul's room. Introducing herself and Robin, Grace asked if there was a chance they could talk.

He was chunky, with a florid face. Checking his watch, he sighed. "I'm waiting for my relief to get here. I need to head back to the station and finish up some paperwork."

Grace nodded in understanding. "I'm hoping this doesn't add to your paperwork. We have information about the man you're guarding." She nodded toward Paul's door.

Robin, seeing he wasn't impressed, added, "There's more to the story than you know."

He sized them up. "Tell you what. I'll call the station. See if someone can take a statement."

In fifteen minutes, they were sitting in a little room off the main floor lobby with a plainclothes policeman who introduced himself as Kovacs. Robin and Grace worked like a tag team, telling what they knew and offering up more than a few speculations. Kovacs's neutral expression, Robin thought, masked his skepticism.

After relating what Paul's son, Peter, told her in the cafeteria, Grace implied Paul had probably been embezzling from the synod funds to pay support for his illegitimate son, Beau. Robin took over to explain about Beau's mother, Sierra, and her supposed suicide.

"We think Sierra must have gotten together with Pastor Paul recently, and asked the father of her child for more money," Grace said, suggesting a motive. "Whether she threatened to expose him, or his guilt and paranoia made him fear retaliation, he must have felt he had to silence her."

Since Matthew had already named Pastor Paul as the one who'd given him a near lethal dose of prescription painkillers, Robin pointed out, "Is it really so far-fetched to think he might have drugged Sierra as well? We think he either drugged her in the house and got her to get into the car, or they were sitting in the car drinking."

Kovacs leaned back in his chair, assessing them.

"He'd just had a hip replacement, so he couldn't have carried her," Robin added. "She must've walked out on her own."

"Right. And when she passed out," said Grace, jumping in, "all he had to do was shut the garage door and wait for the carbon monoxide to do the rest."

Officer Kovacs sighed. Looking at them in turn, his expression was not unkind, but he cut them off, saying, "I'd rather skip all the conjecture."

"Just the facts, ma'am. Is that what you mean?" Robin said, giving him a too sweet smile.

"You might want to listen to what they have to say," said a familiar voice behind them. They turned to see Sheriff Bill Harley walking toward them.

"What are you doing here?" Robin asked, jumping up and throwing her arms around him.

"I came to see Foxy." He looked uncomfortable. "I was just in her room, but she's asleep."

"But how did you—?"

"Your friend Cate. She told me about Foxy's accident and how you all came to her rescue."

Kovacs stood and introduced himself to the sheriff, who said, "These fine women helped me solve a crime a couple years back. It wouldn't hurt to hear them out." He pulled up a chair.

Grace started over from the beginning. This time, the cop took more notes.

Robin told about Pastor Paul showing up at Foxy's apartment on some false pretext. "Maybe he was just on a fishing expedition to find out what she knew," she suggested, adding that in any case, Cate's mother, in her brief interaction with him, had led him right to Foxy. "Vinnie and Matt were probably just collateral damage."

"By the way," Grace said, "we heard someone here talking about Wylie Stuart. What happened to him?"

Kovacs really perked up. "What is your relationship with him?" he asked. When Robin said he was Sierra's ex, Kovacs excused himself.

* * *

OPENING HER EYES, Foxy saw Bill Harley and thought he was just a continuation of her dream in which she was kissing Bill, who became Vinnie in that weird way people and place shifted around. She drifted back to the dream. Vinnie gave her hand a squeeze and spoke to her in Bill's voice. "You scared me to death."

Rousing, she was pleased to see Bill, kind, dependable Bill, holding onto her, keeping her tethered to the present.

# EPILOGUE

A blonde, a brunette, and a redhead went into a bar. They asked for a table for five and ordered a bottle of red wine called The Usual Suspect, from the Big House vineyard, and were soon joined by two more women, another brunette and a champagne-blonde. They obviously had a close relationship. These friends who called themselves the No Ordinary Women talked animatedly and then toasted to the memory of Foxy's friend Sierra.

Summer was just around the corner. It had been a hard winter, beginning with Sierra's death, and they would not soon forget the Christmas blizzard in which Foxy came way too close to dying in a swirl of snow, just as she had in Cate's dreams. But other than Wylie, everyone else had made it through the storm alive.

Foxy had recovered completely from her partial splenectomy, although her ribs still hurt on occasion. For a month, Foxy and her ex-husband talked, both of them testing the possibilities of reuniting. But after all the arguing and crying and reminiscing, it was apparent their love belonged to another time and place, and they finally gave up and decided to put their energy into looking forward without the constant reminder of the mistakes they'd made with each other.

Vinnie had returned to his practice in St. Louis. Foxy missed him. He could still excite her, more than she wanted to admit, but that simply wasn't enough anymore. Her life was here in the Twin

Cities, surrounded by the most amazing women she'd ever met, and even if it wasn't what she'd imagined all those years ago when she'd first set off on her own, fresh out of high school, it was good enough. More than good enough.

In the Ely hospital, Bill had seen what was so obvious to everyone but Foxy—she was still in love with Vinnie. He'd been a good enough friend to pull himself out of the running while she sorted things out. Maybe the "just friends" arrangement would work and maybe not, but they were both content with that relationship, at least for now.

Luckily, Bill had stayed in contact with all of them, the five women of the No Ordinary Women book club, even digging up the information that freed Foxy, once and for all, from her past. Foxy had wasted no time calling Vinnie and Tina, her only two surviving friends from her Las Vegas days, to let them know what he'd discovered.

The murder they'd witnessed so long ago in Las Vegas had been solved almost a decade ago. The dead man was small-time thief who'd had the misfortune to jimmy open the trunk of a car owned by a known drug dealer and pimp. His killer, arrested later in a drug sting, had confessed to his cellmate only days before he was murdered in prison.

Ever since finding out her past couldn't come back and destroy this life she'd made for herself, Foxy had felt more lighthearted than she had in years, but today she was celebrating yet another release.

Today she'd called this impromptu gathering at a coffee and wine bar in St. Paul's Lowertown to share with her friends the above-the-fold article in that morning's *Star Tribune*. There was an air of victory as Foxy held up the copy. The headline read, "Former Pastor Admits to Embezzling."

"Former financial administrator at the Minnesota synod . . ." Foxy began to read out loud. The story told of Paul Niemi, the now disgraced and defrocked minister who had admitted to embezzling not only from the synod but from the church he'd served immediately before that. The total figure for his embezzlement was over a quarter of a million dollars.

A subheading partway down the page was "Robbing Peter to Pay Paul." The paragraph detailed how months after Paul's son, Peter, succeeded his father to the pulpit of a large church in Minneapolis, he'd noticed a discrepancy in the budget, which he'd asked his father about. The elder Pastor Niemi called it an oversight and immediately rectified the shortfall, using synod money. After some investigation, Peter was absolved of any involvement with his father's crime, and according to the article, "Synod representatives and the younger Niemi are cooperating fully with law enforcement and ask prayers that God's grace will extend to all involved."

There was a suggestion the older man's mental health was suffering. "Only recently, Niemi pled guilty to leaving the scene of an accident outside of Ely, MN, in which 51-year old Wylie Stuart was forced off the road and plummeted to his death. According to Niemi's son, the former pastor had been despondent in the past year-and-a-half, causing grave lapses in judgment."

The article did not give motivation or mention that the fallen pastor had fathered a child other than Peter. However, the fifth paragraph left wide open the possibility of criminal charges linking him to Sierra's murder. "Authorities in Rochester, MN, are conducting their own investigation into the recent death of an individual who may have had a close connection to Paul Niemi."

Bill, in a phone call to Foxy, told her he thought the indictments were coming down soon and hinted at the likely scenario. Having already admitted to a hit and run in Wylie's death, Paul would be charged with vehicular homicide to which he'd likely plead guilty. His drugging of Matthew could be charged as attempted murder, but he'd probably plead to a felony drug charge.

Sierra's murder would have been more difficult to prove, but when presented with Sierra's "message in a bottle," the paternity test and Paul's handwritten notes discovered by Cate and her mother, Niemi had talked. "I can't tell you what he said," Bill told Foxy, "but tell Grace and Robin their speculations were, well, just tell them they pretty much nailed it."

The five women talked on and on, and, just as she had again and again in the months since she'd been injured, Foxy said, "I don't want to think what would've happened if you hadn't come. If Paul hadn't finished us off right then and there, I would've died from internal bleeding and Vinnie from exposure. Matt wouldn't have made it either."

It was an ongoing conversation, part of the growing lore that bound them together.

After a while, Grace said. "How about if we quit solving murders and go back to our ordinary lives."

Robin snorted. "Ordinary lives? I don't even know what that means anymore."

"It means we go back to getting together and talking about books," said Cate. "But I wouldn't mind going up north and seeing where it all happened."

"Oh, I forgot." Foxy clapped her hands together and said, "Matt's pulled out of his funk now that he's dating someone new, and wants all of us to come to his resort this summer for as long as we want. He thinks we're a bunch of Superwomen, and says we don't know how lucky we are to have each other." Her eyes misted over as she looked around the table, knowing whatever circuitous path had brought her to this moment in time, it had all been worth it.

THE END

## Acknowledgements

The No Ordinary Women mysteries did not come into being without the help, support and advice of a lot of extraordinary people in my life.

Many thanks to all of you who read the manuscript along the way and helped to make it a better book: My wonderful critique group—Wally Roers, Karen Beltz and Ethan Boatner—plus Carolyn Pittman, Mickie Turk, Christine Glendenning, Dorothy Olson, Mary Ross, Mary Murphy and Bob Deese.

The Twin Cities Chapter of Sisters in Crime has been wonderfully encouraging, informative, and just plain fun. Thank you all.

A special thank you to Doug Wills, retired commander of the St. Paul Police Department and currently Minnesota State Lottery's chief of security. Since I have no personal experience in criminal behavior, I have to rely on the experts. If I've misrepresented anything in describing a crime scene or police behavior in a murder investigation, the fault is all mine.

To Corinne at North Star Press. Your actions in bringing this book to print in the face of a huge time crunch were heroic. Thank you!

To all the readers who have loved the previous books and their characters—Your overwhelmingly positive response is what keeps me writing when I don't feel like it. By recommending the books to friends and inviting me to your book clubs, you've been the reward that makes the work worthwhile.

And speaking of book clubs, my own continues to inspire and support. Dorothy Olson, Jane Anderson, Kay Livingston, Laura Utley, Linnea Stromberg-Wise, Mary Ellen Hennen, Mary Murphy, Mary Pat Ladner, Mary Ross, Pat Almsted: You are every bit as fabulous as the No Ordinary Women of the books.